D0912478

PRAISE FOR
SERGIO CHEJFEC

"Without a doubt, Chejfec deserves greater recognition. *My Two Worlds* paves the way for the novel of the future."—Enrique Vila-Matas

"A novel that is both unique and opportune, it challenges the conventions of Argentine literature."—Rodolfo Enrique Fogwill

"Lean, thoughtful, and keenly observed, the Argentinean Chejfec's first work translated into English packs a great deal of insight into 102 pages. . . . Carson's magnificent translation of Chejfec's latest work should be treated as a significant event."—*Publishers Weekly*

"*My Two Worlds* stands on its own as a vast and complicated work of literature. The book is a substantial achievement, clearly the most interesting, original new work of literature I have read this year. The more I read this book, the more it devours me."—Scott Esposito, *Critical Flame*

"*My Two Worlds* is both a resignation (a wistful sigh of a book) and an endorsement of the instinct to giving oneself over to felicitous discoveries."—Jennifer Croft, *Words Without Borders*

OTHER WORKS BY
SERGIO CHEJFEC
IN ENGLISH TRANSLATION

The Dark
My Two Worlds

SERGIO
CHEJFEC

THE PLANETS

TRANSLATED FROM THE SPANISH BY HEATHER CLEARY

OPEN LETTER
LITERARY TRANSLATIONS FROM THE UNIVERSITY OF ROCHESTER

Copyright © 1999 by Sergio Chejfec
Translation copyright © 2012 by Heather Cleary
Originally published in Spanish as *Los planetas* by Alfaguara, 1999

First edition, 2012
All rights reserved

Library of Congress Cataloging-in-Publication Data: Available.
ISBN-13: 978-1-934824-39-9 / ISBN-10: 1-934824-39-9

Printed on acid-free paper in the United States of America.

Text set in Fournier, a typeface designed by Pierre Simon Fournier (1712–1768),
a French punch-cutter, typefounder, and typographic theoretician.

Design by N. J. Furl

Open Letter is the University of Rochester's nonprofit, literary translation press:
Lattimore Hall 411, Box 270082, Rochester, NY 14627

www.openletterbooks.org

For Graciela Montaldo

Of all invisible countries
the present is the most vast

ONE   Dream, nightmare, truth. To Grino, the series
played itself out like a promise rather than a dream.
Days earlier he had woken to a memory, at the time
still unreal: Sela's little legs, which suggested a future beauty and
inspired a desire inappropriate for her age, ruined by her fall. But
dreams were insatiable, they always demanded more; according
to Grino it was not enough just to dream them, they also sought
some other form, a complementary action to rescue them from the
confusion of the night. It is not only the dream, then, that took
on a new inflection; real incidents—in this case, Sela's fall—were
cast in a nocturnal light, revealing an enigmatic quality. It would
be in keeping with the order of things for a ripe piece of fruit to fall
to the ground under the force of its own weight, but the fact that
the girl should tumble from the tree after he dreamt about her fall
transposed the whole sequence of events, including the backdrop

against which they took place, onto the realm of the fantastic: the causes outnumbered the effects. Grino often wondered about the power of his dreams: whether they simply reflected events or if, perhaps, they catalyzed them. A patio, a few flower pots, a fig tree, and typical tile flooring completed the scene; the bedrooms were off to the side, set back about three meters, and one meter further, half hidden by branches and cans containing the sprouts of future plants, a railing separated the patio itself from the area used for the clotheslines, the laundry room. Little by little, Grino had become accustomed to the details of this scene, in which the girl was only one element; he had decided to call her Sela as soon as he laid eyes on her on his first day of work. Sela could reach the top of the tree in just a few movements, but she climbed slowly, stretching her legs so wide that Grino was afraid that at any moment her delicate body might be torn apart. After a while, she would disappear into the dense foliage, only to reappear further up, perched on a swaying branch. She would sit there for hours, like a sentry. The scene reminded Grino of a photo of a girls' swim team lined up along the edge of an indoor pool, their heads covered by their swim caps and their legs exposed, poised to kick off a government-sponsored competition with their first dive. He had seen these images in magazines as a young boy, had thought about them until they began to feel like part of him: pictures of a row of bodies against a murky, dark background in which one might imagine people, but where there might only have been bleachers, or perhaps nothing at all. Since the water, too, was invisible, the swimmers appeared to be performing some sort of ritual, their joined hands pointing downwards as though invoking a submerged deity. The caption of the photo read "The girls are grateful for their healthy development." Watching Sela climb the tree, Grino would think: She climbs like

4

a swimmer. Her legs reminded him of the bodies of the girls in the picture, but were endowed with all the darkness, danger, and urgency that the others, due to his youth and the nature of photography, had lacked.

Something happens and the scene is transformed. The explosion is right on time. One can imagine the din of shattered stones, broken branches, the shifting of the earth that ends only when, paradoxically, it becomes clear that nothing is as it had been. Changes in nature often seem impermanent; they might be violent, even cataclysmic, but their effects spill out quickly as they fold themselves into the landscape and soon all is quiet again, which means it is time to begin anew. Nonetheless, years ago, when the news reported an explosion out in the countryside, beyond the city limits, I sensed that some aspect of those changes—not a before or an after, but a who, a how, and a how much—would prove to be more intractable, though less perceptible, than the changes in the landscape.

It was an impassive plain, interchangeable: there is infinite countryside just like it. Only in the minds of its inhabitants and in the memory of the animals and that great expanse of dirt, stones, plants, water, and little else did the blast hover like a noise waiting to trail off. Few things seem more gratuitous than setting off an explosion in the middle of nowhere, but in this case the macabre disguised itself as meaningless or innocent, a banality, supplanting the true face of terror. (This turned the danger into something irrational, not because it was too much to comprehend, but because it made itself known by unfolding according to an unfamiliar order.) The article talked about remains scattered over a vast area. There is a word that describes it well: sprayed. Appendages sprayed, spread out in concentric circles from an unequivocal center, the site of the explosion. No matter which direction one went, one would run into remains for hundreds of meters, remnants that had become no more than mute symbols fit only for an epilogue: bodies broken after having suffered, been torn to pieces and dispersed.

I looked up from the newspaper and toward the street. A taxi slowed, affectedly, neither coming to a stop nor advancing. I tried to formulate a thought: This is how we go through time, I said to myself, just barely moving forward. Aside from the lessons that could be culled from it, the taxi's sluggish pace was meant, primarily, to give its passenger a moment. The man was eventually ready to pay, and the driver turned completely around to accept his fare in a gesture that seemed, if not overly obliging, at the very least contrived. Certain insights could be drawn from this, too, I thought. What I mean is that life proliferated itself through these events, while the text of the newspaper was something static, something that speaks of a seemingly inevitable past, a realm in which hope is extinguished, et cetera. While life and time marched forward in unison, branching out into infinite possibilities and consequences, the news stories that effaced the past and left us without hope were like a cynical grimace announcing what was to come, for example, that what once was light was about to fall into darkness.

Like many others, probably, I believed that I knew things the newspaper did not mention. In my case, the explosion had a painful history, which began with the abduction of M (M for Miguel, or Mauricio; it could also be M for Daniel since, as we know, any name at all can reside behind letters). Several days passed between the abduction and its announcement, a length of time I do not dare try to calculate, partly because I am not sure that I could: those days were not days at all—they were a single, interminable mass of time, at once ephemeral and able to reproduce itself without end; in a cruel twist of fate, as they sometimes say, the pages of that newspaper offered the only possibility of an ending, if not in the form of a conclusion then at least as a cessation, a way of giving shape to that mass and thereby opening it up to an after.

I should say that I lacked then, as I do now, any proof that M was in that explosion. But I was not, I am not, in a position to ignore the possibility. Imagining him among the dead served little purpose; in fact, it served no purpose at all. Nevertheless, it was a thought that insinuated itself time and again through association: what once pulsed with life, its own form of abundance, that is, his body, a combination of liquids, nerves or whatever all of that could be called (a typical presence to which the world has grown accustomed and is widely taken for granted, the habit of leaving life unspoken); the thought of something that had been inexhaustibly alive until that moment, the organic life of a body now emptied of its substance, took the shape of an idea marked by necessity, perhaps even by fate.

The pit opened by the memory of M was slowly covered over—days, then weeks and years—by the desolation left in the wake of barbarity. Unlike those of other transgressions, the effects of this crime do not fade immediately, in the short or long term, or ever. A deathly patina covers the faces of the living, their features become a shield against unsuitable gestures, emblems or examples of absent faces; these grimaces are eloquent precisely because the living, overwhelmed by the evidence before them, chose lassitude and dissimilation. (Now I will speak of my country.) I have always had the feeling, when walking anywhere in Argentina, but particularly in Buenos Aires, that I was doing so among people who, surprised by the intimacy of their relationship with death, choose cynicism as their form of atonement (when sincere repentance is such a simple act).

As a result, what follows is a story without an end. Perhaps within the sphere of evil there is a need to complete unfinished stories. When I say the sphere of evil, I am not referring to some sort of absolute complicity, but rather to the fact that its victims, though they belong to the realm of good, have been cast into another—the dominion of evil—by virtue of being victims. Since we know that good may be limitless, perhaps within the sphere of evil the need to bring stories to their conclusion becomes urgent. Maybe this is why I thought of M's abduction when I read the news of the explosion. The time between those two events was an exercise in panic during which I imagined the cruelties he suffered, prior to the moment of that equalizing blast, which ended both life and horror. Looking at the newspaper I imagined that, after those interminable days, reason—though it was a childish and abominable sort of reason—had finally prevailed: his annihilation, of which the abduction was only part, had been fully realized.

I read the story three times, then found myself transfixed by its title. It would be an exaggeration to say that I was thinking about something, but I was not thinking about nothing, either. If there is a moment that precedes the formation of a thought—a moment in which one's consciousness tries to make way for an idea but is impeded by the sheer number of details involved, a moment in which a future thought takes the form of a dream, an involuntary impulse—if such a moment does exist, I experienced it for an inordinately long time. So long that I jumped when the waiter came by to empty my ashtray, startling him. The title read: "Explosion in P." I stared at it without taking in the words, the paper covered with disorganized blotches of ink, like when one stands in front of a mirror and sees the glass instead of one's reflection. The newspaper said that, for a few hours, the locals had heard trucks speeding up and then stopping; unusual noises that somehow failed to draw anyone's attention. (If it had happened during the day they would have seen the whole thing, but since it was night, everything appeared to be in order; night is the embodiment of the clandestine, which in this case allowed many to turn a blind eye.) It had seemed like some sort of public project, roadwork, maybe. Engines running at capacity, something heavy rocking back and forth, banging against metal. Sometimes the trucks could be heard dumping their loads of rubble, the stones flowing out of them like a solid, dissonant stream. Then the activity began to subside, and little by little the noise tapered off until at some point in the middle of the night everything seemed to return to its indifferent state of normalcy. And yet, as would be proven shortly, the process had already been set in motion and was gaining momentum. Having forgotten the trucks, all were shocked by the explosion. Silence spread among them until the following night. (The silence itself was a sign; expressed physically it would have been a grimace, an acknowledgment of the lack of explanations and also a means of excusing the violence. The people's faces.)

A silence less enigmatic and drawn out than the one adopted by M's parents. Despite its eloquence, which did not deign to utter a word, it was a silence composed of gestures as emphatic as blows with a stick. I never fully grasped the meaning of this silence, though I tried in vain several times to understand it. One could say that the absence of the child produced an emptiness in the parents, who lived their lives inside a sphere of glass bombarded by signs from the outside world. Because of the transparency of their enclosure, its interior was visible to all, despite the fact that M's parents felt and acted as though they were living on the dark side of a planet composed of their own pain. They were comfortable in their anguish and consoled by their own desperation. The outside, generally defined as "others," "things," or just "the world," which had always seemed somewhat adverse, revealed itself, after what happened to M, to be openly hostile. As a form of self-defense in the face of so much adversity, they chose to fade away, to become transparent. But the truth was that they were still being observed, perhaps more than ever.

I admired the fact that a drama so intense would, for them, be silent. It was not the hermetic isolation that usually imposes itself after a tragedy, the form of autism adopted by the victim, or the open display of fear and self-pity exhibited by friends. More tangibly, it was the melancholy silence behind which his family would hide, as though each of them were fulfilling a predetermined and accepted religious role that originated in the distant past. But this obedience, because it was born not only of personal conviction but also of their very nature, unfolded against a backdrop of confusion. In this way, even though they did not hear it, the explosion that ended their son's life was still a shock to them, I thought as I sat in a café—a pizzeria, rather—on what was then avenida Canning. It shocked them still. Like stones in a pond, the waves of the explosion reached M's family, actually gaining force as they traveled rather than tapering off, as they would have under other circumstances. Of all the dangers involved in going near M's house, one of the most painful was confessing to his parents and his siblings, without actually saying anything, that chance had been on our side, that of his friends, and not on his. This arbitrary act of evil grieved us as though we were his kin and left us in his debt. M was our martyr, not because his sacrifice was intended to bring about our salvation, but because we were marked by his death. This is why some days I think of him as though he were divine, assigning to him impossible powers, worshipping his memory. Though his existence is slowly slipping away from me, becoming abstract, it continues to be the most vibrant, certain, and immediate thing I know.

Captives of geography, our past is shaped by the city. That earlier city is still our doorstep. A multicolored fabric of extraordinary vastness, woven of shortcuts and straight lines intersecting at outrageous angles, imposed itself as the backdrop of our sojourns. But its surface, known conventionally as the real and as resistant as a scab of asphalt and cement, lost something in M's absence; it was reduced to belated shadows and reflections projected onto that other city, the one etched into the past. The true present faded into the distance, and the city itself, built from substances designed to withstand the effects of time, dissolved into a nucleus of disorder. This degeneration of the city, which spared only the traces of the two of us, making M's absence even more pronounced, devastated me and left me silent for months. It was another who could speak, not I. For weeks on end, the days refused to pass; as I walked I could feel the presence of some remote power, older than time, that kept me from knowing my own destination. It happened in all sorts of situations. And yet the city was not empty; it was full of people who were able to carry on as though nothing had happened. Things like "the 100 neighborhoods of Buenos Aires" and "the Queen of the Río de la Plata" would still come out of their mouths. To me, these phrases revealed, just as more explicit ones did, the spread of misinformation and falsehoods. Nothing escaped, nothing was spared; they even afforded the dead a part in this scene, if only to turn their backs on them. It was a jumble of words in which the memory of its inhabitants was invoked only to be decimated.

He met M when the two had just grown out of childhood. Several years before the abduction, they sealed the friendship with a classic rite of communion: *they exchanged portraits. (It was more than a fad, but not as deeply rooted as a custom; the youth of the time were of a particular sentimentality that combined emotional impulses with a nonconformist—and often heterodox—attitude. Although this could be said of adolescents in general, at the time this energy was directed toward the unification of tastes, opinions, and ideas. They often spoke of whether they could be considered to be under the influence of the masses; they were young, but they were also foreign; they were amphibians. Inhabitants of a secondary nature, they adopted beliefs in a way that immediately exposed them as inauthentic, or mildly or profoundly out of place—depending.) M's portrait was an enlargement of part of another photo, taken on calle Humberto I, in the neighborhood of San Telmo. The magnification of his face blurs his features and the rough grain of the photographic paper lends him a dramatic, if somewhat less than spontaneous, expression; his open mouth reveals his distinguishing feature: the hollow of a missing incisor. Partly because of the enlargement process, and partly due to his expression, his face seems on the verge of forming a grimace; almost, but not quite, due to the very circumstance that produced the effect: the false proximity of the camera.*

Before giving it to me, M wrote the phrase "buffeted by the wind" like a title or an emblem on the back. I turned the photo over and saw him: he was standing on a fence and holding on to the railing, precisely as though he were being buffeted by the wind. In the interest of simulation, someone else might have pretended that he were leaning out over a precipice or some other thing one might expect to find on the wrong side of a fence, but M had chosen the least likely option: a vague idea of questionable representability. Of all the scenarios he could have depicted, his expression hinted at the violence of imagined gusts of wind and his grip on the bars, which were barely visible, spoke of its incredible force.

The day we exchanged pictures, M declared, "I don't believe in photographs." He did not say this to detract from the exchange, but simply to express that, in his opinion, photos did not have any documentary value whatsoever, and for that reason he doubted that they could carry a complementary emotion. As was often the case when he spoke, his words were aimed at refutation rather than persuasion—nevertheless, I was persuaded. I looked at him without understanding: where, if not toward the traces of our lives, private or shared, could we direct our emotions, apart from other people, I silently wondered. M did not hear me, but went on speaking as though he were responding to my question: Photographs are evidence of a momentary reality, inherently archaic and out of place, he repeated (in different words); but for this very reason they are also useless as documentary records. Relics as soon as they are processed, they are mute, a bridge between the past—the circumstance depicted in the photo—and the present—the moment of its viewing. And what is there between the past and the present? he asked, raising his voice. Nothing, just a chasm open at your feet; if we believe photos to be auxiliary truths, either truth itself is nonexistent or reality needs no proof. As we know, there was no wind and that fence is just a collection of posts so thick you can barely tell what they are. The weather that day no longer exists, and the noises we heard have long since faded. We'll keep these photos as talismans, but not as proofs. "Let's keep these photos as talismans, but not as proofs," I repeated, as though the words were a prayer or a line of verse, trying harder to convince myself than the occasion demanded. I could sense, in this insistence and excess, a religious undertone of guardianship. Something between protection and adoration, at least; if the figure in the photo no longer existed, and neither did the sounds of the street or that particular palette of light, as is the case in any place and time, that afternoon the secret value of the image, the photo, lay in its power of conservation rather than in the representation of an origin. Years later, my photo would lack the protective qualities he had tried to assign to both. But "my photo" was not my portrait, but M's. Just like "his" was not his, but mine. Which of the four photos retained that power? His in his possession, mine in my own hands, the picture of me that he held on to, or his in my possession (which I still have)?

After the abduction, I took refuge in the house of a friend who had the same name as M. I met my mother from time to time in a nearby café; she wanted me to leave, I didn't respond. My mother would smooth her hair and ask how long I was going to go on like this. I remained silent. Then it would begin all over again; the same dialogue repeated two or three times in different words, followed by the same silence. Then, with a sudden movement, which in its swiftness conveyed both annoyance and concern, she would take out a little money and tell me that she would not be able to go on offering it for long. I am sure it was not easy for her to come by, but the supposed tact of calling "offering" what was so obviously "giving" seemed both unnecessary and inappropriate; it was the introduction of courtesy into a situation that rendered courtesy trivial, even insulting: the circumstance, as she herself acknowledged with her concern, simply did not allow for social graces or attempts at elegance. How, if not like alms or a tip, was that money handed over to me? I was in no position to turn it down, but she insisted on the word "offering" time and again; in a way, the care with which she tried to protect my supposed pride showed just how far apart we had grown, how divergent our paths had become. It was on one of those days—when I would walk from café to café, my mania fueled by fear, exhaustion, and boredom—after seeing my mother, that I read about the explosion in the newspaper.

M lived on a street that was divided in two by the railroad. Whoever wanted to cross the tracks had to do so by following its old-fashioned walkways in the form of an S, which would force them, precisely, to slow down. The house was thirty meters from the tracks; cars hardly ever drove down his block, which was lined with trees and façades so similar they seemed indistinguishable, interchangeable. To get to M's house, one had to walk down a long hallway that extended almost to the middle of the block. Every few meters a door would appear on the right—these were not only similar, but in fact completely identical. His family lived behind the fourth. The door opened on to a patio, which was the nucleus of the house. There were a few plants and large flowerpots in it, which at first glance seemed to be scattered about at random. M's room was reached by climbing a narrow staircase that rose up from the patio next to a large sink and doubled back above it (so closely you had to stoop over to do the wash). I remember my surprise looking down for the first time through the steps of iron grating, just like the ones found on countless railroad bridges. M should feel lucky to have his own room, I thought the first time I visited, especially one so isolated from the rest of the house.

The residence, which was nothing special in itself, took on an enigmatic quality the moment M's family moved in. It was not just the building or the apartment, as I will explain later on, it was also its location. Even though it was in a mostly Jewish neighborhood, the house was in an area that was not considered as such. The proximity of the two, as is often the case, made the differences between them even more pronounced. The opposite can also occur, as it did with my family, which did not live in a Jewish neighborhood but drew little attention just the same. Invisible from the street, in an area that seemed strange to my inexperienced mind, M's house was ensconced within the very heart of the block, surrounded on all sides by other houses and other families. This confinement, which shaped the family's daily activities, proved that "confinement" was not really the right word for it; more accurately, it was an excessive form of cohabitation and a different sort of abundance, though it was foreign to me. It was the realm of the diverse, the disparate. I should say that the "geographic" oddity of the house represented only my first concern; a second arose when I met M's parents, who spoke without any particular accent. I still remember my surprise at hearing his father speak; his language was unquestionably that of Buenos Aires, utterly *porteño* in usage and intonation, and was, of course, more emphatic than my own. My admiration mingled with suspicion. I had always seen a foreign accent, especially a Yiddish one, as a perceptible mark; because of this, I viewed its absence as a profound ethnic limitation. The way I saw it, a foreigner displayed greater abundance than a local did through his speech, the outward sign of a nucleus that affirmed his identity.

There are, in life, passing moments and pivotal ones—some can be both at once, some, only one or the other. This lack of an accent was one of these: not passing, but pivotal. If the condition of being Jewish were a hollow meant to be filled with distinguishing attributes, in those years I considered flawed speech to be a fundamental element of the mix. We had been taught to set our sights on this, and it is well known that everyone else was doing the same. I sensed, in the lack of an accent among M's family, a diffuse sort of danger, which did not attach itself to anyone or anything in particular; in the worst case, it suggested a threat, in the best, a mistake—the destruction of that which separated them from the rest of the world. The world thrives on difference; it is from this difference that we learn. In this way, language and geography came together in M, highlighting his enigmatic surroundings and forming a complement.

I'll now mention another thing that was important to our friendship: the railroad. The tracks became our territory. To M and his friends, a stroll through the area was an exclusive activity; it meant walking, separately and guided by individual routine, along streets and homes that offered up their hidden corners without resistance. They killed time looking for oddly-shaped rocks, pulling weeds from the sides of the embankments, poking around the fences and walls at the furthest ends of the lot. Over the years, this place would become another shared emblem. I would take the train into Buenos Aires every day from the outskirts of the city, often traveling the same route along which M would walk. As I passed his house, I would stick my head out the window and look back at the short, tree-lined block, its cobblestones in perpetual shade. We spoke with great composure about the trains, not with a sense of admiration that could deteriorate into enthusiasm, nor from a desire to expand upon any meager technical knowledge of the subject, but rather paying particular attention to the details, which were often questionable, as all details are, in an attempt to understand them as part of a real—and apparently unattainable—whole: the one represented by trains of metal, glass, and leather that crisscrossed the city, more noisy than they were fast.

When the world is so dark that the truth seems beyond our reach, it is best to create an efficient, though illusory, system that allows us to represent it as though it were real. These topics of conversation, then, were assured their longevity not only by the fact that the trains were a part of both of our lives, but also by the monotony of those lives, a rut into which we gradually fell. I would mention things I had seen, M would describe others. He would tell me, for example, that the bells on the corner near his house had rung the whole afternoon, that there must have been something wrong with them. I, for my part, would listen, think about what he was saying, and remember, for example, that I had been delayed an hour near Ramos Mejía station. The car I was in—as always, the last—was blocking the street. I could see the frustration of the drivers as they looked out at the obstruction that was arbitrarily blocking their way; they must have thought that it would have made no difference to the train to have stopped a little further along. And maybe they were right, I said, the fact that the last car of the train was exactly as wide as the street made it seem like something that had been done deliberately, maliciously. M thought for a minute, and then asked if there were many people on the train. "On what train?" I replied. The train I said I was on, he explained. I answered him with a wave of my hand that signaled "like this," when what I had wanted to convey was "you know" or "the usual," meaning that I could only speak for the car I was in; as I described to him in detail, the car was about half full but many of the passengers, myself included, were standing, which allowed me a better view of the street. It was no problem for the people riding bicycles or traveling on foot, I continued, they went around the back of the train and crossed the tracks carefully. The drivers of the cars sighed as they watched people on foot pass them by; they were slaves to their vehicles, and they rested their arms on their steering wheels in a gesture, I repeated, of both resignation and impatience. Sometimes a few of them spoke; a pedestrian pointed into the distance.

After thinking for a moment, M wanted to know: Were the crossing gates lowered? "What gates?" asked the other. "The crossing gates, the ones you were just talking about," he answered. "I didn't say anything about any gates." "Where you were stopped," he said. "How did he know about the gates?" the other asked himself, not expecting a response: he looked at M without understanding and answered with a gesture, a widening of the eyes—the train was in the middle of the street, how could they not have been lowered? Even the bells, which had been meant to announce the train's passing, were a platitude and, in some respects, a failure: there it was, stopped in view of everyone. The fact was that the train was full; everyone was pressed together without room to raise their arms. The noise from the alarm, coupled with the lack of space and the closed windows, provoked a general sense of drowsiness, except among those who shouted things like, "We're going to be here all night," "Keep your hands to yourself," and jokes of that nature, before letting out a guffaw. M, listening to the commotion all afternoon, had come to the same conclusion, although by an opposite and incomplete route: it seemed obvious to him that the bells would sound when a train passed, and so he assigned the error to the fact that no train was passing: the cause of the commotion was unclear, but the fact that there was no train coming was an obvious mistake. "But what was the mistake?" asked the other. "What mistake?" replied M. The mistake of sounding the alarm without the train ever passing; was it the error of the train or the alarm? M replied that he couldn't know, just as he couldn't know what was obvious about the situation. In the other's account, he continued, it was different, both train and alarm were implicated, the error was obvious. All afternoon M had watched his neighbors lean out their windows, as if they might identify the cause of the alarm by doing so, but they could not; he had also noticed the care with which the few pedestrians had crossed the tracks. He had not gone down to walk along the tracks—the way they wound through the terrain there, the bells were the only way to know a train was coming. Later that night, they stopped ringing. It was a moment like any other, but different because it marked a change. The other's train had also suddenly begun to move, without warning. Many of their conversations were like this, a vague compendium of news from the railroad. From the comments of the other, M learned about the curve of the tracks at Villa Luro, harder for diesel engines than for electric trains to take, just as the other discovered the nicknames that M and his friends had for the engineers.

M had always had a poor sense of direction; this led to a complete detachment from the geography of the city. It took him the same torturous effort to locate a point five blocks away, as fifty. His gaze would drift off and, absorbed, facing the abyss of which he felt a victim, he would finally ask, "How do you get there?" Great feats of memory allowed him to go to familiar places; it was impossible for him to orient himself if he was forced to set out from anywhere other than his house. To his mind, space was a question without a clear answer. After more than six months of classes in our first year at school, he would still confess some mornings that he did not know how to get home: he knew which bus to take, but since he had forgotten its route he did not know where to get off. A corner two blocks from his house was mute, it said nothing to him. Experience told him that that it was part of the same city, but to his mind, it might as well have been at the antipodes. The names of the streets, like the streets and avenues themselves, did not say much to him either; his understanding of the city was tangled and confused, and therefore naturally unfathomable. Things could be anywhere: they could even occupy the same place, superimposed upon one another. This system, which seemed natural but was actually based on the extremes of absolute dispersion or absolute condensation, condemned him to perpetual uncertainty. One afternoon, on his way back from school, he fell asleep and didn't get home until after midnight; the bus had an unbelievably long route, going as far as G. (Which was very close, in fact, to P; it might even have bordered the area where, it is my belief, his body would fly through the air just seven years later.)

Earlier, I referred to geography as question without an answer in M's mind. This trait—which he was the first to admit: "Give me a map and I'll read it upside down"—was equivalent to the mystery I sensed in his neighborhood: an unusual, if not defective, sort of suburb. His lack of any sense of direction or spatial relation absolved him of all commitments. When it came to the area in which he lived, he could not be held responsible. I did not realize it at the time, but my uneasiness followed from ignorance. Later, as time passed and we remained friends, I would notice the natural feeling and steady rhythm of the neighborhood, which was strange in many ways but also so much like others in Buenos Aires. Everyone thinks of their block as the epicenter of daily life: they leave from and return to it every day. This sense of certainty about space fades as the perimeter grows until it becomes, depending on the individual, a ghostly image. Distance, in this case, is confusion; anything, as I said before, could be anywhere and everything could be everywhere, which is to say that any place could be anyplace. M had a limited radius of movement, which altered his perception, but since he also lacked a sense of direction, experience and routine often translated into greater insecurity rather than understanding.

Earlier I said that M's abduction left us speechless (I should add that my world fell apart). I am going to recount the moment I found out. One afternoon I heard someone knocking at my front door; still, nothing seemed particularly urgent that day. I dressed slowly, wondering who it could be; when I neared the door the knocking began again. I opened the door reluctantly, only halfway. It was my neighbor, who was about to leave. As he turned he said impatiently, "Hurry up, now, you've got a call." We started walking, him in front and me behind. It had been quiet inside my house, but out on the street everything was jarring. I tried to excuse the delay, saying, "For what it's worth . . ." "So don't give out the number," he responded, and he was right. We got to his house and I walked . . . back along the walls; one burned from the hours the sun had been at work on it. I got to the kitchen, where they kept their telephone. Up to that point everything was normal, even predictable: the untended plants, the two old plum trees out behind the house, the smells of the kitchen, where they were just sitting down to eat (my standard joke: I would be there in a minute). A friend was calling, to let me know. That's what he said: To let me know. This friend, named A, sounded like an idiot. How could he say "to let me know"? (Someone, someone else was speaking through him; he could not be saying that.) He said he couldn't believe what he was saying (what he was letting me know). I could not believe him, either. Some of the details were absurd, fragmentary, unclear. We didn't know what to do, him on his side and me on mine, which was demonstrated by the silence we maintained for a few long moments before hanging up. I remember a parenthesis opening up as I put the phone back on the receiver; something was interrupted, for how long, I don't know. Some time had passed when I came around, but my neighbor and his family, who were waiting to eat, the bottle of soda water sweating on the table, were looking at me as though I had just hung up. Something had happened, they could tell, and they were waiting for me to explain it to them. The meal didn't matter; they could wait in silence for hours until I was ready to speak. I regretted the silence, and regretted in advance what I might say. I muttered something about the soda siphon, that it was getting cold; that the bottle was getting cold because the soda, as it warmed up, let go of the cold it had absorbed in the refrigerator. I had wanted to say something about the food, which was steaming (and actually getting cold), and tell them that I didn't want to bother them any further (this is what I was regretting in advance: that I would sound like my mother with her overly emphatic courtesy). I had wanted to say that the food was getting cold, but seeing the perspiration on the siphon, I felt utterly defeated: not only had something terrible happened to M, I thought, but on top of it all the sweat from the bottle was pooling on the table. And so, with those disjointed words I left, flustered and impatient, not knowing where I was headed. I went back through the house. I crossed the stone patio and walked along the wall, which was giving off a more intense heat than before. I stepped into the street and was pained to see that things were going on as usual, when the worst had come to pass. Everything expanded around me; time took on intolerable, immeasurable dimensions and nothing seemed to have an end. I went over what had happened; the notice from my neighbor, our conversation; I was ashamed that I had been so leisurely in the way I dressed and so cavalier when I greeted the family. And, on top of it all, the worst thing imaginable had happened to M. Outside, the sun was hard at work. My mind was an intensely white screen, as bright as the chalky wall behind me. Strangely enough, my first impulse was toward calculation: I wanted to guess how long it would take the bus to reach the corner, how many cobblestones fit on one street, how much heat it would take to melt these walls, and the houses along with them, once and for all. These calculations were a way of stopping the advance of time, anyone could have seen that, but there was still a time that evaded me: it was the moment itself, in which something was beginning that I did not understand, something born of abandonment and also, although it sounds contradictory, a double life. (I mean that I felt M's life in danger within me; of the few duties and sensibilities he had chosen for himself, I decided to follow and complete the greatest number possible. It was a means of survival. Later on, I will explain how.)

One afternoon, weeks after the explosion, I ran into his mother on calle Acevedo. She was distracted, not looking where she was going and wrestling with her bag; one of those that can be used either for shopping or as a briefcase (I remember because it seemed very large to me, empty; a flaccid weight hanging from her arm). This woman, about whom I knew so much, seemed to know very little of herself. The dense trees formed a tunnel of shadow, the exact center of which was occupied by her weary approach. Her disarray did not surprise me; it was the outward sign of a trait shared with something, many would say with someone, that was irrevocably absent. Beginning with M, I had noticed certain attributes in each member of the family, the presence of which affirmed that they belonged to the same clan: disorientation, dishevelment, and a particular vacillation that persisted even after they had made a decision. M's mother remained true to her nature, but there was a nuance to her demeanor that had not been there before. I did not realize it at the time; I only came to recognize it much later, thinking about that encounter in the course of one particularly long night. This new trait was not something commonplace, but a profound weight;

it was the mark of accelerated aging. I am not referring to the signs of her pain, which were evident. To say it in a direct and slightly arbitrary—perhaps even fallacious—way, one sleepless night my mind happened to linger on the memory of that encounter, and the obvious truth that had been hidden finally dawned on me: the body of M's mother was smaller that afternoon; she had been reduced. On Acevedo I had only noticed something strange which, coupled with the familiar, became mysterious. This union of the *strange* and the *familiar* was, I believe, the first effect of the tireless labor of M's absence. The familiar accommodated the strange, and the strange took over the familiar. The former absolved the latter, and the latter pardoned the former. (The familiar was M, the strange, death.) When I saw her, almost at the end of the block, I said "There is R, M's mother," and nothing happened. I recognized her gait, the family's shared demeanor of tribulation and bewilderment; I thought about the son and was saddened by all that familiarity, which had been divested of its origin and purpose. What was I thinking as we approached one another and I tried not to look at her? I remembered the number of times M and I had walked down that street, on that very block and in that same direction, and lamented that chance had brought his mother and me together in that moment. Our paths crossed. She did not see me and I did not stop her, and we passed one another. To speak with her would not only have meant interrupting her distraction—her momentary unawareness of evil—and restoring the absent image of her son, but also drawing attention to a disruption imposed by circumstance; for these reasons, I did not.

Yet it is also true that it was a mistake not to face her. A mistake and, if it does not sound inappropriately elegant, a gaffe. It was to turn my back on M, who had brought about the encounter (I don't mean this only in a figurative sense). Mute, with his mother already behind me and probably on her way home, I immediately regretted what I had done—or, rather, what I had not done. So I ran, wanting to make it all the way around the block—Padilla, Gurruchaga, Camargo—and force a new encounter, which this time would be unequivocal. Despite the fact that it was planned, and something of a ruse, it was more real and natural this way. Distracted, I turned the last corner and saw her walking toward me, as I had moments earlier, watching me. Now she, too, was ready to acknowledge me. Sometimes we need to shield ourselves from spontaneity in order to endow our actions with a measure of truth. Never before that afternoon had I seen a face that showed so much, forgetting modesty, fear, and precaution. A face with nothing to hide and nothing to offer: that was the face of M's mother. Her eyes, fixed on mine, clouded over intermittently, giving her smile an air of melancholy. (We were standing face to face, waiting for who knows what.) All of a sudden, I realized that she was possessed by a deep conviction: that of having lost M forever. This idea, which at the time I myself did not dare to consider, surprised me. I admired this awareness, the certainty of it, because—though morbid—it followed the logic of a profound sense of peace. Yet, strangely, I was unmoved (I felt neither agitation nor grief). She was convinced of the fate of her son: this could be discerned in the veil of uncertainty, of vacillation, that shields people after a loss. Waves of stupefaction swelled from the cobblestones in the street and the trees along the sidewalk. M's mother seemed to be at once a child, an old lady, and unquestionably a grown woman. At last the tears came—this, too, was inevitable—and before saying goodbye she asked me and, through me, the others, to stop by and see them now and then. Again I found myself at a loss for words. I thought that she—to whom I could say nothing, knowing nothing, particularly about what was going on inside her—demonstrated a remarkable, substantial wisdom by asking that we visit her "now and then," mainly because she broke the silence from which I had been unable to free myself. As I clung to her shoulders, I understood that it was of secondary importance whether this wisdom was born from her experience, her intuition, or some other thing; what mattered was that it was wise. Some time passed this way, the street also in silence. Then we each continued on our way; some things, at least, had returned to normal. After a few steps it occurred to me to watch M's mother as she walked away. I imagined that her back could tell me something, who knows, that it might have something to add or a different way of communicating. But I stopped myself before turning; I had the feeling that I was about to ruin something, and that this something was not secondary, but rather meant a great deal. I was only a few meters from her, still within the danger zone that exists between people: R might be able to feel the weight of my gaze from behind her, and doubtless would have considered it crass that I would stop to look at her. She had inspired me to run around the block, that much was clear, and it was she who had rescued me from silence as we embraced. If it had not been for M's mother, I thought as I walked away, we would have remained joined, fossilized there on the sidewalk like one of those statues that commemorate a foundational moment.

Their first conversation took place one afternoon a few days after they met, when the other asked him about the soccer field a few blocks from his house. "What field?" responded M; he was either distracted or had forgotten. The other had to clarify: "Club Atlanta's stadium, it's famous." He wanted to know whether, given how close it was to his house, he could hear the goals, the chanting of the fans, or even the announcer. M said, with affected confidence, that he could; too emphatically to conceal a swell of pride. The other vacillated, saying that he had thought it would depend on the direction of the wind. Even if he lived nearby, he might not be close enough to hear everything. M conceded that of course he couldn't hear everything, that wasn't what the other had asked, but he did live close enough to the field to hear the goals and the chanting, regardless of the wind. When it blew toward his house he heard better and when it blew the other way, not as well, but he could always hear it. In any case, he continued, you couldn't say that he didn't live close enough: "My house is five blocks from the stadium if you follow the streets, but only two hundred meters if you follow the tracks," he explained. The train was the clearest indication of proximity, perhaps even of contiguity, but at the same time, on match days the train's whistle made it hard to hear the sounds of the stadium and so, he acknowledged, sometimes the distance wasn't ideal. The other listened silently. The truth is, continued M as he walked, that even if they are playing an important game on a Sunday, it can be hard to hear anything if it's really windy. Of course, this has nothing to do with the distance; everyone knows that it is impossible to hear in strong wind unless you are very close, even right alongside.

When the match is over, M continued, the fans disperse right away along the surrounding streets. If you're still in the stands you don't notice this: the wait to leave the stadium seems endless. But, at the same time, a crowd has suddenly filled the street. This diffusion is similar to the way the chants, shouts, and noises of the multitude spread through the air, only slower, almost as if each of the spectators were going off in search of the final destination of his own voice. And so they set off on their separate ways. Even the tracks filled with people, the fans covering the whole embankment, walking as a single turbulent mass, surging like a scene from a proletarian epic. So, whether far away or nearby, I live in the stadium's zone of influence, which means hearing what can be heard. M wanted to end the conversation there, but there was still something the other wanted to know. It seemed that M understood this; before the other had a chance to ask him anything, he conceded that, despite its size, the shadow it cast, and the matches that were played within it, the field was not really the center of anything. The noise that swells up from the grounds and the silence—despite the match—beneath which everything seems submerged and that allows no indication from inside to pass, demonstrate the ambiguity of the gaping space, at once receptive and manifest, that is the stadium. The funereal silences that fill the air when the stands suddenly fall quiet imbues its rudimentary architecture with a sense of absence proportional, though inversely, to its size. At first one thinks about it and says, for example, *Well of course the stadium is the center of the neighborhood, the place that gives life to its surroundings, the building that gives the neighborhood its character,* and things like that, referring to the green patch of turf toward which all the surrounding streets and sidewalks seem to be oriented. But the opposite is actually true—the crust of the field is precisely that: an empty space erected on an arbitrary site.

They walked on. Game days, M continued, are saturated by an incongruous mood and sense of time. One hears the noises and is able to identify each one: the cries of joy and indignation, the encouraging cheers, even the gasps—sudden and unanimous—of disappointment or relief at a missed goal; you can hear the din but it is obvious that something fundamental is missing, something overlooked that could explain the cause of the noise and restore its meaning, like gazing out over a landscape in which a light shines so brightly from one point on the horizon that we are not able to see or understand the scene as a whole. Sometimes, the other heard him say, *I'll be sitting at my front door and the fact that I am able to hear the fans seems unjustified; not unreal, but inappropriate, excessive for mere noise: the effect arbitrarily conjoins a single yet disparate, diverse, and even unconnected geography; a strategy of events meant to indicate that, as I sit on my front step, I am connected to something that is happening two hundred meters away. "Space abolished by noise," he concluded, struggling to wrap his left arm around a mass of folders and books held together by elastic bands. A few blocks later, at the corner of calle Sarmiento, each went off his own way.*

Years later that same place, a mixture of neighborhood and suburb, a few blocks crossed by tracks, fatigued by trucks, saturated with stores, family shops, and modest homes joined together in clusters; that same place would contain M's sudden absence as it had once contained his body, as contradictory as this might sound. What had been present until that moment was now gone. M wasn't taken from his home; they took him from a friend's house. It could have been mine or anyone else's, but that day it was his. This element of chance would color his disappearance with a sense of gratuitousness, which in a way undermined the dramatic quality of the circumstances. Many would say that the abduction of a political militant was unjustified but that causality, however cruel and murderous, was still at work. What happened to M, on the other hand, had been pure chance: an unlucky presence that had allowed happenstance to restore death to its final and inalienable place. The combination of political innocence and the coercive force of fate endowed M's disappearance with a sense of error or the failure of destiny, making his innocence seem to reflect back on his abductors, who one could, hypothetically, imagine blaming chance for putting M in their path.

The abduction was followed by a drama that was at once silent, private, and confidential. M's parents, unable to take even the slightest initiative to search for their son or to find out what happened to him, were left in a stupor. Eaten away by passivity, in the end they obeyed their fear, the conviction that it might be possible to save the rest of the family if they did nothing. To this day I am astonished not to have found M's name written anywhere; not in the lists made by organizations or in the press. I say to this day because right after the abduction I, like many others, threw myself into reading legal appeals, denouncements, documents, the testimony of the victims, et cetera. This lasted for years; after that, I simply waited for him to appear in some list or press announcement. I now find myself feeling a combination of fear and adoration: the effect turned back into the cause, M's name was set apart by silence and in this way was able to return to the state of pure incantation in which all names float until we claim them through use, assigning them to an individual. As is well known, it is a fine line that separates this from sorcery.

I am unable to break this pact between absence and reality, made with no one and among all, into which ambiguous words like memory, oblivion, name, and individual insert themselves, as though only half of M had lived on in me. The names of many of the victims are unknown; still, for those of us who knew him, his absence from the lists suggests an emptiness that calls into question his very existence. It is not as though seeing him in some index were necessary to confirm his time on earth, but it would have increased the density of his memory; no one has written his name or read it since. And there you have the anomaly, since this tends to happen with people who have been dead a long time, not with *recent* deaths. Around the time of that first conversation about Club Atlanta's stadium, about noise and distance, I remember the realm of ambiguity a student would enter if he were not included in the class list. Seeing your name there was not only a confirmation of registration, but a magnification of existence: it meant being something more or, occasionally, something different. The anxiety that would set in on those who did not appear on the list was the most convincing evidence of the hypothetical nature of their person. They had to make inquiries, change rooms, come back with signed papers. They passed into a limbo from which they could only be rescued, once they got their papers in order, by their appearance on the list.

It is also true that while many of us may have felt powerless or indignant at his omission from the lists of the abducted (first his body disappeared, then his name), his parents may have seen this absence as natural or even necessary. After all, it was clear how little could be done about it. The accusations, investigations, and protests contributed to the collective reaction through which the victims were reborn and claimed their right to have gone on living. They also allowed the people to touch the horrific medium into which they had sunk. In the meantime, most Argentines, thrilled with questionable accomplishments like the 1978 World Cup and the 1982 war in the Falkland Islands, noticed too late that the flood of kidnappings, torture, and murder had unequivocally renewed its campaign against frivolity and barbarity; in the face of this, they chose to forget.

It is natural that, when confronted with this panorama, the complexity and meaning of which were beyond the average family, so many would choose resignation. M's parents did the same; on one hand because death was natural to them and, on the other, because their meager resources and particular lack of aptitude and personal connections left them not only without tools, but also without the reflexes to deal with the hardship that had been imposed upon them.

What is more, at the time, political violence and death hovered in the air; they were recognized as an everyday occurrence toward which many or few could feel aversion or horror—this did little to reduce its power; in fact, it had the opposite effect, preserving it as part of the normal order of things. This acceptance could have been a result of detachment, consent, or debasement, but either way it meant that death had proliferated through its use; a use that was sanctioned by endowing politics with a functional dimension, turning its morals back into action.

There is the incident that took place a few months after M was abducted. I was about to cross one of the typical, cramped avenues of Greater Buenos Aires, which were roads in the days before the area was populated and only later, with the spread of urbanization, ended up as very narrow avenues. There was no curb; the simulacrum of a sidewalk angled slightly toward the pavement, creating a formless space in which a bit of earth ate away at a fine layer of asphalt. The cars kept coming; I was waiting to let them pass before I crossed, when a hand holding a cigarette emerged from a car window, trying to burn me. I did not jump back, but managed to lean away and watched the bandaged hand, still holding the cigarette, return to the car a few meters down the road. There was a military base a few blocks from there; it was clear, despite its lack of markings, that the car belonged to the so-called security forces. I was not afraid, nor was I angry; again, typically, I felt nothing. Nonetheless, I saw how the coincidence of my crossing as they passed created, momentarily, the setting of a game, of order, organized with ease and pleasure to which the rest of us submitted with a certain natural acquiescence, at the dramatic and even more organized core of which M had met his end. That hand was accustomed to burning, and it found diverse, even incidental, opportunities to exercise the habit. Afterward, I crossed, but I did not forget what had happened. Once more it had become clear that chance is a condition of tragedy.

The relationship between M and the other was based on a mutual—though not always shared—time, within which certain topics, interspersed with actions and events, were advanced through both conversation and silence. As I have written, the railroad was discussed throughout their friendship, but there were other recurrent topics that became more central over time, signs of harmony or danger, the marks of a shared identity. One Saturday morning, as they were going to the house of a classmate, M and the other saw a group of Orthodox Jews; all were male, men and boys, and they walked without any particular hurry. M said, pointing, that they were genuine, real Jews. "They're authentic," he murmured. "Who?" asked the other. "Them, the Orthodox Jews. Don't you think they're more authentic?" M replied. "Why would they be more authentic than us?" retorted the other. He made a gesture to signal his reproach; he felt slighted at his exclusion from a group to which he had been certain he belonged. "I don't mean that they are more Jewish," M continued; only that their condition has retained qualities that speak of a truth and not only of constraint, as in our case. Our nature is marked by loss, by absence; what is left of an abundance that is slowly becoming more remote and somehow exotic: the Yiddish language, the religious holidays, the dances, the food. They, on the other hand, signal a confirmation, affirm a continuity with every step; they operate in time, within the diffuse time in which sons are, in the future, mistaken for their fathers like a convergence of the self, a self-fulfilling prophecy. Their lives find meaning in repetition, turning it into constancy. "But," the other said, "what does repetition have to do with authenticity? It's true that repetition ends up becoming authentic, but that's not just a matter of repetition. On the other hand, how can you turn authenticity into a collective category? Yes, an observant Jew has an image that is easier to assimilate to Judaism than one who is not religious. One aspect of this is appearance (we are talking about them now because we were able to recognize them); no one would recognize us, though in some cases, like yours, certain features do help," the other asserted, avenging himself for M's earlier exclusion. "Every trait, whether visible or spiritual, shows its condition; a condition that is not necessarily religious," he continued. "The truth is, one could say someone is—for example—a gaucho, when he lives the life of a gaucho; when his experience aligns with the model, generally speaking. Still, it is possible to say that the further he gets from that model the less of a gaucho he is, and just as there may be a moment in which he is no longer a gaucho, there may be a moment in which one is no longer a Jew or an Indian or a homosexual. One simply isn't, or one is in a complete and absolute way one moment, only to find that one isn't, the next. There are also moments in which one is so little, when one is at the mercy of the slight pulse that keeps our hearts beating. Perhaps, then, Jews have a more flexible threshold of identity; more accommodating in one sense, but more implacable in another, since someone might no longer belong to a congregation, without knowing it, or the congregation might include someone among its ranks who sees himself as an outsider." "I hadn't thought of all that," answered M, emphasizing the all, "but it doesn't seem like you disagree." At that moment the other got distracted: the bus lurched forward and the sidewalks, filled with pedestrians, slipped into the distance with the sole objective of avoiding scrutiny; he saw vague colors and reflections, neither whole nor essential; the side streets opened up to him only to close in on themselves like dark little wells. After a while M, noticing the silence, asked, "What were you be thinking about?" "When?" the other wanted to know. "Now," said M, "what do you mean, when?" "What should

35

I be thinking about? Nothing," he answered. "The street." So M told a story that the appearance of the authentic Jews had helped him remember. It was an adventure plagued by imprecision, like all fables; or rather, it was a collection of precise imprecisions. This fairy-tale quality extended further still: M did not know how he came to know the story, which seemed not to have an author. At some point he heard it for the first time, yet he already knew all its principal details—just as he already knew its outrageous conclusion.

THE FIRST STORY TOLD BY M

Two boys, classmates, decide one afternoon to play a trick on their parents: upon leaving school each would take the road to the other's house, go in, and greet everyone as though it were their own. They finalized the details as they left the building and, anticipating the illusion they had dreamt up, both laughed happily as they traded names: Sergio called Miguel *Sergio*, Miguel called Sergio *Miguel*. Until they arrived, neither wanted to give up their role; the routine of the journey home, coupled with the novelty of the route and particularly the new identity, intensified both impressions and thoughts. It was a kind of emotional tourism; similar to, though the opposite of, the way children imagine their own death and actually feel afflicted. They got their first surprise when the mothers welcomed them naturally, as though they really were their sons and had been at school since the morning. The second setback was encountering the same attitude in the fathers when they got home from work later on. In the meantime, everything seemed at once strange and familiar because, even though they had been over innumerable times before—their parents were also friends—they realized that they knew nothing beyond the superficial. One generally associates the unknown with terror, especially during childhood: silence, darkness, or being around strangers produces a singular sense of anxiety that is immediately dissipated by turning on a light, hearing familiar sounds, seeing familiar faces. This was something similar, though not exactly the same, given that experiencing the extraordinary in the company of people close to them—and the fact that those very people would be the primary actors in the nightmare—allowed them to deliberately immerse themselves in confusion and represented a kind of ironic terror. Both boys spoke little while they ate, but the parents did not stop talking; they even seemed more talkative than normal—though, of course, they were comparing these parents with their real ones. The boys were asked the usual questions about their time at school, their assignments, and the material they might have learned, then they all talked about their days: work, acquaintances, the neighborhood, politics, whatever came to mind, until the conversation turned to the coming weekend and the many choices of things to do, as they said. In one case, they were leaning toward the rose gardens in Palermo, and in the other, toward La Boca and the Costanera Sur preserve. Miguel and Sergio realized the persuasive power their words had over the other, as well as the influence of their real parents over the other ones, since those had been their own excursions the week before. Now they were faced with the prospect of repeating them, after having spoken enthusiastically about the activities of the other.

Later that night, in the solitude of the other's room, each grew more uneasy with every passing hour; they felt the unchecked growth of something that, despite their having initiated it, was strange to them. They could make no sense of it. Just a few hours earlier they had still been themselves, but now a simple, innocent event threatened to become the soft crackling that announces the onset of an avalanche. Due to the strange nature of catastrophes, they, who had pushed the stone and had been full of delighted anticipation at the prospect of watching the complex effects of their joke from the side of the cliff, suddenly understood that not only would the avalanche exceed their plans and permanently distort the landscape, but that they would be buried *up there*, on the mountain, contrary to the laws of physics. But these fears seemed premature and too bleak to keep worrying about, and the next morning they awoke with a new hypothesis: they decided that they were being taught a lesson, that it was a tacit form of punishment. Nonetheless, they would have been closer to the truth if they had stayed with the theory about the avalanche, as they would discover later when fate stepped in to prove it.

Meanwhile, the thought of punishment or lessons did not even occur to their parents, who were even more lost within their naivety than their sons: they simply did not notice the change. The anguish of that first night, born of the certainty that only terror can produce, brought Miguel and Sergio close to the truth, though it also made them retreat from it in favor of a more comfortable—albeit false—theory: that of punishment. And so, as tends to be the case, the more exhilarating the start—that unfortunate act of trading names—the closer they would get to the truth, from which they would in turn distance themselves the further they got from that inaugural rite. Meanwhile, the following night would be torturous for both of them. They missed their parents. They wanted to sit on the floor of their houses and never get up again, to breathe in the natural scent of home. Dinner on the third day found them quiet and depressed; not sullen—they lacked the confidence to be rude; at the end of the day, they saw themselves as guests—but solemn.

The next day, in school, each saw his own desperation reflected in the face of the other. They thought they were dreaming, but their reciprocal experiences confirmed the simple, very real nature of what was happening. During recess they went over a number of strategies; by the time they said their goodbyes in the street, they had already decided to do something drastic in the hope of bringing things back to normal: they were going to admit to the prank. If the adults wanted their humiliation, they would have it. That afternoon they could hardly sit still. They had decided to broach the topic that night, so that was what they did. Decisive moments tended to come at night, during dinner: this was yet another of these important changes. They talked, confessed, admitted; they even considered an appropriate punishment for the offense. But nothing happened. There was no reaction at all. The parents looked at them in wonder, taking in what they thought to be a completely imagined account, an almost mystical illusion too fantastic to be taken seriously and too unbelievable to be understood. Miguel and Sergio insisted, swearing that they were not themselves, but the other, and that the people they were talking to were not their parents, but their friend's. One pair or the other, when confronted with these flights of fancy, laughed in their faces; as mentioned, the couples were joined by a close friendship and felt flattered by the amusing fantasy of the little ones, which in some way held them as equals in their affections. But the boys insisted and, as might have been expected, the night ended badly: they cried, they begged, and fixated on the idea of going home to their real parents, until one set of parents or the other ended up dragging them to their beds, where they nearly needed to be restrained as a result of their intense nervous state. The fifth day was nostalgia and despair: they just couldn't understand it. The future seemed uncertain and they asked each other about their parents, the smells of the house, the floors, meaningless details, and about the boxes in which they hid prized objects, amulets, and talismans. The sixth day brought envy: the beauty and intelligence of the mothers was directed at the wrong person, just like the strength and the sympathy of the fathers.

From that time on, whenever the families would visit one another, Miguel and Sergio would feel joined again in brotherhood, although every time it was their despair that brought them together. They saw themselves as victims of a cruel conspiracy that, if not the product of nature, was all the more cruel for being their parents' idea. It goes without saying that the moment arrived when their names seemed unreal to them, both the previous (Miguel and Sergio) and current ones (Sergio and Miguel). When they heard them, they saw only an equivocal extension of the other and not of themselves. But the problem was also that the extension was evident; the evidence was right there in the names. At the same time, the friendship between their parents revealed its own ambiguities: for example, Miguel and Sergio were able to see, one night when the two families got together, how the ex-father of the first—making an elaborate effort to conceal the gesture, which only highlighted the transgression—grabbed the waist of the boy's current mother as he asked her to let him pass, despite the fact that he had the whole width of the house at his disposal. After a few bottles of wine the conversation turned to the mysteries of romantic affinities and how, when they fizzle out, they tend to redirect themselves toward a person of the same social circle as a means of staying faithful, if only to some basic and primordial sense of community without which we all would feel lost, orphaned in the void. They were, evidently, talking about themselves and their own crossed desires, which had been aroused by the alcohol: as though they belonged to a shared but unknown past, they longed for a galaxy in which those affinities could be realized. It was then that the four, without the prompting of anything concrete, looked over at their children, who were watching them in silence. In this way, Miguel and Sergio sensed, without fully comprehending, that they were the manifestations of their parents' desire. Not so much as people, bodies—that seemed obvious—but as subjects whose identity constituted a relative and unverifiable gift, conferred or withdrawn according to circumstance or the emotional state of the adults. The friendship that once could have joined them had been eclipsed by domestic ambiguity; at the same time, this confusion would seem redundant to anyone who understood that it was simply a friendship.

One might say that time passed and the friends grew up, but even something as straightforward as that would be complicated by the circumstances: time did not pass and they did not grow up, in the true sense of the word, despite the fact that the years advanced and before they knew it they were adults. The misunderstanding they created had opened the gates to a darker nature, with its own rules and conditions (just as natural as any others, but different). This fact, their being at the mercy of something and knowing what it meant but not what it was or how it worked, led them to wander around in a state of absolute confusion, impervious, despite their physical maturity, to events and experiences. One was the origin of the other, the source of his identity and the proof of a deviation. They were sensible enough to admit how deeply they relied on their mutual friendship and did all they could to maintain it, but were slow to notice the mystery that, though created by them, existed independent of their feelings, their will, and their intelligence, and threatened to make them indistinguishable from one another. They were tired of being themselves, but also of being each other.

Identity—which, as they both knew, was one of the most difficult things to discover, obey, preserve, and understand—pulsed erratically within them, moving from one body to the other, shuffled in among names, memories, and beliefs: a commingling only heightened by the friendship. They were equivalents. *Sergio*, for example, meant one and the other at the same time; so did *Miguel*. Experience was shared. The four parents, relegated to a diabolical world by the adult memories of their children, became increasingly diffuse, distant, and imprecise figures. Had they existed? On the other hand, both—each imperceptibly puritanical—had their own theories and conclusions about certain memories of family get-togethers.

They looked back over the past and found only one essential moment. By baptizing themselves in jest, by exclaiming in the sharp and unwitting voice of a child, *Ciao, Sergio* and *Ciao, Miguel* as they left the schoolhouse, a ritual whose outcome their immature minds were unable to grasp, Miguel and Sergio did nothing less than create themselves. Everything that followed would be secondary to this. Yesterday, when everything was positive, black and white, didn't matter; what mattered was today, the invisible present in which differences were erased and everything seemed unreal. Like those charmed lives which were able to mitigate failures and thereby free themselves from a precipitous downfall, Miguel and Sergio held on to the hope of restoring the plenitude they had lost in the prehistory of their youth. But they were unable to resist the slow collapse—the true operation of time—that added a sense of ambiguity to their mutual indistinguishability.

In the end they took to walking. They would choose a street and follow it from one end to the other, navigating changes in its name, and even changes to the street (if the one they had chosen came to an end, they would follow the nearest one that ran in the same direction). To return, they would cross the street and follow the same route all the way back. Seeing them together one would almost think they were siblings, yet something did not quite fit. In their movements, in the distance they kept between themselves, and in the monosyllables they used to communicate, one could sense an unfulfilled promise; a promise that sustained them, yet did not unite them completely. As though they were indeed siblings, but were brother and sister. That was their problem: a slight but radical difference. What could they do now to regain their autonomy? The streets offered no solution: it was only the truly desperate, those given over to the mercy of God, who searched for answers in the streets. Still, they had no choice. The solution was neither in their homes nor inside them, nor could it be found in the past; in fact, that was where the drama began.

Sad, bewildered, and powerless against their luck, as they walked along avenida Garay one day waiting for the afternoon to end, they would come across a beggar resting against a wall that surrounded a municipal building. From far away he looked like a bundle of clothes; drawing nearer, he appeared to be asleep. It was only from within a few meters that his alert stillness became visible. Before, in the past, the human form used to be more clearly defined, thought Miguel and Sergio; heaps like that were never thought to be anything but people, due in part to the fact that one didn't tend to find bundles of clothing or fabric left out in the street. (The mass of cloth only appeared to be defenseless, within it breathed a life on guard within its nest.) It was an old man with pale skin and thick eyebrows, into the shadow of which his eyes, gazing out as though from the greatest depths, seemed to recede. Miguel and Sergio froze at the sight of his face, which was veiled by short, sparse stubble discolored by tiny flecks of silver that caught the light. One of them realized that he was not asleep and immediately thought that it was not only poverty or indigence that had put the old man in their path. This old man was one of those whose age is concentrated in their eyes, suggesting a wisdom that transcends experience. He might have had poor vision; perhaps this was the reason for the intensity of his gaze, but the eyes themselves were enough: they would have been wise at any time or in any circumstance. He looked at them, they stopped. A casual remark about a distant street and a bitter one about the state of his back did the rest; they served as a pretext to start a conversation with Miguel and Sergio who, as tends to happen, found themselves under his spell before they knew it.

They found that the words of the old man transcended their literal meaning. Colors, for example, became sharper when he spoke of them; they took on a shine that was able to stand out through the quality of his speech. At one point Miguel and Sergio felt the same shudder run through them both: it occurred to them that perhaps this old man could help them. And as though the air were condensing in an unusual way—unusual for the climate and circumstance, somewhat theatrical—they noticed a rough incandescence surrounding his shadowy figure (the nimbus of intelligence). And so they started to recount their whole misadventure from the beginning. The old man kept silent as he listened. Voices, saying more or less incomprehensible things, could occasionally be heard from the other side of the wall. When someone spoke really loudly, Miguel and Sergio would stop talking and look up to see that the wall was only a bit taller than they were, and that there was probably an expanse on the other side, an enclosed area, perhaps a garden, where the voices and the people to whom they belonged could walk around. Seen from the street, Miguel and Sergio probably seemed to be talking to a pile of clothes; whoever came a bit closer would think that they were conversing with someone who was asleep. They alone could see the attention with which the old man listened to them, deaf to all other voices and sounds. They went on like that for a long time. The encounter took on such meaning for them that Miguel and Sergio forgot that it might only be a coincidence; they imagined that someone or something—even they themselves, though they found it hard to believe—had guided their steps toward that place. When they finished their story, they waited for the old man's verdict. The noise of the street returned, distant but vital. While the man reflected, they gave themselves over to the gradual diffusion of their surroundings: the plastic bags and bits of cloth, the dirty wall on which he leaned, the municipal building and its complex, the dilapidated neighborhood and the city as a whole, with all its flattened expanses, were held in suspense. But it was not that the scene was actually dissolving; it simply was not of interest. What mattered was the two of them, after so many years, finally being understood for the very first time. Perhaps the old man had the answer. After talking for a long time, mostly about a few strange moral episodes that he had experienced in own life, he made his decree: "Go to the river. If one of you catches something, come back right away, but if three hours go by without a bite, you won't have anything to worry about anymore." Miguel and Sergio looked at each other. They were disappointed by the enigmatic nature of the task; having expected a solution, even if only a bit of advice, they found themselves confronted with an order. They gathered from the words of their maestro that it would be preferable not to catch anything, so they chose to go at night, when they thought there would be less chance of landing a fish.

They arrived after midnight. The wind was blowing from the east, off the banks of the river, making the darkness even more still.

Impassive, they supported the weight of their bodies on the rails of the jetty charged with protecting them from the abyss. Anyone would have realized that they were not fishermen and that, if they were fishing, they were doing so against their will. Gradually, they grew bored, observed the serenity of the air, the water lapping an unknown distance below, the unmatched depth of the darkness. A life of indeterminacy had emptied them of all interests, nothing really mattered; it had been a long time since the future held any tension for them. Five minutes were the same as two weeks, and two weeks the same as three years. But it was also true, as they had proven, that an essential element of friendship was tedium: knowing how to share it and how to tolerate it. This brought them back to the original problem, their mutual indistinguishability. And so, as they ruminated, they allowed themselves to be distracted by the lights they saw nearby: the wavering lanterns of the fishermen, and the ones further off that belonged to the ships.

At one point, an unexpected movement jerked Sergio's line. He froze, unable to react. The silence and the darkness would have kept the secret, but the pressure on his finger would not allow him to ignore the situation. After a while he exhaled and said, shakily, "I think something bit." "What do you mean, something?" Miguel asked, unsettled. "How should I know? Something, I don't know." "What is it doing?" "What is what doing?" "It, the thing you caught," said Miguel, "it must be doing something." "Nothing" replied Sergio, "it's tugging." They started to reel the line in slowly, hoping that their prey would break free; so slowly it did not seem like they were bringing anything in at all. The fish could have grown old and Sergio, in his anguish, would have offered it some of his own time—entire years, if it would have made a difference—for it not to appear. These lines seem short, he thought.

They were both nervous; a profound shock heaved them out of the dark night they knew and into a darker one they did not. Miguel prayed that he would not have to take Sergio's place although, in reality, it was actually Miguel who was reeling in and Sergio who was grateful he had not had a bite. They finally saw, tangled in the line, a rain boot. It was hard not to be disappointed by the climax. Having expected, though it would have complicated matters, a real fish, a real body thrashing about in a fight for its life, the river answered their hopes with a rubber boot filled with mud. They immediately began to analyze the nature of their trophy; while on one hand it could hardly be considered the spoils of fishing, it had, on the other hand, obviously come from the river. Fear, and the desire be free of their problems, as the maestro had predicted they would be if they failed to catch anything in three hours, impelled them to continue fishing. That was their mistake: they stayed there with their poles at the ready until—once the three hours had come to an end—a storm surged up along the river. The wind blew with an extraordinary force and the water turned rough, threatening to topple the jetty. The waves seemed to be reaching out for something: they broke high and scattered like horizontal rain. Miguel and Sergio wanted to leave, to go back to that which could be called "the city" (so different, under the circumstances, from the place they found themselves, which could not be named). But going back was the last thing they could do; the darkness had closed in around them so completely that the rain, the wind, and the howling of the storm cut them off from any spatial referent. Even the location of the river: it could have been at their backs, alongside, or even in front of them. And so it was that the water took over everything; by now the river was flooding. The two obeyed their mandate: they did not move, staying with their equipment until the last moment, but at the height of the storm a wave dragged them down to the riverbed. And so it was that Sergio and Miguel met their anonymous end, absorbed by a confusion not unlike the one to which they had exposed themselves as children, and which had perhaps marked them for a long time before that. With the boot, the wise old man would have solved the mystery for them: the one who was able to put it on and walk in it would be Miguel, since he had lost it in a previous life and it had later been thrown into the river by an angel so that one fateful night, if he passed the test, he would be able to recover it. But since this required the trust of both—they were still indistinguishable from one another—and such a thing did not exist, the two ended up being punished by an undefined, though evidently quite effective, authority. This authority may have been religious, or it may have been nature in general, their own desperation, or anything, really; the problem, if there was one, resided in the fact that it was both superfluous and inevitable, just like the lives of our two heroes.

The other listened to M with particular attention throughout the story. From time to time the bus would slow down, until the driver noticed the delay and drove at full speed for a few blocks, only to slow down again later. When M finished, the other reflected on the obvious: that he could not find any connection between the story and the matter of more or less authentic Jews. It's strange that you don't see it, said M. It's not the story itself, but the insecurity about one's own nature, one's own identity. The Jews are like Sergio and Miguel, each believing he's the other, before or after, less or more than himself; they pass through life in this indecision, some with faith and others in puzzlement. When they take steps to discover the truth, everything becomes distorted. The universe that brought them to question their condition is disturbed and they remain adrift, somewhere in the expanse, while fear goes to work inside them. The Jews were never certain of their origins, which is why they found themselves surrounded by insecurity: both that of the world they believed they were observing and to which, despite everything, they were certain they belonged, and that of a more palpable and menacing sort, the kind represented by hostility.

The Orthodox Jews had passed and their long coats were probably already being illuminated by a different light, but they were nonetheless still among us, summoned by the narrative and the conversation. M could make any number of arguments, including contradictory ones, in favor of the authentic nature of religious Jews, but I sensed something in everything he said that exceeded the literal: a desire for the words to become something else, to reach another level, an auxiliary plane on which they did not need any proof to assert their truth. The subaltern and equivocal character of his language, paradoxically, turned the moment into an absolute truth. It may seem mysterious, but the excess borne by that which accompanies the voice is the substance to which images, commentaries, and influence yield. In this way, more than for what he actually said, M was credible because of these intimations, despite that fact that one—in this case, me—was only in a position to judge what was actually heard. *"It is the phrase,"* he would say to the other on more than one occasion when they returned to the subject, *"not the word, that establishes a prior truth"* (understanding a phrase to be the combination of things that accompany the word).

The religious Jews could have been anywhere at that moment, but there was no question that an imagined pattern connected their bodies with ours, which were now walking down the wide sidewalks of Villa Urquiza along calle Altolaguirre, as though we—them and us—were figures, entities that were equally vital to this constellation. And so, he continued, even within time we are joined with them in solidarity as we define space. The story of Miguel and Sergio was not enigmatic because of its ending, but rather because of the way in which it unfolded, which has no end. And because of the old man, who puts his wisdom into practice at the same time he renounces it through the use of magic. A boot is, after all, a boot, and very few would be able to assign special powers to it or introduce it to the realm of the enchanted; that it should fit Miguel's foot was not only a question of faith, it was also a matter of sacrificing the cause in order to give life to the effect.

TWO

The punishment obeyed the laws of oblivion. One would think that, had his powers been greater, the old man would have been able to avoid that particular outcome; but it is also true, as is often the case in these circumstances, that magic only exercises its power in a realm enriched by the upright conduct of man. This fact, which in most cases would have been an insurmountable obstacle, seemed like a secondary issue, a simple lapse, when it came to Miguel and Sergio. That they had decided to exchange identities did not matter; the real problem was that, by doing so, they would forget the essence of their own, their name. While they were not to blame for this error, they would suffer its consequences as though they had been. The parents, probably infected by the insightful fantasy of the children—and who watched, in the most uncomplicated way, the emergence of that which they themselves desired with such intensity and which they fought so hard, being adults, to define and overcome—seeing them come home one day transformed into the other, said "Why not?" to the inspired idea and, by doing so, condemned them both. Not even forgetting, in so many ways a necessity and even a virtue, could describe the circumstance, because it also meant uncertainty. So many things are called forgetting, and the confusion among these does not align with the concrete ambiguity of the problem. For a long time, Miguel and Sergio asked themselves if perhaps they were, in fact, brothers—the four adults got along so well that it was natural to consider themselves the offspring of the same community—but a shiver would run through them if they pursued these suspicions too far. Brother and friend have never been incompatible conditions, though in this case the nature of their friendship, so intimate and so problematic, clouded the idea of brotherhood with an inexplicable sense of incest. Meanwhile their parents drank wine at a rate of six bottles per night and squeezed each others' waists as they passed, thought Miguel and Sergio once they reached adulthood, remembering intermittent but recurring scenes from their childhood, when the atmosphere would become more relaxed before the two were sent to bed.

Perhaps the parents received their punishment through their children, whose role, in that case, would be unclear; more precisely, what would be unclear would be their autonomy or responsibility for their actions. "What actions? They barely did anything," I asked. M did not respond. He seemed to be lost in solitude; at that moment either he or I, but one of us, was invisible. It might also have been that the parents did not experience punishment at all, but rather the opposite: life as absolute paradise. In that case, the children would have been punished in place of their parents, but without knowing it. Maybe punishment, like forgetting, was the wrong word. Either way, however it is formulated, the debt is passed on to the children, M continued. Sometimes, without meaning to, the parents would torture them with their jokes, especially when they called them by the other's name, that is, their original one. For a moment, Miguel and Sergio would imagine that everything had been set right—after all, things always happened that way; everything can be restored or destroyed in one brief moment—but then they would catch the irony in their parents' gaze, a nuance in the tone of their voices, and would resign themselves once again to their permanent state of self-imposed error.

I asked him several times about the origins of the story; at first, M would answer evasively, then end up admitting what to him was just as obvious as it was enigmatic: that, as I have already written, he heard it once and felt absolutely sure that he already knew it. He knew all the details, even the most obscure: the ones that were, despite being problematic, impossible to forget or to set aside. And of course, he knew the ending. Yet each time he heard it, it seemed as though it were for the first time, or as though it prefigured a dream. On the other hand, if the story were interrupted he would sit there in suspense, unable to react, as though he suddenly found himself abandoned in an unfathomable landscape without any means of orientation. These conditions may seem contradictory, but in M they proved their correlation: the same spatial perception was at work. In this case it was simply directed at a story, which made it fluctuate between conjecture, confusion, and ignorance. His mind was organized according to recollections; there was an ideal state or territory to which he was certain he belonged and from which emerged the collection of impressions, and even experiences, that made their way to him.

This might lend existence an inexact and, above all, a symbolic quality—depending on the moment, the situation, and the need—but did not strip it of its ineffable reality. A balance like this hardly seems compatible with everyday life, but M maintained it, partially because his beliefs had always been hypothetical, stopping just on the verge of certainty. The absolute meant destruction: the absolute collapsed under its own weight. It was his deepest conviction that forests should never be too dense or plains entirely flat, that peaks could never be too steep or days utterly bright; nature always maintained an excess: nothing was completely anything, there was always something more that could be added. This was the circumstance, this absence, that kept dissolution at bay. For this reason, and much like the time he found an eye, he paid uneven attention to, and was perhaps even a little negligent of, the signs and symbols handed down to him by reality.

One Sunday morning, the embankment seemed like a surface expanding. (The embankment is bigger on Sunday mornings, M would repeat before describing his walks along the train tracks.) Perhaps the light, sharp under clear skies, was the cause of this amplitude. An invisible tunnel saturated with silence and transparency rose up from the sides of the embankment; it was an illusory radius, but it was almost palpable. M walked along the tracks, lengthening his steps, trying to make them match the railroad ties. He was focused on the shapes on the track—thin oil stains—and the industrious plants along the rails, and was halfway attentive to the murmurs emitted by his surroundings. The boredom that, according to him, had driven him from his house moments before had evolved into calmness, hope, but not eagerness. Four walls, he said, would have driven him crazy; on the other hand, the open countryside would have crushed him—too much space for just one person, as he used to say. What he meant was that the parallel glint of the rails, and the houses so low they seemed crushed against the ground, created an ideal frame for contemplation and thought. Generally, he did not stray far from his house, although he did not stay very close, either; sometimes, because of the curves, he was closer—along a straight line—than the distance created by the tracks.

That morning, the tall grass, bent slightly by the breeze and a bit more by its own weight, caught the light, and from time to time the late call of a rooster could be heard from some nearby property or another. "What a morning!" thought M. "Such a hypnotic intelligence to it." Clarity, air, silence; light. Walking along the tracks stimulates thought. I'm in my room and notice the time, I can hear the sounds of cleaning—my mother and the neighbors—I hear a television—nothing irritates me more than the sound of a television in the morning—and with all of Sunday ahead of me, I feel a sense of terror at the monotony to come: I am bored in advance. So I get up and go for a walk. One imagines that things reach a limit at the tracks, even go beyond it, particularly at night, but that all signs are erased by the morning. Everything that has occurred either belongs to the obscurity of oblivion or was once harmonious (but that never happens). Being young, M believed that at night evil—pure horror, according to his imagination—occupied space in such a way as to saturate it without leaving a trace; the disruption of the landscape was so great that not even the most patient efforts of man would be enough to restore it, and yet every day the morning set about its reconstruction and, in fact, did so without any help at all. Partial measures would have been no match for evil's absolute power of devastation. Terror nested there at night, but nonetheless during the day it inspired the calm confidence of a well-maintained park.

Dying cats and dogs come to the tracks, he continued, to lie down in the vegetation and wait; other times people bring them there, already lifeless. Dead bodies. Someone is walking along and he catches a scent, heavy and sweet, that quickly turns into the undeniable smell of decomposition. As he gets closer, discerning the body and being overtaken by its intolerable stench are one and the same thing. He needs to quicken his pace and get past the critical area, to cross through the field of odor and feel as though he's gone back to the beginning, the sweet air as an advance toward normalcy. A strange feeling because, even as he keeps moving forward, the return down the scale of odor makes it seem as though he were going back the way he came. But, as also happens with noise, the direction of the wind has an effect.

That morning there was no wind or any dead animals, or at least none that stank. At the most, a faint breeze rustled the vegetation. What a prodigious morning, what extraordinary light, he repeated. The thought that a train might approach seemed unrealistic, not because it was impossible—in fact, one must have been headed that way—but because the tumult of vibrations, noise, and air, the rupture, however fleeting, of the peace of that morning, would have seemed like something from another world. M paused to listen more closely and without realizing it looked up into the sky, as though he were expressing gratitude to a god, then back down at a jumble of weeds that looked as though they had been embedded in the soil by a giant fist. Curved against the blue sky, they wavered just slightly under their own weight, an effect distributed along the line. Further down, the wind could not so much as stir the leaves on the trees; any agitation, like that of the grass, should have shown its cause; otherwise, it would not have been perceived at all. Meanwhile, deafening noises emanated from the houses. On Sundays the neighborhood turned industrial; workshops became factories, there were storehouses where lathes and grinders, if not power saws and sanders, were kept running all day. Mechanics revved motors just to see what they could do. "Shut off" was not part of their vocabulary: the entire neighborhood seemed to have its generators going. You could even hear the sound of hammers on metal. The clamor of machinery was concentrated near the plateau of the tracks and spread upward from there. The silence was an illusion, but the noise, being so frenetic, also turned out to be illusory, like those Sunday afternoons when the stadium seemed to roar.

M, absorbed in his thoughts, might hear nothing for a long stretch, and then, out of nowhere, he would hear everything a few steps later—not just the sum of the noises, but each of them, at full volume. Always inclined to frustrate desires, the trains had refused to run for hours, he told me, perplexed. At the dead ends he stopped to look left and right at the other tunnels of shadow formed by the branches of the trees that met several meters above the street. The absence of trains amplified the brightness of the tracks to the point that it made them seem impractical: the train could be eliminated and the rails would go on gleaming for all time; two long, straight, silver lanterns, M added. It was this gleam and nothing else that made the trains run, but it also frightened them (another of his theories). "I went alone, the boys from the block didn't come with me" (I remember his voice, like that of an adult, and which I struggle to hold on to, saying that childish phrase I doubt belonged to him; nonetheless, he said it). He thought about the weight of the trains relative to the width of the tracks, about how strange it was that, on other vehicles, the widest were the most light. What I am trying to say with these examples is that M proceeded through the transparent dust of the tracks, lost in his thoughts but in some way already aware of what would soon catch his attention, when he stopped with the intuition of having seen something a few meters ahead, something he had not yet made out, but which would—once he had covered a considerable distance—come to the forefront of his perception. It was the eye. From that moment on, though he would not understand it, he would be at the mercy of the search.

The layer of dust left by the trains, the invisible shavings that come loose with the friction, the organic remnants the wind has torn from the trees; these were and are the only things on the tracks, and they're incapable of rousing anyone's interest. Nonetheless, M was interested. Very. His steps seemed to be driven by something outside himself, but it was actually something internal. The gravel, covered by a waxy grey that announced its own passivity, played a prominent role. Prominent and undeserved. M retraced his steps without knowing what he was looking for, leaning forward as though he had lost something. He couldn't help but feel ridiculous and embarrassed. Someone, hidden in the shadows of one of the many attic rooms around him, might have been laughing at his every move as he bent pathetically over a stretch of land that could never hold anything worth looking for. Ever since he was a child, he said, as though he were no longer one, he had known how to choose at first glance the perfect stone for whatever game he was going to play; this knowledge, like all others, is not easily lost. At most it is forgotten, but it is always recovered. Now, however, those same stones refused to take on any particular shape, or rather, they organized themselves according to an unexpected order, taking on a quality beyond any classification or meaning. He stumbled twice. There was no question that they were stones, but the fact that he did not know what he was looking at, or for, meant that they could have been anything at all while still remaining themselves. After a few meters it finally appeared, close to one of the rails and on top of a small mound: nestled alongside two pebbles as though it were a third, there was the eye, looking out toward the horizon.

M told this story one Monday morning before class, and I still have my doubts about it. At the time I didn't believe him—how could I? It was so strange: the absolute solitude, the radiant day, the discovery, which seemed so outlandish. Then I thought the opposite: Why not? I said to myself. What is the difference between an eye and a stone? (Discoveries of any kind are always somewhat exceptional.) Later it was the rest of it, everything surrounding the eye, that seemed unconvincing: finding an eye might not be that unusual, but filling the scene with a combination of primordial elements like the weather, the light, the noises, and the smells—all fairly vague and only halfway comprehensible—seemed a bit gratuitous and tenuous. The eye to which M wanted to call attention was invisible; it was hidden in a chasm of nature. For this reason, I didn't listen to him at the time; I thought about other things while M went over the minute details, for example, the morning light on translucent leaves, the struggle between the sun and the raised branches of the trees; this scene of harmony and natural tranquility seemed more unrealistic than the discovery itself. A scene that did not actually end up being harmonious because the machines thundered on continually, the distorted voices of the neighbors splintered the air, and the tumult of the clouds, their urgency, was palpable; three or four times during his walk, M watched the sky darken, the light fade, and a storm almost erupt. If all these things remained on the verge of happening, even those that would have been by all counts mutually exclusive, without any of them actually taking place, it was natural to think that the eye itself had a limited, if not shadowy, existence.

And yet that was not how it happened; the discovery was real. M was filled with panic, but he did not run. "I was scared," I remember him saying, "but I didn't run." An eye silently calls out for its complements: the lid, the lashes, eyebrows, even the rest of the face (a face, in turn, would demand a head, and the head a body, the body a life, et cetera; something is always missing, in that moment). The solitude of the solitary eye keeps it from being an eye in the broad sense of the word: it is a lost eye, which is a different thing. M did not know what to do. Somewhere nearby, perhaps no more than a few meters away, was an empty socket. Up close, it was bigger than he would have imagined; it blended with its surroundings, seemed like another stone. Its solitary nature was useful in this respect. M studied the eye until another burst of silence drew his attention away. "I couldn't hear a train, or any other noise, just like I couldn't feel my tongue resting in the space where my tooth used to be." The eye had him in its power, its sphere of influence extending for several meters in all directions, making no distinction between animals and minerals. M amused himself by imagining its perspective, which lacked a focal point; so much so that he got the idea of lying down and looking in the same direction: the rail, a steel fence, the ground, craggy with stones, and a sphere too high above him, the sky. Now, for example, if someone were to look over they would see M lying across the tracks, his face resting on the sharp pebbles, looking off to the side. He thinks about people who commit suicide: maybe the eye he is trying to imitate belonged to one of them. M remembers: He once saw a mother who was unable to commit suicide without her son. The child was trying to get away from her, but she held on to him, impatiently awaiting the arrival of the train. The two were behaving normally; they did not draw any attention. No one noticed them. Did the child know the mother's intentions? There is no way for M to know. They were seated on a bench in the station, wearing long coats that covered their bodies. It was winter, and although M has no memory of the cold, he can still see the swollen and flushed faces of mother and child, the watery eyes, the lips pressed tightly together. He also *sees* the breath that the mother expels from her nostrils; the child does not give any off. It is strange that, even when faced with the elemental state that is suicide, people tend to behave according to habit. There was nothing unusual about the scene of a fussy child, restless for whatever reason, and the mother forcing him to stay near to her. In those moments, according to M, the mother forgot about suicide. What mattered to her was not drawing any attention to herself; to her, composure was a gift, not just a behavior—it was a deep-seated value that opened the door to other virtues. Whether or not it came naturally was secondary, it was a gift that must have been ingrained, a deep conviction. M saw then that people's natural actions served as a pretense to conceal self-destruction. It is true that this is the definition of pretending, doing something without calling attention to it, but M was not sure that the mother was pretending at all: to her it was essential that the child behave himself. It was everyone else that was concealing something, the situation as a whole. The mother's efforts brought several jokes to mind: for example, the one about the prisoner condemned to death who, as he steps up to the gallows, turns down a final cigarette because they are bad for the health. Still, it is understandable that she would want to die in full possession of her convictions, not just her faculties. There was also a practical concern: the child could escape just as the train was coming, which would have meant waiting for another. But did the child know the mother's intentions? Could he sense the danger? M thinks not. Mother and child were unaware of each other, even though they were together; he was used to expecting the worst and she to giving it to him. The child's gestures were those someone would make around an unfamiliar person, a stranger, even. The mother bored him, so he grew restless. For her part, the mother was filled with two intermingling desires: not dying alone and not being accused of leaving the child to fend for himself. Abandoning the child meant recognizing that she could have chosen life; taking him with her affirmed her decision, made it unequivocal. She had little to think about, then, as these desires clearly indicated what should be done. Still, M kept returning to one thought: there was something so natural about the mother's impatience at the child's fussiness that it suspended the notion of death. M demonstrated this by turning it around, suggesting that the emotions were the individuals and the individuals the emotions. On one had, the desire for suicide: on the other, childish agitation. The first is the mother of the second. Suicide is ashamed of the effects of agitation; it does not show itself as it is because in those moments the desire for suicide forgets itself, becomes more concerned with not making a scene and shows a hidden sense of maternal propriety, wanting agitation to behave itself, not to be rude. If we believe this, that these two states have taken on form and that mother and child—two beings only half protected from the cold—are no more than the vague ideas known as Suicide and Agitation that inhabit bodies of flesh and bone, what name can we give the remains scattered on the tracks once the train had passed? What do you call the torn overcoat, the lone shoe with a foot still inside it, the crimson scarf? The desire for suicide cannot put on a jacket, nor can childhood agitation carry sweets in its pocket. Laid out across the tracks, M thought about that day when the whole station froze in an expression of horror as it watched the mother run, clutching on to the child.

M stood up and observed the eye from above. If it came from a suicide, it had not stopped pretending, he thought, except that now it had chosen to be a stone. He thought for a moment about his missing tooth. Only for a moment, but it was enough: he picked up his foot and brought down the heel of his shoe on the eye, as hard as he could. The rite had reached its apex; the sacrifice was complete. A white liquid splattered his other foot with such force that it seemed to come from something living. The delicate resistance of the eye was, for a few chaotic instants, a vivid and lasting memory; stepping on something rarely has such a contradictory effect. He observed the colloidal remains, which were just as disquieting as they had been a moment earlier, even though their origin was, by then, difficult to discern; a new, undefined state. He was afraid. "I must have been afraid, I don't know" he clarified; either way, he found it intolerable. The eye, that solitary presence, left the body that had served as its vessel and its protection exposed; far from establishing its autonomy, this produced only confusion. It was like the sudden jolt caused by the presence of an insect, only in this case it was not precipitous, but belated. With the eye smashed, a change had taken place. It was striking: though the morning was not yet over, M sensed the premature decline of the day; the light began to withdraw and shadows stretched languidly across the ground.

Later, he continued, it occurred to him that he should tell his friends, but there was nothing left to show them; he had destroyed the evidence. So he began to look for its mate: if he found one eye, he thought, he should be able to find the other. He inspected the stones again. The railroad ties, especially that day, were dead trees that could not exist in any form but as railroad ties. He looked up and saw the rails extending toward the center of the horizon, cutting the city in two. He could sense, to the right and the left of him, the world spreading out symmetrically on either side of the tracks, just as the Red Sea parted before Moses. "The planet divided by the San Martín line, who would have believed it?" he asked that frozen morning before heading into school, amusing himself with his witticism before the sun had yet warmed the space we occupied on the very planet he was talking about. "Why should anyone believe it?" I responded. "Believe what?" he asked. I looked at him without understanding. "What you're saying, that the tracks divide the planet." "No one has to believe it; they only have to understand it. You don't know why I said that?" he asked. "Since when do I ever know what you're trying to say?" I retorted. As an answer, he regarded me silently. Our conversations were occasionally that mangled.

M was lost in his thoughts about endless train tracks when he heard the whimper of a dog coming from the vegetation. The machines faded away; he forgot the impassive advance of the day, just as he had noticed it a moment earlier. It was not a pitiful howl like that of most dogs, but a feeble wail. Orienting himself by the sound, he advanced with caution. He saw a white head and a grey back in the tangle of vegetation; he went a little closer. The dog had its back to him. M had a sudden and devastating intuition: that was where the eye came from, he thought, that poor animal must have just lost it. To confirm this he would have to get it to turn around. He yelled, throwing stones at it, but in vain. The dog drew further into the vegetation, probably lamenting the bitter fate that had imposed the hostility of a child upon it. M was happy with the solution to the mystery. Finding the owner of the eye explained the discovery and therefore made it more real. But the irritation with which he had crushed the eye returned, only this time it was directed at the animal as a whole, as though there were an unfinished task he needed to complete. Meanwhile, the dog was moving away. "I could accept it if it runs away," said M, "but not if it ignored me." He quickened his pace and, when he got close enough, grabbed its tail and pulled, hard. This time the animal would react: it forgot the reason for its whimpers and let out a howl, forceful this time, as it turned its head to defend itself. Then M could see both eyes, which fixed on his for a moment.

He got out of there immediately; this time he was the one that fled. He climbed up toward the tracks as though he were returning to a brightly lit summit, to clear skies, from a place of nightmares and dreams. He didn't know which of the two things (the eye or the dog) affected him more, but he could not imagine what use knowing would be, anyway. Perhaps affected was not the right word. They were two mysteries from which he should have retreated, even as a means of solving them. But by acting he had revealed them and, in his weakness, had found himself. He did not know what to do: he had been walking for the past few hours to kill time, and now, in the middle of the day, he was overwhelmed once more by boredom. The secret of the bored is that things always begin over for them. The sun loomed above him once again, he asserted, unlike a few moments earlier—as though it ever could have done anything else. Again he walked along one of the rails, balancing without trying to do anything in particular. Bewildered and receptive, he went along like someone calling forth on his return the same path he had traveled on the way, remembering details as suggestions that could finally be confirmed. Yesterday morning, M commented, ideas, discoveries, and impressions had a knack for turning back on themselves. Interest turned into apathy, fear into recklessness, audacity into caution, enthusiasm into tedium, and plenitude into nothingness. The very geography of the tracks confirmed the disposition of the place (because the place did have a disposition, there was no question of that): the events of the night, described by the neighbors with shock and fascination, extended through the air like the rays of a fable until they were diluted by the even light of day; the noises, extraordinarily loud, ceased a few meters further, defeated by the silence. The intense vapors, an attribute of the area, dissipated in the neutral air (in the scent of the air itself). Yet at the same time, as anything could become its opposite, this combination of things hinted at a menacing atmosphere whose violence sometimes manifested itself without warning when, within this more or less menacing and more or less peaceful environment, the sound of an approaching train could be heard, that calamitous disruption that plunged oblivion and serenity into a convulsive state of disorder with its din and its vibrations.

"As soon as I left the tracks I wondered if the eye had been real." In the street, in the shade of the trees—M continued, using other words—I felt relieved that I had gotten out of the glaring sun. The eye seemed like something illusory, even false. The dog, too. Still, he had no reason to be surprised. "I had no reason to be surprised," he explained, being so used to hearing stories about mutilated bodies on the tracks. It was rare for a week to go by without something turning up, but now, as the protagonist of one of these discoveries, M simply could not believe it. Things were always being found—it could be a limb, part of a limb, organs, et cetera—but now that it was his turn, he simply could not believe it. Nonetheless, it would not have been an exaggeration for him to say that he had already forgotten it by the time he stepped into his house (insofar as exaggeration means little when it comes to forgetting, as is well known). As soon as he left the tracks and stepped back onto the sidewalk, he was beset by doubt (not the garden-variety doubt suggested by the word beset; it was a dynamic sort of doubt) as to whether the eye had existed or not. A neighbor was repairing his car, his head, arms, and torso hidden under the hood; before reaching him, M noticed the frenzy of hammering, which sounded as though he were trying to break it to pieces. It was not the first time he had seen someone destroy his car. Surprisingly, the further away he got, the more clearly he could hear the banging.

The tracks, the eye—none of it mattered to him anymore; he just wanted to return to the peace of his room. The memories, despite their immediacy, seemed unreliable; later they would be untrue. He did not know how to explain where he had been. He said, "I saw an eye, and then a dog, which I followed," and could not believe it; as a thought, it had an eloquent simplicity to it. Consequently, it was soon lost to him as a memory. It doesn't seem like you've forgotten it, given the way you just told the story, I reasoned. At this point M began a long explanation, a rationale of the varied, contradictory, and often tyrannical forms of forgetting, finally concluding, "I only remembered at night, when I told everyone about it and no one believed me; no one but Sito. For the rest of the afternoon, though, I didn't remember anything." Wasted Sundays, he declared; mornings lost in the sun and afternoons locked up inside. Just like at dawn, when everything enters my perception at once as I sit up— the creaking of the bed and the striated light in the doorway—noise and light enter without warning, as though they had been waiting outside the whole time, readying the machinery of oblivion.

The first time I went to his house, I noticed that his room matched the simple eccentricity of its owner. There was nothing particularly unusual about the correspondence—it was, after all, where he slept—but the truth was that, as I later observed, both room and inhabitant maintained an unawareness of one another, which is what allowed for their harmonious coexistence. M thought of his room as a private, even confidential, backdrop upon which his image could be reflected without the tiresome and obedient passivity of a mirror (and without its eloquence). In contrast, the room—in which there was neither a desk nor any sort of table, and which accommodated only a bed, two chairs, and a crooked wardrobe whose doors could only be opened by pushing up on one side—put up obstinate resistance, as compensation for its simplicity. As I mentioned before, the room was up high; accessible only by a narrow iron staircase. This was not particularly unusual, either. At the end of the day, an infinite number of houses had rooms built into their attics; the strange thing was that, instead of being above his own house, it was built above his neighbor's. You went up the stairs and the wall that originally divided the two served as a landing, which meant that by walking into M's room you were standing, irrefutably, on top of the house next door. This displacement was, I believe, the reason for the sense of resistance coming from the walls, from which an invisible and foreign substance seemed to flow. Although nothing looked out of the ordinary, you could always sense a presence not yet realized, as happens when we know the words that will be spoken to us before they are uttered. In this way, by passing through the door to his room I felt myself transported to a new expanse that was peaceful and yet enigmatic, foreign and welcoming. The most clearly discernible smells, for example, were those that came from the other house, and if a human presence could be felt nearby, it was usually that of the neighbors, not of M's family. In this way, the very idea of contiguity—as he would explain, in different words— was challenged, since the house next door was actually his own, and vice versa; the room belonged to the neighbor's house, though it was actually part of his own. You could still see the traces of a door that had been covered over, the frame of the original aperture half-hidden by plaster and paint, at the foot of which was a worn-down wooden sill that seemed unusual now, in front of a wall. Over on the other side of the wall, M explained, the first stairway—the original one—still led up to the door that had been sealed over.

His room offered other surprises, and not necessarily topological ones. I remember how, one morning when we had off from school, we were working on a project when my pencil fell from my hand, and, strangely, it rolled all the way across the floor. It is true that the room only appeared to be level; in any case, whether it had been caused by force or an incline, the accident resulted in a singular discovery. I crouched down to pick up the pencil and saw four or five plates and several sets of cutlery, all used, stacked precariously under the bed. He would forget to bring them down, and no one came up to collect them until their absence was noticed in the kitchen. I asked M about them, wanting to know what they were doing there. "What can I do? I forget to bring them down," he said, smiling. Today I would assign it another name but, at the time, this recklessness—though I would not quite call it recklessness, just as I did not then—was extraordinary to me. Later, as time passed, how often I would eat there and feel myself taken over by a sense of urgency and uncomplicated happiness at the possibility of being the first to put his plate under the bed and look up at the walls with an air of defiance (evidently this possibility was nothing special to M; it belonged to the inventory of actions he performed day after day).

In this way, M possessed a unique autonomy that allowed him to arrange his room as though it were a separate residence. The organization of the space was in his favor, in this regard. It is necessary to exercise autonomy in order to determine its limits: sometimes it proves illusory, sometimes too limited. We never encounter a sense of autonomy radical enough to separate us from the world, apart from death. Even the stars and celestial bodies we often discussed, trying to excuse our ignorance with our enthusiastic veneration, which seem to travel through space with liberated precision millions of kilometers from our precarious influence, are actually subject to a complex network of forces that is always at work upon them, such that their movements are easily anticipated. Consequently, doubt and disillusionment about autonomy are understandable. Instead of being one, his room—because of its two entryways, the first closed off and the other in use—was two at once. This was the value of the scene—so far from ornamental and yet, at the risk of being redundant, so scenic—which endowed it with a combination of real, concrete elements, so long as no one stepped beyond the limits of the room.

THE SECOND STORY TOLD BY M

In the end, the pair from Formosa endowed their memories with a greater freedom than the modest one offered, even involuntarily, by life itself. They had come to wear the label of drifters affixed to their bodies, a mark found nowhere yet which nonetheless spoke volumes; they were stigmatized and the people around them acted accordingly. Their transitory routine (walking, being rejected more or less explicitly, which in turn pushed them not to linger) proliferated, not so much in events as in reminiscences more painful than any actual episode. And this made them withdraw, impervious to their surroundings. We are used to thinking about individual memories, but fall silent in the face of shared ones. Thrown out of their home, they traveled the city without looking for a place to stay; they returned to the old custom that, as they understood it, belonged to the natural realm alone. The vague intuition that they were in the wrong place did not discourage them, nor did it prevent them from enjoying the simple, portable pleasure of memories.

A neurasthenic juxtaposition of cornices, innumerable focal points within fragmented space: that was Buenos Aires. And that wasn't the half of it: reliefs could be counted by the hundreds, planes, by the thousands. Just as when they had wandered through the provinces, and unlike their time spent in confinement, the streets, buildings, and spaces now amplified—in the sense that they multiplied—experience. Walking for half a day along an avenue might be more exhausting than, but was definitely equivalent to, spending a week anywhere in the countryside among the simple and isolated scenery of the interior. Yet they were not able to draw anything palpable from this urban plenitude, because it was deceptive: experience in the city might be more varied and abundant, but it was always less significant. There was no room for imagination (or the other way around: they could not find the imagination necessary for places that had already been defined and categorized). They did not find it necessary, as they had in the country, to compress either time or space: events unfolded at a normal rhythm, the time spent on a block blended with its length. Life in the city occurred on a grand scale ample enough to contain, without threat of disintegration, the geography in which events took place—streets and blocks—while dividing time to an extreme. They remembered their excitement at the promise of becoming someone else with each new town they visited, a desire to which they always surrendered; this memory consoled them when the fiction was interrupted by their arrival in Buenos Aires, where they were always the same. Marta,

Sela, Mirta, Lesa, or whoever she really was, could have existed under any other name, but to them—though she took on various forms and images—she was a unique symbol.

The story begins like this: Unsettled by the lack of activity in the furthest reaches of their native province, they were driven by a shared passion for itinerancy. Back issues of any magazine, any fuzzy photograph, could become a promise of the oft-postponed odyssey, especially when the stories were about exotic lands. The photos, better than nature itself, preserved their hope and aroused their desire. According to these, leaving the city meant finding oneself at the edge of a dense African jungle, a few meters from pyramids of yellow sand, or in the land of the kangaroo. Distance was not overcome but was, rather, ignored; the clearest examples of this were the reports from visiting travelers who arrived in the country as though they had simply made a little detour, were just passing by, as they say. In magazines of the region, Argentina, the continent, seemed the place prescribed for little detours, where anything that could happen would, and to which all visitors from the exterior arrived as a result of absentminded and persistent displacements. This fact, which might seem mundane, made both the visits and the desire to travel even more real.

In Formosa, as in the rest of the world, there was unanimous agreement on the benefits of settling down in one place; yet some are not satisfied by this coziness, and these two were among them. Their bodies occupied such a small space compared to the one promised by travel that, from the virtual epicenter they represented, nature could not help but be an expanse that offered no resistance. The moment arrived one morning after months of preparation that was more verbal than practical: feverish conversations that seemed to exhaust the very experiences they were hoping to have. One morning the cardinal points extended in subtle combinations to form a range of real possibilities, and they departed.

Formosa, a land without a sea, offered no obstacles to its crossing. They avoided unnecessary goodbyes and headed north, following the widespread belief that things would be closer at hand. In those days few things mitigated the hostility of the roads, one of these being that, because they were so bad, a day's travel was forcibly reduced. But since the two were not trying to get anywhere in particular, their days always lasted the same amount of time; weariness was their only limitation. Public transportation did not exist; every now and then a sympathetic truck would bring them a little closer. Under these conditions, hardship and danger were commonplace. When faced with adversity, they would look at one another and immediately recover the spark of that first day when they left the city, which they thought they could see in the eyes of the other like a faint line on the horizon, out beyond the suburbs. In this way, they overcame weakness. They rarely ran into other travelers, but if someone asked them where they were going, they would lift their eyes toward the clouds and sigh uncomprehendingly. Such an infinite range of possibilities rendered specific goals irrelevant—and also unnecessary. It seemed as though they had been driven mad by their pursuit. In reality, they desired neither to go anywhere nor simply to wander around. The journey, paradoxically, consisted of a sort of tranquility that sought to adapt itself, with the least amount of movement possible, to the gradual shifts in perspective of which walking was the principal effect. They were not proud, but they were envious of wealth; particularly the kind which, being poor, they associated with variations in the landscape.

Their first great disappointment took place in Paraguay, where they were disheartened by a panorama overwhelmingly similar to that of Formosa; if they distanced themselves from the memory of the days spent walking and resting, it was as though they had never left. The names of places, which—according to them—should identify particular and distinct environments whose variety would be grounded in difference, were simply denominations of the State. The identical was superimposed over the same; not only was the toponymy astonishingly consistent, it was so precise that it became useless: for example, a gully that had been baptized a gully. Yet nothing made any mention of the horizon. It was the State that baptized the horizon; along that line difference was neither recognized nor represented, the proof of which could be seen precisely in the similarity between Paraguay and Formosa, they complained, indignant. Though they had not set out in search of diversity, they were disappointed by similarity; it made sense that they would wait, expectantly, for the road to provide adventures previously unknown to them.

They had reached a turning point. Afraid that the similarity would only increase the further north they traveled, they decided to change directions and head south. But they had trouble at the border with Argentina; they simply were not allowed in. No one had slowed them down when they were leaving, but now that they wanted to return, they were bombarded with questions. They were taken for illegal immigrants, two of the many Paraguayans who turned up with the hope of living in a shack in Clorinda before moving on to legality or escape. Thus, once more because of the State, they realized that it was not only the landscape that was the same, but also the people. Their papers were examined in great detail in search of the error that would reveal the truth, the detail that would uncover the lie. Nowhere else had they been detained or asked their nationality, but they were immediately viewed as suspicious for wanting to enter the country, even though there is nothing less mysterious than the desire to return. Through this contradiction they came to understand the mistrust that surrounds travelers. Until that moment, rest and movement had been parallel conditions; something like mutual exclusivity confirmed the implication of one by the other. Now a separate conviction arose, an independent truth of which each felt himself the bearer: stillness and movement were the interchangeable poles of disorder and that everything—the static and the dynamic, the two of them, the people they would meet and the mirages that would catch their attention—would belong to a new kinetic category. Something like a state of perpetual creation in whose breast everything expanded and contracted without interruption, like a heartbeat. The immediate implications of this discovery were also the most profound: the journey as a progression, a collection of actions that seek to realize a goal, was invalidated, as was its opposite: the idea of the detour also became useless. The ideal, then, would be to proceed without pausing at the obvious and, rather than overcoming an obstacle, to ignore it. Though this belief could, in many cases, provoke a lasting feeling of anguish, in theirs it simply resulted in a sense of bewilderment.

They did not understand the weeks of waiting; every day under the merciless tropical sun with the other immigrants while someone—who knows who—carried on with the examination of their documents. They thought they were being detained not because of something related to them or to their condition, but because of a circumstance—singular, perhaps, but also certainly arbitrary—which, at the end of the day, was external to them: the fact that they had displaced themselves. In reality, they had not been detained for their nature, but rather for their condition. If you think the life of a lawman is hard, it's nothing compared to what they inflict upon the immigrants, they consoled themselves by whispering into the wire fence of the camp before the evening came to separate them. They watched a flock of parrots approach; as soon as they had passed, their low flight turned into a memory made of light—a few spots of green cut out from the sky—and the fading echo of their raucous calls. They longed for their past freedom, which they had seen as an inexhaustible resource, not realizing that it had actually run out too soon. It may have been brief, but it was of an immeasurable intensity.

After a few weeks they would learn the customs and limitations of Formosa's immigration policy. The camp, with its progressive stages of detention—indictment, confinement, freedom—and its rhythms adapted to the arrival of new immigrants, was nothing more than a simulacrum of control. There was no such thing as deportation. The inmates that had been there the longest, having passed through all the stages, were given priority to leave as more people came; in that moment, they were no longer illegal immigrants, but legal ones. The groups of Paraguayans were perfectly happy to accommodate this system, but to citizens of Formosa, like the two protagonists of this story, these machinations bordered on the absurd. After a while they made up their minds: nationality was of secondary importance—they would be Bolivians, Turks, or Paraguayans; they just wanted to get out of there. Their determination was so great that, even if they had needed to declare themselves citizens of Formosa, they would not have hesitated to tell the truth. From time to time a corporal would appear and comment jovially, anticipating some groveling plea for freedom, "Stop your complaining, we'll kick you out of here soon enough." He was like a ghost or an angel. These assurances could be repeated for months, but they always came true in the end. It actually did happen that way: one night they were given back their documents, and the next morning, along with hundreds of other prisoners, they saw the cloudless Formosa horizon stretch out before them like the promise of a journey. Without realizing that they had finally made it back to their native land, the vast expanse brought to mind the pictures of the Siberian steppe they had seen so often in their illustrated magazines, though they had to ignore the vegetation—now the silence of midday coincided strikingly with the awed silence that fell over them as they pored over the images. Everyone dispersed through the deserted streets of Clorinda, though only to pass through; soon there was nothing left of the group.

It happened just as it had on the way, only in reverse: once at the outskirts of town, they thought they were still in Paraguay. Just as nature showed wisdom in its diversity, it was also predictable in its similarity. They rejected the idea of passing through the city of Formosa; they hated the thought of anything that might delay them from getting back on their way. Without border controls, the land to the south seemed limitless; Paraguay represented a stage they had to pass through, while Argentina seemed to swell with opportunities for adventure. And so it was. Over kilometers and kilometers of open countryside, they honed their skills as itinerants. Apart from greater physical resilience and a sense of sight that grew sharper with the passage of time, the first virtue they acquired was that of forgetting the notion of speed and, along with it, any sense of hurry or delay. Just as it would be risky to say that a planet completed its orbit quickly or slowly, time no longer presented itself as a measure applicable to space; distance was anticipation, which, like existence, was pure duration. The momentary could last for days and the permanent, only seconds. Like events, which lacked any finality apart from unfolding and simply "occurring," the idea of velocity lost its meaning. Sometimes, excited by their new qualities, they would imagine themselves as a group (tribe, clan, family, or sect) that paid no mind to obstacles and for whom the essential thing was the direction in which they were headed, or perhaps the movement itself, but never a destination; the essential could never be a destination. A group that would build a barge rather than go around a lake that blocked their path, or which, if they came upon a mountain, would immediately begin digging a tunnel.

The second virtue they cultivated was frugality. There is nothing like a journey to foster ascetic tendencies; in their case, the privations of the impassive landscape forced them to subsist on a diet of bland, unvaried roots for days on end. Still, they did not suffer from these hardships; a balance existed between hunger and movement, under the force of which these two forms of abundance converged. This sustained them and cemented the harmony between them. They were made of lightness. Their fast was not imposed as a precaution: they carried only enough food to keep them until their next meal, and this was sometimes days in coming.

The third virtue was indecision. They did not hesitate to set out along the road, or when they had to choose between paths, but they did hesitate later; they deferred their actions in a way that went against their own will, though it had nothing to do with that. They also vacillated if they had to read the signs presented by their surroundings: to say that something was to their right or their left revealed an inaccuracy, more than a falsehood, as soon as they turned around; the red sun of the late afternoon was just like that of daybreak. The fact that the landscape changed as they advanced was a secondary detail. The simple tent they were occasionally forced to improvise in the open countryside had a limitless and unknown sphere of influence that was, as such, irrelevant when it came to undertaking any initiative. These two, who invaded all with their wanderings, felt themselves invaded by nothing. They felt insubstantial, transparent, and in this sense saw any decision they could make as secondary and any incident as deeply inconsequential. When they crossed paths with someone, they would exchange greetings and then get the customary question: whether they belonged to a circus or, sometimes, if they were looking for work. No one noticed that they were simply vagabonds. Sighing had become a reflex for them, so they sighed, not seeing the point of the question in light of the fact, so obvious to them, that they lived under the sign of itinerancy. Over time these sighs became automatic, like compulsive blinking.

One morning, just as they were just setting out, they saw a point in the distance that was stationary, but which looked like a person. They had not come across anyone for quite some time but knew that someone would eventually appear, despite the inhospitable nature of the place. And that was the appointed day. At first they thought only eyes as sharp as their own could discern something so tiny; later they realized that it—or, rather, she—was something naturally small: a little girl. Perhaps it was because she was abandoned or that she was in the wilderness, or because, among nomads, differences in age—among other things—tend to disappear. What was certain was that they saw a distinctly un-childlike disposition in her eyes. The girl paused when she saw them, unsure whether to keep going, turn around, or leave the road and cut across the terrain. The two sensed a kinship in this indecision, and decided to help her. Accustomed to being asked questions, they looked forward to the chance to formulate them. After so many unpleasant experiences, this might be a positive encounter. The little girl realized that she was in no danger and approached them slowly; she was thirsty. They handed her a jar—a rudimentary glass—and waited. The water trickled over the corners of her mouth like a river flooding its banks. Once she had quenched her thirst, she spoke. As soon as they heard her voice, they thought: that same slowness, that same indifferent lassitude. The girl explained that her house was nearby, that she only needed time to find it. She hadn't seen anyone, not even an animal, for weeks; they were the first. It was right around here, she repeated, but she had been wandering for some time. Her parents and brothers must be out looking for her; she wondered why they hadn't found her yet. She sat down on a petrified log and said that she once heard a story about a boy who tripped and hit his head on a rock. He wakes up a few hours later in a place he only half recognizes; it is the same one he had walked through before, but now slight changes, especially in its coloring and vegetation, make it seem different. A community of hardworking and, in their way, wise people lives there, but because the boy does not understand their language, he never realizes how aware they are of their own advantages. It was not that they lived in a realm of abundance, but rather that they lived according to their basic human needs. This simple trait, more than the sum of any riches, made the place a paradise. The boy has to change his name, become another, in order to join them; from that moment on, the most profound and personal things in his past seem unreal to him, in that they expressed the present in his old language.

The girl's name was Marta. She did not know whether she had wanted to be stopped; without rushing, she had simply started to walk. In the same way, she did not hide, but tried not to attract attention, to make herself invisible, to see without being seen and exist without being present. The night before she left, something had kept her from sleeping; she heard noises. One of the animals must be restless, she thought, as she tossed and turned in her bed. After a while she got up, wondering why no one else had woken. When she reached the shed, her attention was caught by the sudden stillness, which had neither cause nor effect, as though normalcy had returned to stay until the morning. She vacillated between turning back and pressing on, but her curiosity won out. When she opened the door she saw that nothing had ended; in fact, the action was at its apex. There was her favorite older brother, on his knees, pressing a hen to his abdomen. Marta was not shocked. She admired the harmony between skin and shed, between her naked brother and the backdrop of chicken wire, planks, hay, earth, feathers, and excrement; there was more truth in that combination than clothing could ever provide. This surprise would serve as an initiation. She slept badly the rest of the night, not knowing whether she was thinking in her sleep or dreaming while awake. Her innocence kept her from fully understanding the scene, but her intuition hinted at the inescapable presence of a revelation. Early the next morning, the din of the birds reached its usual pitch. She woke up not knowing how she had gotten back to bed. She remembered the unclothed figure of her brother trying to disappear behind the hen, and she was filled with a confused sense of anxiety. After a while, she got up and started walking; she would not be coming back. She walked past her parents, her brothers, even a few neighbors. No one noticed her, each went about their daily activities; she seemed transparent. That was how she left.

Marta handed back the glass and waited. They did not speak. The sky was turning pale, the afternoon coming to an end; the night would soon impose its own style, that of suspension. She was not afraid of what might come, she insisted, she just wanted to keep going. A little while later they would watch her fade slowly into the horizon, a reversal of how she had appeared. Of all their encounters, this had been the most intriguing. They did not overlook the affinities between them—a mysterious shared disposition, the same penchant for migration, the same diffuse violence enacted upon them by forces they could not name—to the extent that they imagined a life shared between them. Two were simply a pair, but three made the beginning of a tribe. Why not ask her to join them? Why had they not adopted her, even if they had to do so by force? They reproached themselves too late. They blamed their timidity and bemoaned their lack of initiative; sometimes, they thought, a bit of decisiveness is in order (though they forgot this right away).

The next day was cloudy; the clouds formed an armor-plated ceiling under which not the slightest breeze stirred. The stillness was so complete that they immediately thought of the cold, of those polar days on which everything, time and air, seem to stop. It was sad to see the wind, perhaps the closest natural simile of itinerancy, conspire against them, the consummate wanderers, with its absence. A few days' journeys followed, one after the other, according to the custom of the road. The trace left by the girl began to dissipate, gradually turning into an imprecise figure and a vague sense of nostalgia. Nonetheless, they occasionally suspended their silence to wonder about her out loud; she was, of course, just a girl, they thought with regret. In those moments, the excuses stuttered by one or the other did little to absolve them; explanations explain, but they rarely justify.

They would see just how right they were a few days later, shortly after discerning the forms of several people on the unhurried horizon. They were Marta's parents and brothers, who were shocked to hear that they had let her go on her way alone—she was just a girl, they couldn't believe it. They asked where she was headed. The two responded with the truth: nowhere in particular. The road, in fact, was straight and there was no other; unless she crossed through the countryside she would not have left it. This answer surprised Marta's family, who took it as a provocation. They found it shocking that the two had nothing else to add. No one passed through there for days on end, there was no way the girl had not given them some explanation. The mother added her own touch of drama: Marta was her only daughter and, as they could see, who knew if she could have any more children. She would not lose her. This argument moved them, so they mentioned the story about the hen, in case they could deduce something from it. The family was unaffected, like someone who, hearing a familiar story, wants only to verify a few of its details. It was always the same dream, they said at the end. Standing in the middle of the road, all seemed to realize at once that there was nothing more to say; their silence took on the shape of a truth. Marta was one, her family, many; they were two. Thanks to divisions such as these, which so often translated into running away, insomnia, or persecution, tribes are formed and continents joined. They said their goodbyes wishing one another luck; they would be sure to share any news.

Our pair was silent for several days. What Marta had confided in them as a tragic revelation was actually the retelling of a dream (as such, her flight from home might also have been a habitual bit of mischief). On the fourth day, once they had recovered, they picked up their dialogue and reached their own conclusions: just as the girl had made them participants in the dramatic account of her discovery, the family had not only expelled them from that drama, but destroyed it altogether. The days began to blend together again; the color of the countryside varied imperceptibly. In one area they noticed an unusual number of towns named after saints. One evening they came across a sign, but it was dark so they decided to wait; in the morning they were able to read: "Area under Dispute." This was the sort of thing that would happen. They were far from Marta's country when a form appeared on the horizon, just as indistinct as on that other day. Their pulse immediately quickened: the scene was exactly the same, it seemed like a repetition. Their impulse was to start running, to hurry the embrace, but the girl's vacillation left them once again at a loss, preventing any outburst. They kept quiet and waited for her to speak. Lesa sat down on a pile of lustrous bones, skeletal remains that had probably been there for thousands of years, and spoke: Later that same evening, she had felt genuine terror as night began to fall. The countryside that had seemed so limitless during the day turned, in the dark, into a magical cell whose walls were slowly closing in and would eventually crush her. It was impossible to move of her own volition; a secret, industrious force pressed her forward, while the silence and the heavy sky kept her from making out even the slightest reflection among the shadows. On top of all this, it was getting colder and she was afraid of going mad before freezing to death. She called desperately for help for a long time, but could only remember the blow that knocked her over—she hit her head on a rock and slid, unconscious, into a ditch. It would have been the perfect opportunity to dream in colors of a different hue, she remarked, or about a community of wise men, but instead she would awaken the next day as though nothing had happened, with the sun scuttling across her face.

They wanted to know where all this had happened. Marta remembered nothing, except that she had been walking all day. She was still lost, but was no longer running away: now she was walking in order to find her parents. She felt strange in her own skin, as though a new—but not necessarily strange—body had taken over parts of her own. At the same time, everything seemed so recent: the anxiety, the memories of the night before. She thought about her name. There was something about it that she could not quite define, but which seemed not to fit: she did not know why, but she was convinced that "Marta," as a sign, as a verbal substitute for her person, was hardly the right word. The name belonged to a recent past, that much was true, but a past that was also remote, before she ran away and before her fall; maybe her name was Mirta. The two regarded her in silence. They were about to correct the error of their previous encounter, when they did not invite her to join them, but their intuition held them back yet again. Something had made Marta unrecognizable, though not on a superficial, or even a deep, level; it was something essential. They noticed it in the tone of her voice, and also in a change in her gaze and the way she walked. This transformation, though unclear, manifested itself in Marta with a touch of innocence, even beatitude. They vacillated between baptizing her and convincing her that her name should be something else—Lesa, for example—or, the other way around: convincing her first and baptizing her later. Either way, they said, they should keep her with them. Who, except someone trying to start a cult, would baptize a person only to abandon them?

They immediately reconsidered. They were prepared to venerate Marta, but could not live with either Mirta or Lesa. And if they were going to venerate, they preferred their memory of the Girl a thousand times over. With this conviction, they sank into an uncomfortable silence and, again, deep into regret. They didn't want to seem insensitive but, at the same time, could not make that mistake knowingly. Meanwhile, the girl waited longingly for some sign, even the most ambiguous, even part of a word; she could have waited there for hours and at the slightest hint of an invitation would have said yes, she would love to join them. The two, for their part, knew that they would never see her again. They no longer had the will to console her, aside from telling her how worried her family was. Then they wished her luck. Forgetting that both their lives and the landscape contradicted the excuse of haste, they said their goodbyes in a rush: it was urgent; they had to get going right away. And so, once again, they left a little girl alone in the middle of nature. But, just like the word *urgent*, the word *left* rang hollow to them, as drifters. Both words, against the desolate backdrop of nature that surrounded them, took on a hue of irrelevance—though they were familiar with the word abandon. Still, since they had certainly never possessed Marta, they did not know which sense to adopt. Mirta, Sela, or whoever she would be from then on, would hold a special place in their hearts. How perfect it would have been had things gone differently: if Marta had woken up in a way that would have allowed them to adopt her. But nothing ever happens according to plan.

They continued down the road. Sometimes they would come across train tracks and follow them for weeks, stopping to cook on the crossties and spending the night off to one side. Life went on as usual, which is why they did not notice how long it had been that any image of a girl—a photo, a drawing, any portrait on any surface—would bring the oval of Marta's face back to them. Every morning they woke up not knowing where they were. This happened to both of them. They had been sharing feelings for some time; these almost certainly passed through their skin and were transmitted through the air. Sometimes they surprised themselves by thinking the same thing; other times one noticed that the other's thought was not new to him, but was rather the memory of another, similar one. They never quarreled, never separated. Yet even recognizing that few other unions could be as harmonious, the memory of Marta proved to them that no relationship could ever be intense enough, profound enough. Her memory reproduced itself on an industrial scale. Photos of schoolgirls, illustrations of small female athletes, simple and anonymous charcoal portraits: any image of a girl produced a passionate feeling of devotion and kindness. Yet, strangely, they were impervious to girls of flesh and bone. This detail caught their attention right away—they interpreted it as yet another aspect of their own eccentricity—then, little by little, it took on a menacing air. The fact that Marta was not called into presence by the living and corporeal, a person, but rather by these images, made them wonder whether the world of travel that they had chosen might not also belong to a secondary order, a reflection or shadow of the real one. A world built by the imagination might be limitless, of this there was extensive proof, their own inexhaustible, intense experiences included; yet in order to last it needed the calm of the other world—the real, tangible one—because when it erupts, whether under the sign of condemnation or redemption, the other surface of the planet—the hemisphere of the imagination— becomes the substance of that breach, the fuel for the fire. Sometimes truth and imagination seemed like two fairly harmonious hemispheres, other times they could seem like different moments in the cycle of the same one; yet the fall of one always meant the rise of the other, as they consumed one another. This was the amorphous substance of which their vague intuitions were formed.

It was so easy and entertaining to formulate theories that a few years later, unaware of any danger, they were detained as vagrants outside Buenos Aires. They had not been arrested since Clorinda, nor had they spent much time in any one place. At first they were taken to the famous prison Villa Devoto. They would be moved often after that, though not as often as they would have liked. What is more, the places they were taken were increasingly unsubstantial; the last ones, little barracks scattered at random across a field zigzagged by barbed wire, barely sealed them off from the outside. Their time in prison was a time of stillness, of the lack of movement. This conclusion, obvious to anyone, held for them the inverse meaning, as well: that stillness was a prison. They had been locked up for two years more than they had spent on the road. They came to understand that if, in the country, the poor had a right to wander, in the city they had to follow a prescribed circuit; the rich, on the other hand, who stayed still in the country, were the ones who commanded the surface of the city, constantly moving from one place to the next. They could hear tango music all the time, no matter where they were inside the prison. It was better not to think in there; wide eyes wakefully dreaming and a blank mind made it possible for time to pass more quickly, for little to happen and, at the end of it all, to leave behind a lean life, with few things to remember. When they were finally released, it took them a long time to recognize themselves. They had to reconstruct the image from memory. They saw their own suffering in the eyes of the other; as consolation they walked away from the prison reliving the heights of their wanderings.

Buenos Aires accomplished what Clorinda could not: it did not even occur to them to go back to their old life. They preferred to hold on to the memory of a countryside "of our own," as they would say, that nonetheless was as neutral as the sea, as ephemeral as time and as undefined as Marta. When they moved into the house that would become their home, they were surprised at how young the trees on the block were. The train, whose tracks were just a few meters away, also embodied the ideas of travel, freedom, and migration: this was a comfort to them, as well. The first thing that happened to them was finding a large image of a certain virgin. They adopted it, as they had not done with Marta. There, from the living room, she would oversee the daily activities of the pair, who had gone from being perambulatory to being sedentary and, what is more, to being still. In a language so secret that it was never even expressed as sound, they called her "the colossal virgin" (or something like that): the lack of space, territory, and mobility lapsed into a pious devotion. They also lit candles to the memory of Marta, for whose presence they were able to find no better image than that of a girl about to dive into a pool, her hands folded together as though praying downwards, cut from an old magazine of current events. Marta's innocence became atemporal; even the vocabulary that described it changed, swelling with mysticism, something like a beatitude. If they had, up to a certain point, referred to their first encounter as her "arrival" and their second as her "return," now they spoke of an enduring presence, albeit one that chose to manifest itself only occasionally. Marta had shown herself at one moment or another, though she had—since they had met her—always been present; she still was, only in absence.

It was inconceivable to anyone who saw them that they had been consummate, slightly diffuse travelers (a passing difference). The hostile air of the city, which was intangible but nonetheless verifiable, forced them into their home, pressing them into its corners. They never went downtown, or anywhere too many people got together or too many things happened at once. They knew only the streetcars and buses that took them to work. They were not aware that the city was changing; had they known, they would not have cared. When they would think back on their glorious past, the whistle of a train would save them from sadness, transporting the imagination of both to the great open spaces of the North.

As time went by and their religious life expanded, they would attract the attention of the neighborhood; first as two people unusually attached to their vigils, and then for their demeanor, which gradually grew more cautious and reserved. They wanted to be invisible but they could not, and so the care with which they moved and the way they directed their gaze recalled the behavior of certain animals. At a time when the city was filled with Paraguayans, they were unable to distinguish themselves as natives of Formosa; if they did manage to do so, it was only a little while before the simple and ruthless judgment of the people, which assigned nationality by association, would render the distinction irrelevant. Apparently, this situation reproduced the one in Clorinda. They were suspicious in the eyes of others, regardless of the situation. The fact that they retained, even after living in the city for years, the traits of vagrancy—an inability to distinguish between the fleeting and the permanent, a penchant for long periods of fasting, a tendency toward vacillation—would make things even worse. A cult was attributed to them that was much more exotic and, in its way, much more provocative than the innocent, private one that they practiced.

The emptiness was palpable, with the exception of a few old-timers annoyed at having to walk all the way to church when there was a perfectly good altar nearby. There, in the tiny room that crowned the courtyard and was reached by a narrow flight of stairs with bowed slats, the habit of prayer and of honoring the memory of relics and beliefs they had shared throughout their life together created a unique sanctuary. What causes a cult to grow, to expand? It's hard to say, exactly. The cult grew. When it was private, the room presented no problem; once it acquired a certain reputation, however, a window would have to be opened to air out the smoke from all the candles the people brought in. And that is how an individual, or dual, cult came to expand. The hosts, whose sense of hospitality at first led them to politely explain the images to which the place was dedicated—alluding to a divine intervention in the midst of their prolonged itinerancy, offering proof of Marta's story—would later watch strangers arrive who were already initiated, in a wayward sense, in the details and events of the iconography. The cult took on a life of its own, as did the worship in the chapel; they said that three hundred was an ideal number of followers. Peering in from a landing on the stairs, the heads drew back as before a mystery: this was the reason they were there. But since that mystery also attracted them, it kept them from withdrawing enough to forget.

Their worship could not be kept secret; little by little it would be rejected by the community and its churches. What did they get out of their cult? The freedom they had lost in the prison in Buenos Aires, the abstract pleasure found in the proliferation of the air and the landscape. Looking at the images that hung from delicate nails, they were able to breathe the rich and enigmatic aroma of nature once more. Standing before the photos of Marta and the pictures of the virgin, they caught their breath, began to dream again. Veneration, as both a credo and an experience, was the next best thing to itinerancy; the key to both was less a matter of continuity than it was of persistence.

One day they had a dream: They were at the foot of a mountain. They looked up and were overwhelmed by the climb ahead of them. They turned and saw a peaceful valley, with lazy little foothills spilling over into a river, a narrow and sinuous strip that reminded them of a snake. The noise of beasts hidden in the underbrush filtered down along the dense face of the mountain; from the valley they could hear the whisper of the breeze, an anxious whistle. The plain stretched on and became a narrow crate that made the wind rear up in frustration. In the dream they remembered moments from real life. These moments no longer belonged to their past, but rather to that of the dream: they were planes superimposed upon one another, searching for a framework that could accommodate them all. In the meantime, they needed to decide. They didn't have all day. Above them was the mountain, below them, the valley. The dream repeated this over and over, highlighting a difference that disconcerted them, first and foremost because it was so obvious, and secondarily because it revealed to them that they were nowhere. At first they thought that the moments of their shared past were coming from above and prepared themselves for the climb, but then they saw that they were coming from the river and started their descent. Every call they heard was followed by its opposite. All of a sudden, someone wearing a uniform came down—he looked like the agent or guard of something—someone who protected a good or goods. They thought maybe a forest ranger (but that was ridiculous, there were no forests). They asked him about the truth, but he turned away before he could say anything. And so they came to know a kind of terror not born of fear, but of confusion.

The pressure grew; combined with the prevailing climate in the community, it would end up destroying the chapel. They had to lock it up and turn it over to the house next door for use as a bedroom. They sealed off the door and made another, facing the back and opening on to an empty space where a flight of stairs would soon be built from the neighboring courtyard. But it was not enough. Their persecution ended up consecrating the place, and a religious multitude chose it as the site of their gatherings. The story would end shortly thereafter when the two decided to run off in the middle of the night and were never heard from again. Some have said they've seen them off to the side of the train tracks with their packs, looking like vagrants; others say they've passed them walking up and down the avenues with a blank stare and an absorbed look on their faces, paying no attention to the world evolving around them. Either way, it is hard to imagine two more innocent souls.

Unlike in nature, where everything is explicit and categorical, in the city, they remarked, the abstract imposes itself upon the concrete. In the city, mental operations come before facts. At the very least, said M, the streets are an entelechy, defined by what they are not. It is the space of withdrawal, the scene of mental operations. The names of the streets are the greatest proof of this misunderstanding and the origin of the most notable exercise in abstraction of all, M continued: the routes of public transportation, which arbitrarily unite remote points. One can imagine, in an instant, the slow trajectory of a bus—have its entire route in one's mind. ("I wish I could do that," said M. Make connections, establish confines not only in thought, but also in practice.) The way the line refers to a specific geography is just as arbitrary as the names of the streets, but of a greater complexity; if the former suggest a trajectory, the bus routes also assume the complication of obstacles, traffic regulations, unevenness in the terrain and in neural centers, which are also pathways. He would be overcome with excitement as he named a line for the other to translate. It could have been the 109 (Liniers-Luna Park), the 96 (San Justo-Constitución), the 53 (Boca-José C. Paz) or the 61/62; when he described the return route, he provoked outbursts of admiration from M, who would stare at him wide-eyed. The lines that had been shut down remained as traces, as living furrows in memory, as did those that came before the ordinances that would transform them, the ones that had belonged to trolleys or streetcars. The various names of certain streets were also a source of mystery and happenstance; as tends to be the case, chance was obscured by reality. "Uruguay becomes San José," they recited, "Cobo de Caseros, Yatay de Muñiz," and so on.

The houses, whose façades constituted the exterior, were—according to M—pure reality, the backdrop of private experience and real life that nonetheless depended on the street to define itself as such. Safe within their homes, people entered a realm of shadow day after day, like the planets; here, however, shadow was a rhetorical quirk that meant isolation. And light meant the presence of others, of witnesses, in the street.

THREE

The story about the pair of nomads absorbed me just as much as the one about the eye. Unlike me, who was unable to describe the events of the previous day except in the most confused terms, M abounded in stories and anecdotes that not only concerned him directly, relating to his own experience like the episode of the eye, but also encompassed broader, more diffuse—and therefore more debatable and controversial—material, which reached him from who knows where to adopt a new form through his voice. This is why it is clear to me that, were he still alive, he would have been the writer, the novelist. (The surrogate that I believe myself to be at times does not represent a fault; I do not see it as such. I cannot say, "I failed," I am not myself, et cetera.) On the other hand, writing is the order best suited to take up error and even simulation, converting them first into chance and then into fortune; I can hardly mistrust my affinity for replacement and substitution, as I have been convinced for years that if there were something to be said in my—particular—language, not the words or the facts, but rather the morals behind some and the value of others, it would be dictated in some way by the memory of M.

A sense of loyalty to his memory leads me to write. At times I have thought that with this work I abandon myself, submit myself to an unclear condition in which personal feelings and the ideas derived from them are mixed together. Yet it is also true, I believe, that there are few things as amorphous as identity, in terms of both depth and breadth, and that it is therefore pointless to wonder about its limits. I am here right now, but suddenly I cease to be; I am another, or simply *less*. Imagine the strain of someone trying to be himself all the time. M taught me to recognize the moments in which our identity appears, becomes a category, emits energy, and then subsides into a lethargic state of anticipation that lasts who knows how long. In less than five minutes we are able to oscillate among an infinite number of states, from abundance to saturation to emptiness. It is also true that we are not aware of *when* we are; those around us notice this when our signs become visible to them. Identity is gradual, cumulative; because there is no need for it to manifest itself, it shows itself intermittently, the way a star hints at the pulse of its being by means of its flickering light. But at what moment in this oscillation is our true self manifested? In the darkness or the twinkle? M and I achieved solidarity, a bond through which our own intermittence was able to develop with neither pressure nor strain, but with a sense of union. If there were a dominant state (climate) in my memory of the friendship, it would be that of harmony and serenity, a nucleus of emotions, from the bosom of which emerged the certainty of creating something unconditional and everlasting, the loss of which I have never overcome.

The real illusion that is space, or, more accurately, the confined, familiar city in which our reciprocal identity manifested itself, disappeared in M's absence. There was no sense trying to recapture it through intermittent, inevitably anonymous, and more or less melancholy visits to his neighborhood or the places we used to go because, unlike objects—which, like photos, can at any moment become talismans or relics—space has its own ephemeral hierarchy. Space is silent, it says nothing to us; it has no surface and yet, paradoxically, it is the most lasting of times. Armed with this proof, after circling the blocks around his house in the months that followed the abduction and returning every day empty-handed, as tends to happen, I understood the bewilderment of the two drifters who were dazzled by their surroundings but were blind to its successive manifestations. An event unfolds before our eyes; we attempt to uncover it, but cannot because it has taken the form of a landscape. There will always be an element of disappointment, just as happens with noises, which are always too loud or too soft for our consciousness. This frequent disappointment was the force that pushed the pair to want more countryside, more space, horizon, views; through the innocent—in that it was derived from their own movement—succession of these, their fantasy of the journey was returned to them. This fantasy shaped the pliable material of which they were made. The vast territory they crossed over the years was, and is, legendary, but their vague sense of distraction failed to take in these legends, which touched upon them in one way or another nonetheless. Occupation, conquest, camping, residence, property: these words were foreign not only to them, but also to nature. They were satisfied simply to cross. In this way, at the mercy of their indecision and to the rhythm of their footfall, a reciprocal being and identity grew to their own measure in the form of outbursts and lulls that flared and languished with fits of clarity and withdrawals into opacity. Similar oscillations between geography and consciousness would shape our friendship, as well.

One day, something very strange happened, something that would have a double effect, lasting into the future and decisive with regard to our shared past. M and I were walking through a neighborhood where the streets, as full of Tipa trees as a park and as bright and as wide as avenues, seemed to want to hide their double excess by tending toward a categorical magnitude. We had come to prepare something like a class project on the climate. We had to choose two *phenomena*. Far from the chilly snow or the malevolent hurricane, and negating any misplaced inclination toward exoticism, our preference tended toward the fog and the mist. Two phenomena that were both diurnal and nocturnal—the former less so than the latter—and were as common, though not as frequent, as the breeze. We were supposed to produce charts to adorn the walls of our classroom: this was the "special" part of the class and the artifice that made the exercise "didactic." Aside from graphs of isobars, isohumes, isotherms, other diagrams and charts, et cetera, we set ourselves the task of representing the mist and the fog. Wanting to elevate their mystery—the common trait of all atmospheric phenomena—we tended toward exaggeration: the mist looked like a downpour; the fog, like a dense sponge stuck to the ground that blocked out the light. There was no violence to this enterprise: the drawing belonged to the field of interpretation. Carefully considered, the fact that mist was not a deluge and fog was not a dense cloud was only a matter of scale. "To an ant, a drop of dew is enough to cover his head and a light mist can seem like an impenetrable fog," M argued innocently. A light mist or a drop of dew could be as devastating as a tropical storm; how, then, could the real nature of the mist and the fog not give one pause? Added to this were connections that presented alternatives to those of global topographies: maps organized according to intangible affinities, such as variations in climate, revealed a living network of relations that exceeded their expectations. *El tiempo*, in the most ambiguous and enigmatic of the word's dual meanings of time and weather— that is, as it refers to the weather—evinced not only an extreme relativism by positing various parallel systems, all integrated with reality, but also offered us the possibility of presenting these as both simultaneous and verifiable. And so we walked along, making absentminded comments about the climate and the atmosphere. (Those dialogues, I believe, were the most complete testament to our friendship; I have never had one like them in spirit or, for that matter, in substance, with anyone else.)

The meaning of those long, conversational walks may have been figurative, but that would not make them any less substantial—quite the opposite, because it was to the rhythm of these steps and these words that M and the other grew together, learning how to think, even how to converse; one could also say that they learned how to walk, in the broadest sense. For various reasons they both lacked adults, parents, who could pass down to them an image, a formation in the true sense of the word. Though it may seem like an overstatement, it is likely that if they had not met, they would not have been able to draw from themselves that which was discarded and contested by their elders. The lines of the isotherms, juxtaposed with those of the continents, indicated that the truth was comprised of many maps at once, enveloping reality like a delicate sheath. Everything that moves, thought M, everything that loses or gains heat, leaves its indelible mark. "If the routes we take through the city, together or apart, were to be written out, they would make an incredible picture: each one coming together to form an orderly tangle," *said M. Sometimes they would be far apart, other times not; they would be near one another or even on the verge of collision, without knowing it. Other times they would be somewhat distant, neither really far nor particularly close. But the figure itself, or at least the nature of the changes and movements, would remain forever.*

It might also happen that they would be close while thinking they were far apart, or vice versa, in which case the direction of the wind, as with noise, or the layout of the streets or tracks, as with the trains, would either indicate actual distances and degrees of separation or, on the contrary, simply confuse them. In a city, M continued, distance did not mean separation ("we surrender ourselves to obstacles"); in the countryside, either, though it is different there because of irregularities in the terrain. But at sea, it does. At one point they stopped, and M turned halfway around, saying, "Let's look back along the street, straight through the trees. The sidewalk looks like a tunnel carved out of the ground, the houses, and the branches." They had walked the length of the tunnel, from a distant point upon which they now set their gaze, but there was no trace of their passing. Footsteps don't leave a mark, he added. Is there a place where our trajectories can speak for us, without our intervention? The other did not respond. If it does exist, we don't know where it is; if it doesn't, we should invent it.

We saw a couple kissing; a little while later, a man switched his ring from one finger to another; not long after, a bus with only a few passengers aboard stopped at a corner. These sorts of things were signs of the journey's progress. The bus slowly pulled away from the curb, the man studied his finger, now bare; the couple embraced, ignoring the presence of their clothes. We registered it all with detachment (almost boredom). A train could be heard in the distance; this, strangely, was not cause for comment. Perhaps it was the place, so luminous and calm, or the topics that arose according to the autonomous manner of these walks, or perhaps it was, as I said earlier, that formative afternoon as a whole, during which we came to feel unique for the very first time, to feel like ourselves in an obvious and decisive sense, without fear of error. We might have known all this before, without being aware of it. For a long time, we assume we know who we are, until the moment we fully realize who that is; in that moment, identity is no longer predictable, but rather takes the form of a truth that, like any other, can become a sentence with no more than a change of perspective. We are condemned to the truth and, as such, are subject to its rule—to me, the most tangible evidence of this is precisely M and his absence. I'll describe the strange event.

A little while later, we ran into each other. We had said goodbye earlier on, and I still remember the way we turned away from one another at the same time, heading in opposite directions. But then, a half hour later, we practically collided in front of a corner newsstand. Neither of us wanted to admit that he had taken a wrong turn; M insisted with a conviction matched only by his disorientation, while I tried to explain to him that he was lost, without really being able to see it clearly myself. I also remember how, for a moment (a moment marked by a peculiar sensation that would linger on), that encounter—at once real, because we were face to face, and impossible—disoriented me and was able to temporarily disrupt geography. That one street should come after the next, that a few blocks past any avenue, there would always be another, was a truth that was bound to outlive us (as proven by the fact that this already happened to M). Yet at the time, as I wondered how it could have happened, I did not sense one but rather many distortions, a generalized disorder: the streets no longer appeared as a succession, as streets, and could be bunched together within the same confines. Another example: west was an idea that was exiled from reality, a repudiated notion. And there we were, standing calmly beside a kiosk looking at the magazines, receiving signs of a disaster in the form of a coincidence. What a strange thing to have happened, said M. Sometimes I think that we move through the city like planets, following our individual trajectories while we maintain our relative positions and trace out uniform patterns. But the planets don't move that way—I corrected him—it would have to be "stars" or "astral bodies." (M wasn't listening.) And so the apparent movement of what is found in the heavens and which we generally call stars became, by pure coincidence, the key and emblem of our bond: despite the gaps and distances that might emerge, there would ultimately and always be, between the two of us, a reciprocal influence marked by the simple tenets of balance and compensation—the fundamental law of our walks and trajectories, which were, at the same time, shaped by the organizing principle of solidarity.

I sometimes wonder whether this solidarity might still exert its force. External space, for instance, is acted upon by processes and forces of uncertain origin, impossible to attribute to any one body, as though the existential proof of all things were not in their mass, but in the indirect effects of their mysterious operations: that which we call an organizing principle, or reality, among other things. Bodies, then, belong to an essentially negative existential category, defined by consequences or signs rather than by materiality. As such, influence would be invisible, but effective; because, as is well known, every force or effect has a cause, we are haunted by the notion that perhaps we just don't not know how to look. Perhaps we live in a world that is evident to all beings—animal, vegetable, and mineral—but us.

A few months ago, while looking for an address near the intersection of Tucumán and Reconquista, I heard someone calling to me. There are always so many people and so much noise on that corner that I thought the shouting could not possibly have been directed at me. But that was a mistake: it was. Someone was trying to signal me as he approached the top of the incline, but he could not go any faster. I remembered his name when he was practically right in front of me, when his vacillation between extending a hand and stepping forward to embrace me became obvious. It was Sito, a friend of M's from the neighborhood. "Hey, how are you, how are you," we said, exchanging similar greetings. Since he had to catch his breath—"This hill gets steeper every day"—it was up to me to speak. I remarked how exceptional it was that we should run into each other, not only because of how many years it had been, but because it was completely by chance that I was there at all; aside from that, with all the cars and all the people it was almost impossible to notice anyone in particular, and yet he had. A minute earlier or a minute later and everything would have been different, I added, no one would have seen me or called to me and perhaps we would not have another chance to meet for years, as many years as had passed since the last time we had seen one another. He said yes, it was remarkable, not only had fate intervened to bring us both to that place, but also to point his gaze in my direction and allow him to recognize me almost immediately; he had always had very good eyesight and an impeccable memory for physiognomy, he added—and I agreed.

As he spoke, I remembered things about Sito. An only child, he lived with his mother long ago, in the days of M. His father had died, or left, before being able to leave a tangible or lasting impression on him, just after his first birthday. Despite having no siblings and being practically an orphan, as a child he found, in his mother, a repository for his cruelty, a deep-seated bitterness that he would cast onto her in the form of arrogance, deception, and even disdain, as though he were trying to make himself disappear. This translated into a pronounced dominance. He lacked the resources of the spoiled child; instead, he made use of a power that anticipated that of an adult, only saturated with innocence, which made it all the more ruthless. Every time his mother would come out into the street to look for him—having to call out "Sito" again and again even though he had not only heard her the first time but had also, like every child, sensed her physical presence—you could hear an abject tone in her voice that belied her wisdom; her entire being was submitted to the ignorant rule of the boy, to his innocent and brutal authority.

A little while after I met him, as he passed into adolescence, mother and son reversed roles: then it was she who was ruthless, Sito who was submissive. It should have been the other way around, but it was not. The mother accused him of being just like his father, when in reality it was she, who drank more and more, that best recreated his memory. Sito had to keep a small sideboard in the living room, which I saw on more than one occasion—closed, of course—well stocked. To this end, he would go out in search of cheap liquor, usually liters of vodka; his mother told him which brand. He would return slowly, doubled over by the weight of his purchases. I remember, on those rare occasions when the three of us were at his house, the silent disposition of that sideboard, as intimidating as a person lying in wait, a figure that at once concealed and signaled the drama of the household. We could have been talking or doing anything at all when that imperious voice would ring out from a tiny room in the attic. As though propelled by a sudden force, Sito would instantly jump to his feet and run up the stairs; it was nothing like the waiting he inflicted on her just a few years earlier. At one point we even saw him dodge his mother's fists and struggle to hold her back; something kept him from using his full strength, which was obviously greater than hers, even simply to restrain her: it was as though her superiority was carried in her voice; shrieks and movement came together in the body of the mother to break down the defenses of the son.

Years later, as tends to happen and as they tend to say, I lost track of Sito; every now and then our paths would cross near his house and we would exchange a few jokes, then go our separate ways. As was now reflected in our mutual and confused discomfort, we had not seen each other since M's disappearance. "I couldn't get work until the war in the Falklands—it was only after I got married that I found something." "With my father-in-law," he added. He helped out in a bar off the turnpike, the Acesso Oeste, which also offered room and board (the Acesso Oeste just past Haedo, he explained). A few years later his father-in-law died, and they had to close it down because he had so many brothers-in-law. The experience had done him some good: since then he had been working as a waiter at a café in the area, on Reconquista; soon they would make him a manager. People passed by us in a rush, indifferent to the decisive encounter Sito and I were having there, on the sidewalk. He invited me to join him for a cup of coffee. "But not where you work," I said. Who said anything about that? he responded, naturally. (To this day I can find no explanation for my awkwardness.) I asked about his mother. She had died, as well, but he was still living in the same place—now with a wife and children. Those blocks around the train tracks never change, it's remarkable, he said. As he approached his house, he would try to find something that had changed, sighing with disappointment when he could not. He felt as though he were still in his childhood or youth: any change—the passage of time in general, his children—having no outward sign, seemed to exist only in his head; it became unreal to him. He said the following: Time moves so quickly that before I know it I'm a man, what they call an adult; my father did not reach the age I am now, and I think I've lasted longer than I deserve to or should have. I look at my children, he continued, and they seem like people, not children. I tend to my customers without seeing any trace of humanity in those I serve: they are just posts attached to the tables. The same thing happens to taxi drivers, he rationalized, many of them have said so. I agreed and looked away. His words sounded harsh; I couldn't tell whether this was due to my presence, if they were trying to convey something beyond what they were saying, or whether this was an effect of his general nervousness, of which I could be a victim just like any other person in any other place. Perhaps it was both. Yet it was not only time—the effects of which he had such trouble perceiving when they were right in front of him—that separated us, no matter how long it had been since we had seen one another, but also the absence of M, so clearly omni-present—in that he was, and continues to be, the reason that we know each other—that lent an air of sadness, distrust, and even inappropriateness to the encounter.

Just as had happened with M's mother years earlier, that day after the abduction when the weight of his disappearance would have kept us on that sidewalk forever had it not been for her wisdom in acknowledging, in different words, that M was gone; just as had happened years earlier, Sito and I were playing a part that was not only unpleasant, but also unclear. Any change of tone, any word half-said or said with undue emphasis, and we might freeze up and remain there, at the corner of Tucumán and Reconquista, for all time—the preserved relics of an encounter immortalized in its impossibility. In light of the disappearance, his absence, every comment, even those not about M, took on a valence of inadequacy, incorrectness, as though some weight were keeping it from achieving any real significance. And yet Sito, with his chattiness and gestures of fatigue, which were actually just a product of his laziness, conveyed something of the image I had of M from those years, no doubt with the spontaneous assistance of memory. In a way, it is those feelings that I am trying to represent now. (Sito greatly influenced my decision to write this account; though the idea existed before, it was one of those vague promises, caught halfway between commitment and resignation. Our meeting was decisive in this regard. Sito was the final impetus.)

Today one might see in Sito—in his robust figure, his agitation as he approached, climbing the hill like some tired animal—M's consent to divulge some aspect of his story, even if that were only his existence. This may seem like magic, or superstition, but it is also hard to refute. Before his death, I had never suspected that a person's substance or spirit could manifest itself from time to time; this was the outcome of M's leaving (I say that he left in the way someone might say I never saw him again, he died, et cetera). But at no moment since have I come so close to feeling M's presence, perceiving it as a sign unto itself. While Sito spoke, I went over the chance nature of the encounter and was even more convinced of the direct intervention of M. Any witness would have said that two old acquaintances ran into each other, but the reality, as usual, turned out to be something less serendipitous and more lasting. A permission had been granted to me, almost a gift, the benefit of which depended on the way it was used. I realized this as Sito's words followed their course, though I was still listening to him. There were two paths: the straight one of his words and the winding one of M's intervention, which, despite its twists and turns, kept up with the other. This is why I believe that, whether irrational, fantastic, or serendipitous, the encounter was a sign. M's presence showed itself to be fleeting and without gradation; one could say that, though perhaps he had always been present; only now, fleeting, did he choose to show himself.

If one can speak of a thing called candor, a virtue some people supposedly possess, I should say that Sito's was somewhat questionable. I realized this when he chose a meandering route to recall that M had not been abducted from his house. Sito's roundabout remarks had something ceremonial to them; in order to speak he resorted to preambles and clarifications whose meaning, if they had any purpose at all, had been lost in a memory overcrowded by time and the—often purely mental—reiterations to which he subjected his own story. (As is well known, repetition does not simplify; on the contrary, it distorts.) What Sito said was more or less this: A kidnapping on the block, with no witnesses. Like nearly everyone else, M lived somewhere: his house. But he was somewhere else, far from there, when he was taken. This meant that the significance of the event dissipated almost immediately; it was not easy to absorb something that had happened outside the neighborhood. Something as decisive as a man's life had closed itself off within its own virtuality, without leaving a trace. His family, especially his parents, by not acting in any ostensible way, seemed to give themselves over to the lack of coincidence between event and geography. And so began the delayed reactions for which they would, gradually, become known; more absorbed than they usually were by the familial penchant for distraction, they were now so slow to turn when someone called to them, for example, that they were already being hailed for the second time when they finally did. Their thoughts and reactions, said Sito, appeared to reach them from the back of their heads, rather than the front. The neighbors gradually found out about the painstaking, short-lived inquiries—which were not worthy of the name and never met with any success—but Sito could not remember how, he said as we drank the coffee to which he had invited me, since no one in the family talked about it with anyone.

One day the father went to the police station. *Went* says too much: the truth was that he simply stepped inside. He was walking along an avenue when he crossed paths with a patrol officer. Something inspired in him a vague sense of duty; he could not pass by the authorities without asking about his son. Information, like life, is sometimes so random that it is impossible to know what path might lead to the truth. In the police station they misled him despicably. They made him wait for hours, saying that the person who could help him wasn't in. All the while, the father watched people arrive who had been in an accident, or who came to report a noise, a theft, or a scam; people who came for a certificate of residence. Every now and then the police would mention a prisoner in the back, in the cells. Only just before he left did he discover that they were not prisoners, but detainees. It was strange; the word remained etched in his memory. Under the circumstances, there was little difference between one (prisoner) and the other (detainee), yet the second was more optimistic. From that moment on, he had the hope that M was a detainee. As long as that was all, he thought; detention can last years, decades, but it is always only temporary, as long as he is alive. The thought of seeing M appear at the far side of the station, from the third wing, as the police called it, excited him. It is so easy for one to believe that reality is directed at them. After a while a sharp pain in his chest made him lean his head against the cold wall. He left the police station at dawn, after another officer, who had just arrived and was supposedly the one assigned to help him, questioned him about everything, absolutely everything, and told him nothing at all; he simply ordered him to leave.

The neighbors, said Sito, offered to help with "anything they might need." M's parents thanked them evasively, as though they did not understand, or as though accepting any help would be to turn their backs on their son, to evade the guilt that had tormented them since the kidnapping and whose weight they felt obligated to bear. There was nothing they could have done, Sito pointed out, how could they have contributed anything more than what they already did anyway? Neighbors help one another with ordinary things, common to all, unless some catastrophe strikes. Nonetheless, there is no extraordinary assistance for extraordinary events; the help available was the usual, the neighborly: a supplemental solidarity that was, given its magnitude, rarely decisive. Half a year after the abduction, in the opposite season—that was how M and I used to break up annual cycles, according to opposing landmarks on a circle, the year—the father nearly died of another pain in his chest. The family's accounts, always in terrible shape, collapsed irreparably. It seemed as though they had all been struck over the head, lost their bearings. They wandered aimlessly through the neighborhood day after day, always disoriented; that much was clear at first glance.

Soda water, said Sito abruptly, putting down his cup of coffee. It was because of soda siphons that he came to know more about M's abduction. An old friend of his from school had showed him the siphons full of gasoline that he kept in his house. He led him into the kitchen and drew back a short floral curtain, with a flourish. A few plates embellished with gondolas, birds, and mountains rested on the cabinet. Sito did not count the bottles, nor did he try to verify any of it; instead he amused himself with the thought of the cloud of boats, feathers, ceramic, and water they would create if they exploded. Preparing the siphons required artisanal zeal. He remembered the care it took to prepare them and the naivety of his friend for showing them off. He could still see the innocent dedication that drove him; his idea of armed struggle, for which those explosives had been made, as something like a carnival, a pageant whose winner would be declared against a backdrop of exploding siphons. Sito remembered, at that moment, the last brigades to use carrier pigeons, whose devotion to their pets and to the virtues of their art led them to overlook the somewhat more decisive aspects of the war. World War II, to them, was a competition between legions of carrier pigeons. Speed, strength, adaptability, and intelligence were the qualities that would decide the victory; only, they were talking about pigeons. The same way that now, as Sito described in the café to which we had gone for a coffee, the strength, quality, and security of the siphons spilled over to the outcome of the struggle. That friend of mine ended up like M, Sito continued. One day he was absorbed in tightening a spout and didn't hear the kidnappers knocking; I guess he imagined it didn't seem like he was home. But what happened to M was different, since he didn't do anything, right? Sito asked, fixing his eyes, as they say, on mine.

And so on that afternoon, months ago, as we drank our coffee I grasped the nature of Sito's doubt. In his memory, the figure of M, who was always distracted to the point of appearing indifferent, retained an aura of innocence, even one of absence or ignorance; in this way, his disappearance represented not only a question about his fate, but also a mystery surrounding his past. M's past, as Sito understood it, could have somehow caused the abduction—or, on the contrary, politics could have been completely foreign to it, which would make him the victim of a circumstance that was neither anticipated nor sought out. This might seem gratuitous; an abduction is, of course, an abduction under any circumstance, just as a murder is always a murder, regardless of the circumstance or place. Still, Sito believed that one's behavior could influence one's fortunes, the way his old classmate had encountered, in his kidnapping and death, the outcome of a process that began when he twisted the first spout on a bottle of soda water; he needed to know whether M was absolutely innocent, that is, according to his measure, an absolute victim. He was, I told him, by answering with a "right."

He made a gesture of relief; he had not been able to ask anyone for such a long time, and now his years of waiting were crowned not only with certainty, but also with peace. That was what he had thought. M's memory became more complete: the truth had elevated it. Sito recounted the utter confusion in which his other friend lived, the one with the siphons, who had once enthusiastically told him that, if he ever needed to flee from his home, the Born money (from that famous kidnapping) would be at his disposal for expenses. The idea that it would be like a paid vacation fit perfectly with the image of a war of soda siphons, Sito observed. The phrase "the Born money" was a symbol of power, albeit a trivial power;

it crossed his lips all the time. It was that money that paid for the gasoline, paid the vendor for the siphons, and covered other necessary expenses. Sito recalled his friend saying, with a childish ironic flourish, that they sometimes just poured out the soda.

Later, we left the bar and walked to avenida Corrientes, where the sun occupied nearly the entire width of the street with an exemplary sunset, reclining against the west at an angle too steep for the city. I asked Sito if he had heard anything about M's parents and brothers, of whom I had not had any news in years. According to him, things went badly for a time: not only badly, but worse. As I already knew, one of the brothers had left his studies in high school. Then there were the undertakings of the father, which rarely succeeded—on the contrary, sooner or later they always failed. I could imagine these projects, impossible to call businesses, which in practice left their success or failure utterly to chance: before, when M was alive, it could have been the wholesale of old-fashioned pantyhose, or the purchase of a batch of defective housewares. It wasn't until five years after the kidnapping that they had any luck; they rented a storefront, filled it with refrigerators and used furniture, and set it up as a self-serve—it didn't go out of business as far as I know, Sito clarified, since they had to move shortly thereafter. That was the last he heard. When he was taken, the group from the neighborhood stopped getting together, he continued: no more talking on the corner or walking together. They went back to being neighbors, exchanging greetings and the occasional joke.

We walked along Corrientes toward the Obelisk for a while, talking about his children and about childhood in general. Sito commented that one never stops being a child—an opinion shared by many. For me, I said, childhood was the most forgettable part; I only sensed the continuity of my character when I left it behind, in a moment that coincided with my finding M. Childhood, that dynamic, foreign land. A broad, ascending stroke illuminated at the far end, in the west, by the sun—that was Corrientes. We were only a few blocks and a few minutes from watching, projected on the pavement, the shadow of the Obelisk grow longer and longer. Sito asked what I did, where I worked. I'm an executive now, I lied. I'm running an Argentine transnational. He was not inclined to believe me. "Yeah, and I'm a millionaire," he said. Had I told him the truth from the start he might not have questioned it, but when I told him that I was a writer he warned me to stop jerking him around. To be honest, I hadn't really believed that he worked in a café; now, with his vacillation, each individual deceit gave itself over to mutual distrust.

Anyone familiar with the weather in Buenos Aires, a fairly predictable climate that adds to the melancholy, indolent air of the city, could both marvel at and question what I am about to say, but it really happened. After going back and forth with Sito about our real or imagined occupations for a few blocks, he ended up saying that he was a mattress salesman; he had a little shop that sold foam rubber. It was what mattresses, pillows, and stuffed animals were made of, he said, but I don't believe he was telling the truth about that, either. I, for my part, indicated that I had been living abroad, as though I were still trying to overcome his mistrust. And so, while we were going back and forth about our occupations and things of that nature, the sky was covered over with a cloud so dense that night seemed to fall in a moment. A metallic truss, at once subtle and impenetrable, settled over Corrientes. It was easy to predict an imminent deluge, yet everyone knew it was not going to rain. That sky, in the particular way it organized itself—a way that, despite its fleeting nature, gave us the full sense of the extraordinary force behind it—seemed to render all other climatic phenomena, all other states, obsolete. In that moment, all believed that they were looking at a vanished past, recovered only by some unusual combination of chance events: it was a phenomenon to be marveled at, if not immediately associated with the miraculous. Still, it lasted no more than thirty seconds. Sito and I discussed this; he reacted with similar surprise. "What a fog!" he exclaimed several times, looking upward. (This surprised me, and I thought back on that special class about the climate.) A few moments later, the sky cleared up and the afternoon continued its serene progress. We had agreed earlier to walk together to the Obelisk, and now that we were there we realized the conversation was coming to an end; we were forced to scour our imaginations in the hope that some new topic might arise. And so the encounter with Sito drew to a close. It was a farewell with neither a particular focus nor a future, like when one closes the wardrobe of someone who has died knowing that happenstance, and nothing else, will be the reason it is opened next. This is why we pretended to be so unsettled by the weather: in order to avoid having to go over it all again and say something formulaic befitting the occasion. And also why, as the darkness suddenly lifted, Sito and I rushed to say our goodbyes.

I waited at the corner of Corrientes and Carlos Pellegrini as Sito walked away. I wanted to see his back, the labored mechanics that moved that enormous body. He seemed relaxed; he even stopped a few times to look at the shop windows he passed. It had not been two minutes since we parted—that is, some particularly brief period of time; barring the absurd, let's assume one can go two minutes without breathing—and it was obvious that Sito had already forgotten the encounter. I disdained and—though it may seem excessive—detested the passive, brutish availability that submitted to my appearance as a way of passing a few afternoon hours. There was no question that both M and I were far from Sito's mind. The effects of apathy could be seen on his body the same way I had heard the indolence in his voice. His mother was still alive, that much was obvious; he had lied to me about that, too, without any restraint or fear. He stopped at a kiosk, and I watched him buy a pack of caramels. How perfect, I thought. Sito likes candy. He unwrapped one and raised it to his lips as he walked. He was pretty far away, which may be why I was tempted to follow him. But all of a sudden, doubtless prompted by my own nerves, he turned around to look for me in the crowd that filled the length of the block. He eventually saw me and raised an arm. In spite of his exceptional height, he stood on his tiptoes to wave to me, holding the candy wrapper between his fingers like some kind of semaphore. This good-natured gesture dispelled my mistrust: no one could turn and wave like that, in such a casual way, without also being a simple, transparent individual. I did my part, in turn; I moved my arm back and forth two or three times until he went on his way. And that was my encounter with Sito: so serendipitous it seemed like a dream, which made it obvious that M had been involved. The Obelisk finally stretched out its shadow, which glided along the sidewalk where I stood, still trying to make out a head—Sito's—despite the distance. As night began to fall, this time unmistakably, I crossed Corrientes and followed Carlos Pellegrini south.

Earlier I said that Sito's intervention was decisive in my writing all this. Now I see that Sito was important, even beyond his words, in that he paid for our coffee. It might seem ridiculous or inappropriate—for a number of reasons—but Sito's gesture served to make me feel that something good could come from M that did not necessarily have to belong to the past. This is why I recount it from time to time: the invitation did not correspond to any mundane sense of courtesy, but was rather a protective gesture, a backward-looking nod of support.

Night arrived quickly: in the city, the sun knows neither patience nor lassitude. It's strange, when I think of those streets I remember the width of the sidewalks, the façades of the buildings and the breadth of the avenue, all of it punctuated by trees, yet that is not what I saw as I walked. At the time I was focused on the people around me and above all the parking lots, which the press was saying were in contract for millions; I have long since forgotten the details and circumstances of these things. Despite how long it had been since last we saw one another, and the slow pace of the conversation that was kept alive, at times, only through halting and painstaking effort, I had the feeling that we had not remembered M. Hours spent talking with Sito, and at no point did we speak of him fully, I realized, astonished. What kept us from evoking his voice, the way he walked, his kindness? How could we not have talked about his intelligence, his modesty, his generosity? M was completely theatrical: the faces he made could signal both happiness and oblivion, distraction and enchantment; M had a knowing sense of humor that inspired reflection, but Sito and I didn't talk about that, either. At Belgrano I thought about the cruel memory those who survive keep of those who did not, not because it eventually fades away, as they all do, but because it is *distorted*; changing things with this transformation, abandoning them before their time. This fact, which is simply the mechanics of memory and is seen all the time, took on a dramatic, doubly cruel, twist in M's case, in that we had nowhere to assign his presence, that is, his body—we know how important place is in the adoption of customs and the interpretation of events, as evidenced by my absolute certainty of M's intervention in the encounter with Sito (as though he were capable of being anywhere).

Later, as I crossed calle Chile, I realized something else: the reason for our silence could be found in the excessive nature of M's disappearance. I will illustrate this with an example. We sigh in different ways, according to different circumstances. We know many different types of sighs, most of which are recognizable: sighs of fatigue, impatience, pleasure, boredom, languor, surprise, and even of terror, but never of excess (in that case what is produced is a silence: people fall quiet before the excessive—this is the *silence of excess*). Shock or fear can leave us at a loss for words, but excess takes away our ability to speak: we don't want to scream, but rather vanish, disappear, die. Neither Sito nor I, I said to myself as I crossed Chile, was ready to know what had happened to M, and so the facts left a wake behind them that was dense, lasting, and difficult to assimilate. If the fatefulness of his absence exaggerated what had happened, the lack of a space, a site, as I said, made it incomprehensible. It might have been a matter of just one person, as was the case, but it was infinite in scope. Paradoxically, it was so excessive that it became something simple and absolute, the way one might say something is both childish and appalling. In this way, we did not give ourselves over to silence, which would have been a pointless and gratuitous gesture; instead, silence chose us, enveloping us from within.

Enveloping us from within. Sito had used those words a little earlier but, strangely, only now as I repeated them was I able to remember them and ask myself what they might mean. He said them in the café where we had gone for a cup of coffee, on his invitation, as he described a fishing trip he had taken with a friend to a lake in the country.

By that point, Sito had gone back to his circumlocutions: There are few things more eerie than spending a night beside a lake, he assured me: a noiseless sea, a river that makes no sound and has no opposite shore. The gentle lapping of the water seems to announce that someone is out there, emerging from the silence to attack us. Even if one believes that no danger is going to come from the depths, one immediately realizes that it is across the surface, of the land, that is, where it could appear. This certainty, so strange in its way, creates a greater sense of anxiety than that experienced by someone who spends a night out in the country, with neither sea nor lake nearby. In the country, Sito explained, the attack could come from any angle of the imaginary circle formed around one's body: 360 degrees suitable to aggression. At the water's edge, however, if one admits that nothing bad will come from that direction, the angle of exposure is noticeably reduced, generally to between 120 and 180 degrees. The security that follows this calculation is misleading, because though there is less possibility of aggression, the likelihood of its effectiveness, given the reduced radius, is much greater. So: the combination of the decreased probability and increased effectiveness of the attack, the motive of which would no doubt be ascertained once the aggressors end our lives, produces great anxiety and fear.

In any event, none of that matters, Sito asserted; not as much as an episode that took place the next morning, as one might expect, at the water's edge. The sunrise promised a picture-perfect morning. The slow and tenuous illumination of the dawn, far from the tropic, flattened colors and textures, just as it did to the elements around us: the water was less like water, the mud less like mud. The moisture from the dew began to evaporate, spreading jumbled and vaguely agreeable vegetal smells; as the nascent morning advanced, the uneasy sounds of the night faded away like the unpleasant memory of a forced silence. We stuck our heads out of our sleeping bags, Sito continued, to make sure that nature had given us the gift of another perfect day, but a reflection sparked our concern: a few meters ahead of us, at the water's edge, a shapeless mass was moving, or trembling, too cautiously to be anything natural. Sito and his friend were afraid the lucky star that had kept them through the night was about to run out right at the break of dawn, and they did not risk saying a word for fear of rousing the monster. Half upright, partially reclined, leaned a little to one side, expectant, their position was unusual and, what is worse, it was uncomfortable. They felt a sharp pain in their necks and yet they could not give up their observation. The fact that the morning mist, which—contrary to the way things should have been—was getting denser as the minutes passed, didn't help things, either. Once more they proved that paying complete attention to one thing detracts from the senses and impedes one's ability to notice other things; the morning and the place were stripped of their positive attributes and recoiled in the face of the threat. They stayed like that for an indefinite period: not long, the sky did not lighten all the way, but not a short time, either, because they were left with the memory of an endless vigil. All of a sudden they saw new shadows emerging, rapidly, from the underbrush to join the pulsating mass in the lake; this, together with the articulation of the forms they had been able to make out despite the confusion and the speed with which they moved, made them suspect that they might be looking at a group of people.

And so they were. In the light of day they would be able to perceive things little by little, eventually discerning a compact nucleus of bodies leaned over the water, as well as others that lay back against the shore, forming a protective arch. They wore coarse loincloths that barely covered their nakedness; many of them, the vast majority, were children. Their backs all had the same shape to them: square and broad at the shoulders, they proceeded straight down without tapering until they reached the waist, where a sudden stroke of reality seemed to remind them of the imminent expanse of the hips. Sito and his friend took care not to startle them; they approached cautiously, afraid they might be violent. They did not manage to avoid the former, Sito clarified, though thankfully they were mistaken about the latter; it was the others that panicked at what the two of them might do. What had appeared to be a protective human shield did not, in fact, do any protecting: it was a mass searching for warmth, which dispersed in a flurry of mud and barbaric exclamations. It was then that the two friends discovered the origin of the lapping they had attributed during the night to the swell of the lake: though they kept their mouths close to the surface, they drank with their hands, using them like little pitchers. It was their up and down motion, their splashing, that produced the melody. Once they reached the group, they realized something else that would surprise them: the water had mixed with the mud, which all were eating, as well. They approached someone who appeared to be the leader, who was about forty years old and wore a pair of pants tied at the waist, the holes in which revealed exceptionally pale skin. He stood up, wiped his mouth with the back of his arm to make it obvious that they were interrupting his breakfast, and greeted them. Sito and the other felt it was their right to ask questions—various measures indicated that they could consider themselves superior—and so they got right to the point. "Why do you eat mud?" they asked. "We're very poor," he said, adjusting the strap that held up his pants. Before that moment, Sito continued, he never would have believed it if someone had told him about gangs of the poor, but now he was face to face with one, and a big one at that. He and his friend had gone there to fish, which implied—as did their dinner the night before and the lunch they would have that day—that fish did exist there, though the others preferred the mud. Their organization was tribal. The leader said that they had been walking—and occasionally running—for three days without pause, not stopping to rest or to eat. They avoided towns, they only wanted to pass through; they had a savage industriousness to them that tended toward boring through hills and filling in gullies. As such, lakes were their favorite havens. They could stay there for a day or two, gather their strength, and relax. Their preference for mud was so obvious that it would be pointless to dwell on it, thought Sito, so they didn't say anything else about it. Moments later, when the conversation lagged, they tried to pick it back up by asking his age. "Twenty," he said, and in the difference between reality and appearance they saw the effects of hunger—or of mud. This was a good topic, and they took as much advantage as they could: they mentioned the strange combination of age and appearance, that though these are almost always linked, they rarely coincide, such that there are those who look somewhat younger than they are, others who look a lot younger or only a little. Still, they continued, there are also those who look somewhat or a little older than they are, and then there are those who look *a lot* older. As they said this, they emphasized its significance by looking him straight in the eye. The chief made no effort to respond; his gaze seemed transparent. He probably did not catch the allusion, suggested Sito. On the other hand, aside from leaning over the water, it had probably been a long time since he had seen himself in a mirror. It might also have been that twenty just meant "old," whether that be thirty-five, fifty, or seventy. But all he said, moments later, was, "The mud envelops us from within." These words were a mystery to Sito for a long time, he remarked that afternoon in the café where we had gone for a chat, but a little while ago it became clear to him, and now it seemed both accurate and evident. The mud was a premise; it was the earth that, once they were dead and buried, would tighten around them from outside. Sito was not interested in making conjectures about their diet: whether it was a collective suicide or a hygienic routine, whether it was a premonition translated into action, the portent of a final truth, or whether it was the memory or the embryo of some ritual; all and none of these possibilities were of interest to him. But he was sure that, beyond its own meaning, it had many others that were equally true.

"The mud envelops us from within. It is enveloping us from within," the leader of this indigenous or impoverished tribe, though maybe it was both, had said in his plain, coarse, and somewhat cryptic way beside the lake, offering Sito a justification for his diet. It was a phrase that seemed utterly appropriate, I thought as I stepped onto the curb on the far side of Chile, as the slogan of that place inside us that had been occupied by silence ever since we learned that M had been taken. What I mean is that the silence was, in the first place, self-fulfilling, like a promise that is kept in its making ("I promise to promise" or "I swear to swear"); second, it was descriptive: it was part of our—new or old—nature and, as such, we could not escape its influence. Third, because there is always a third, it was also prescient in that it spoke of the silence in which we would all end up sooner or later, indistinguishable from one another. Half a block from San Juan, I thought: It is likely that Sito neither works in a café nor sells foam rubber; his mother might not be dead and may never have touched a drink, in spite of my memories. Still, there is no question that he has been reached, and invaded by, a silence just like my own. The lack of place, I thought, the absence of a space where M's poor body might be.

It had grown dark by the time I reached Constitución; it was one of those summer nights that are cooler than usual thanks to the breeze coming off the river. From the morning we found out that M had been taken, from that moment on, we been invaded and silenced by excess. The confusion did not last long, the hesitation was brief; it was the lack of moderation that left us without words, just as M was left without a place. I forgot to ask Sito, I thought, whether he moved out of his house for a while after the abduction. But there was no need, I realized; it was obvious that he had not felt obliged to do so.

One is sometimes moved by the effects of time; while on one hand these promote continuity and endurance, often through the work of memory, on the other hand, they also induce forgetting. This forgetting is, after all, mundane and fairly banal, yet it is confusing, and sometimes disappointing, to acknowledge the particularities hidden in the past. We often speak of forgetting when we really mean to say distress, amnesia, mistrust, fear, indifference, distraction, doubt, weariness, omission. My mind oscillates within this narrow range of emotions when, on occasions like the evening after my encounter with Sito, despite the constant allusions in our conversation, which were largely indirect but were always concrete, I feel unable to attribute any tangible trait, even a trivial one, to M; a feature, a gesture or expression, a past, a family, affect, et cetera. A reflected image that has slowly given way to negation, to shadow. The effect is unreal, and this unreal effect makes his life seem not only improbable, but also incidental. Did M exist? Yes, I say. But what was his time on earth like? It is all conjecture, I reasoned, the more time passes, the less I know. This lack of knowledge has nothing to do with forgetting, though that is what we call it, nor with the length of his absence, but rather with its *excess*.

Constitución station, with its open platforms, its soaring ceiling, and its iron girders studded with colossal bolts, looked more like the hangar of a blimp. At that moment, all the train routes sounded far-fetched to me. Remedios de Escalada seemed just as distant as Bahía Blanca; beyond a certain point space began to dissolve, and that point was not far away. Concepts like near and far are derived from useless categories, I thought.

M and the other often had conflicting opinions about the differences between the capital and the suburbs. Though they took it for what it was, which was truly secondary, for ages this subject interested them more than other questions that were, from several points of view, more vital. Their discussions could last for weeks, with periods of greater emphasis and ones of apparent disinterest. And yet, though it was not mentioned, the subject was not cast aside: it followed its tortuous path without leaving them. M and the other were approaching an axis of coincidences that might seem fragile or weak, but which was useful as a foundation, like a moveable border, to propose new problems in response to a question—this was the basic implication, to which no one objected—that seemed to be both complex and impossible to resolve yet, at the same time, clear and simple. This question might seem pointless now, but the other would not be exaggerating if he said that, until a little while ago it was obvious to him as he passed from the suburbs into the capital, or vice versa, that he was passing into a contiguous order that was similar in appearance but was marked by difference (and certainly still is).

One tends to define both the location and the nature of limits; it is no different with cities. They were captivated by the idea of Buenos Aires as

a never-ending city, but this trait was, in fact, disproven by its periph-
ery: the proof of its supposed proliferation and, at the same time, of its
limits could be found in the expansion of the suburbs, a complex built
on contiguity that did not necessarily correspond to the city, and which
changed it into something else. There are parts of the so-called suburbs
that turn out to be just as incomprehensible as an unfamiliar, unknown
city—so incomprehensible, in fact, that they defy comparison—but in
general, passing through them, one acknowledges that their inhabitants
live partially in our city and partially in another; in a border zone in
which difference sometimes appears as a distortion, a substitution, or a
replica. There exists a collective scene that this dissonance calls into ques-
tion, though it rarely contests and sometimes even reinforces it. Because
of this, at least in part, M and the other always walked around Greater
Buenos Aires with a vague feeling of curiosity, adventure, anxiety, aban-
don, pleasure, freedom, and compassion. It was a difference that returned
to them the sense that the familiar was both certain and decisive.

Sometimes, I recalled that night in Constitución station, M and I
would make fun of Sito. One day, I remember it well, while we
were talking about the tragic state his mother was in, M let slip a
pobre Sito. We found this particularly funny, despite the seriousness
of the subject. The association of his name with the grammatical
diminutive never caused him any problems, I thought as I stood
on the sidewalk; on the contrary, if often made things easier for
him. Like Ada—or Sita—it was a name whose merits anyone could
acknowledge or infer. Sito did not appear to be wealthy, nor did
he seem down on his luck. To pay for the coffees he had taken out
a wad of money that was so thick I found it hard to conceal my
surprise. He could barely hold it in one hand; however, it was made
up of small bills. "Today's tips," he explained. He had been one of

the ones who believed the story about the eye—I remembered M saying that Monday before we went in to school. I had asked him, incredulously, if anyone had believed him, and he told me that, yes, Sito was the least hesitant. That same Sunday afternoon, before the end of the day, he decided to leave his room and headed out into the street. A few hours of sleep had been enough to recover from his collapse and to go back over the meaning of the day's events, M told me the next morning ("if the events had any meaning"). Near the tracks at the end of the block, leaning against the rails of one of their circuitous walkways, the neighborhood assembly was in session. He went over and told them. No one seemed surprised, though several might have thought it inconsistent; they did not object to the discovery, they simply did not believe it had happened, given that the evidence rested precisely on the absence of proof, on the fact that M had not brought the eye back to show them. A conversation without anything special or relevant to it, M observed as we entered the school. Just one of the many that advanced impassively as a way to pass the time as the afternoon advanced and the trees grew darker, that is, until it occurred to Sito to suggest a test of veracity: if M could repeat, in the exact same words, the story about the eye, that would mean that he was not lying. They looked at him blankly and were quiet for a long time; they could not see the point of something so gratuitous, so ridiculous. Eventually a few of them saw the need to voice their objections: "You can make something up, and then repeat it." That ended the discussion, or so it seemed. "No one can repeat a made-up story," Sito countered. Everyone, including M, looked at him cautiously; the argument seemed solid. At that point Sito started rubbing his eye, as he sometimes did.

After that Monday morning—once inside the school, we stopped talking—though it may seem strange, we never spoke of the matter again. Now, as I watched an empty train pull into an abandoned platform, I regretted not having remembered the story that afternoon, so I could have asked Sito how he had come up with that line of reasoning. Not only that, I thought, standing in Constitución, Sito might have been able to explain things to me that I still didn't know or understand. But I didn't ask him anything, I said to myself, which was an error and a gaffe. We spent most of the afternoon in a café; at his invitation we had two coffees each, we even made small talk, as they say, and I was incapable of asking a thing about M. Standing there in the station, I honestly could not believe it. As I said, it is true that Sito did not ask any questions, either, but it was certainly I who should have made the first move, as corresponded to his invitation. He must have been thinking, with all assurance, as he walked away along Carlos Pellegrini and later, when he stopped at the kiosk and waved to me, "What a cretin. Talking all afternoon and never once bringing up the memory of his friend." Evidently, if this was what he was thinking, he was not wrong. I thought I had seen a condescending smile in that long-distance greeting, though at the time I had considered it an effect of the caramel he was eating. Now, on a platform in Constitución station, where I had walked for no reason in particular other than to watch the trains come and go, the gesture seemed both completely reasonable and unmistakably lucid.

FOUR

For those who give themselves over to a territorial friendship, time—even space—is an excuse, secondary to a single, essential element: the indirect path, often sinuous and always arbitrary, along which the traces and labors of distance accumulate as silt does beneath water. It is paradoxical that territory, a spatial concept, should see its own condition dispelled as it grows unfathomable and manifests itself in the form of a delay or of an often irrecoverable past, a lapsed apogee or a liberated present able to change form and occupy another place at any moment, under any circumstance. Sometimes on our walks, the day—despite its clumsy and forced evolution—would not progress. The light, the weather, or the set of sensorial tools one uses to locate oneself within the jumble might change, but there was a residue that literally stopped the passage of time; one felt one might remain there forever. At those moments it was as though we were in a painting over which a faint vapor hovered, or was perceived: some sort of shadow or mist at the horizon, a mix of light and color—or cold and heat—through which an imprecise form, probably that of trees or houses, could just barely be discerned.

For months we walked around different parts of the suburbs almost every day. Both before and after that time—a period in which we were searching for something, something that would become a symbol of salvation, as I will explain in a moment—both before and after that time we walked around intermittently, almost always casually and often without any particular reason but, as I have said, with the same feeling of recklessness and the same excitement, the same combination of abundance and delirium. At that time, when we would go on the walks I am about to describe, it was still four years before M would disappear. If I say now that the future to come would have seemed unreal, unthinkable in that moment, I am truly not exaggerating. No one thinks about the future; we are ignorant of what is to come and abandon ourselves to the void of its mystery. It is also true that, while no one can see the future, we attempt in vain to anticipate it. Those with foresight think about what is to come, those without it think about the *moment*. At the end of the day, everyone belongs to one of these two groups; yet the idea that M would disappear within a few years would have sounded far-fetched to anyone. As a concept, we expect nothing of the future, which is a good thing, but we expect everything of the moment and of what is to come. (This everything has a literal value here: I mean that "everything" includes the word change, as well.)

Something about the city brings us to accept transformations; this thing becomes familiar, and in that moment we acknowledge, or rather, embrace it. Change, novelty—despite being beyond our grasp because, in the city, things happen without our knowledge—are the proofs offered to us by the present in an unremitting stream.

The proliferation of events, the propagation of signs, those forms in which the city expresses itself are the language used by the present to renew itself and, in this way, construct its simulacrum of the future. How else would the future manifest itself, if not in the image of the contemporary? And what is the contemporary, par excellence, if not life in the city? City, future, proliferation, truth: the four ends of an equilateral cross, at the top of which figures the word "city." The other three are interchangeable.

Just as the geography of the city conditions us to accept change or novelty despite the fact that change and novelty are rarely within our grasp, assigning to the present the fantastic ability to contain infinite occurrences, people feel compelled to make their predictions: the city as an innumerable series of events that take place within a defined space, and what is to come as a hypothetical realm in which occurrences proliferate at the heart of a hidden moment, impossible but nonetheless concrete, similar to those that occur all the time on the streets of distant neighborhoods. Even this seemingly forced metaphor between the future and the city allows for the idea of proximity and its effects: nearness and immediacy—essential relations for those anxious about what is to come. On the other hand, the city offers validation to those who do not make predictions: change, the bustle that grows more or less feverish depending on the hour and the circumstance, which can be represented—and contemplated—from a single point. This observation often takes place from a café table or—in the neighborhood—from chairs set up on the sidewalk, open windows, et cetera. The city is not only simultaneous—we know that at any moment, in any place, there are always a number of different things happening—but also *spontaneous*: events unfold without reason or accord, which makes them appear autonomous and random. Those who live in the moment find, in this exercise, the natural model for their lack of foresight. The same thing happens with noise: noises do not fade into the distance, die out, or grow, they simply stop or are drowned out by another, stronger one. Yet the city—which, if one must define it, could be said to be the place in which the greatest number of obstacles comes together—finds its promise of privacy eradicated by sound. M's meticulous observations about the clamor of the trains and the cheers coming from the soccer stadium on Sundays are definitive proof of this. From bombs to the clap of thunder, via the drip of a faucet or the crackling sound of cars inching forward on the wet pavement—these noises moderate the inevitability of its construction. Geography is an art of vision; it is in its profound independence from geography, which is condemned to absorb it, that the difficulty of sound resides. Sound is equivalent to the future: that which one cannot see. This is why the first thing we forget about a person is their voice. M and I used to listen for sounds and reflect on this dubious philosophy, usually on our walks without a set destination—or with a destination that was so unknown that it ceased to be such—while we thought of ourselves as planets. It seems to me today that Buenos Aires had, at the time, a certain essential quality; it was a crystalline city. Now, though, its inhabitants are made of liquid.

At first, and for a long time, M's father did not understand what had happened when he turned his head to discover that his car was gone. He had just left a small grocery store in the suburbs (at the time he worked as a cookie wholesaler) and was going over the list of clients he still had to call on; he was startled to see nothing at the curb. He thought there had been a mistake, that he had left the car somewhere else, et cetera. He took stock, walked the few paces to the corner, and looked up and down the street. Each scan of the desolate block, however, brought him a little closer to the truth. Then he understood that he had been robbed. He went back into the store, to "let them know," as he said, though in truth he didn't know what to say. As he spoke, he felt that there was little, almost nothing, he could do. Then he saw that his world was falling apart and was so mortified that he began to cry. They comforted him at the store; later, as though they were revealing some great secret, they suggested that he report it to the police. In anticipation of his experience years later, they offered him no hope at the police station, so he went back to the office, where they comforted him even more and offered him something to eat. M's father spoke angrily, but ate without any hurry. When he finished, he took a walk around the neighboring blocks, asking if anyone had seen his car. He was out there for hours, getting answers like, "I don't know," "Yes," and "No." At one point he gleaned that the people, surprised by the strength of his conviction, were actually answering at random—not with the first thing that came to their minds, but with the most statistically likely answer, the effect of probability; it was a pre-cerebral response. This realization did not lead him to abandon his inquiry, on the contrary, he told himself that if there were an order beyond experience that determined the answers he was getting, it was also likely that this was close to the truth; certainly, the order with which he was now coming into contact had been the one that dictated the moment his car was stolen. Though the light was beginning to dim, the afternoon seemed to him as though it were fading to white. He thought about that evening, about his return home and about going inside with the news, and told himself that he still had plenty of time, getting his hopes back up to continue the search. He had lingered a bit with the client, he conceded; since no one else was coming in, they had spoken for nearly two hours. When he got bored, he looked at his watch and feigned surprise at the time, but he already knew he had wasted half the morning. As he left he thought: I've been here two hours and not a soul has come into this poor guy's shop. Then all of a sudden he became the poor guy, when he realized that he had left the car alone too long. That's how it happened, M said to me the next day. He was late getting home; everyone was already at the table. "The car was stolen," he managed to stammer as he crossed the floor toward his room.

M and I were in our third year of high school. The next morning, his father began to walk around the suburbs, swearing that he would not give up until he found it. He would abandon his dedication to the car a few years later, because of his son (in this sense I still remember the father, his figure, under a sign of mystery). M would go out with him some days, and on occasion I would accompany them. We were going out to wander around, according to the mother. Despite the lack of signs—or hope, for that matter—and the discouragement that brought down our spirits, especially those of the father, I still have a clear and, I would almost say, happy memory of those walks. In the first place, the likelihood that the search would succeed was so slight that, far from being a duty, it took on the quality of an adventure, of frivolity: there is nothing better than an unlikely objective to make a task that might appear important seem gratuitous. In the second place, I have never again had that feeling, except in memory, of setting in motion the proliferation of whitewashed houses and perfectly regular blocks that unfolded before us as we walked at a leisurely pace. Even poverty, which can often seem unexpected and overwhelming, as one might imagine, proved to be gradual in that territory. Entire blocks of indecision or timidity, and occasionally of cowardice or bashfulness, regulated any contrasts. As it was, the geography of Buenos Aires could not be thought of in terms of depth, but only of breadth—we had not actually entered into anything in particular, but were rather crossing a surface that lacked any real variation—these were poor areas in which the deterioration was so aligned with its medium that it seemed as though they might never end. Surface and poverty were two complementary echoes coming together to create a concrete reality, each multiplying the effect of the other. In the meantime, it seemed as though we—alert, attentive to the appearance of that blue car—were skirting the outer reaches of a territory, an ever-changing yet boundless country. I would not be exaggerating if I said that, despite the difficulty of the operation, we were able to take note of the balance of things, like that of our heads and our bodies as we moved, which was similar to the undulating line of the horizon discerned by a camel. As we advanced, I went over my doubts about the endeavor: it was like trying to find a needle in a haystack, I had said to M, without any originality. Now, however, I had no regrets about joining the committee—"the investigative committee," as the father would joke; despite the growing concern that overwhelmed him, he was always at the ready to amuse the two of us, who were still boys in his mind. I had no regrets; on the contrary, I wanted more streets to walk down, and was happy to have the chance to wander without boundaries, as though Greater Buenos Aires were truly the territory of vastness.

Sometimes M's father would plan our routes to coincide with stores where he could solicit orders. M and I would wait outside, hiding from the sun under a tree, silently surprised that not a soul would come down the street. Other times we would go in, and the father would introduce us to the owner in a way that seemed excessive, not so much because his remarks were particularly fawning, but for the profusion of details he used to describe us. Later, the shopkeepers would ask how the search was going. The father would answer reproachfully with an oath I have not been able to recall exactly for some time now, perhaps because of the jarring effect that it produced, swearing that he would wear out all his shoes before he gave up. Almost imperiously, he insisted that we go in with him when he made use of the walks to sign on new clients; our presence was a force that was hard for the owners of these businesses to overcome. They were flattered by the fact that three people were engaged in the effort to sell them a few little things; they were grateful for the service and, caught somewhere between confusion and pretension, ended up buying more than was expected. The father often used the phrase "poor guy," and on more than one occasion said, "Everyone in Greater Buenos Aires is down on his luck," usually without noticing my presence as I walked beside him through the vastness like one more of those, according to him, poor guys from the suburbs. When he did notice, too infrequently for my taste, he would improvise some gesture of surprise and excuse himself, patting me on the back. First he would say my name, and then add, "Nothing personal" (the order never changed).

Though we might be inclined to talk about it as something common, it is always startling to see the effect displacement has on the organization of space. Scale and trajectory, the tools necessary to organize a route, depend on movement rather than geography; speed is the determining factor. When one walks, one moves within an environment on a tremendous scale; when one travels by train or car, the environment is reduced to a moderate scale; the airplane, on the other hand, belongs to the small scale. To cross half a continent in a few hours, or to walk on both shores of an ocean in the same day, not only contradicts anyone skeptical of movement, but also means the compression of a seemingly impossible distance. Forced by the theft to walk day after day with a double purpose, M's father would discover a parallel essence in the suburbs, supplementary to the one he had observed from his car. The deferred realm of the large-scale, paradoxically, individualized the streets and multiplied the businesses. In this way, he experienced—or rather relived, since this is, as I recall, a characteristic of children—a communion with the minor and the microscopic: fleeting moments, brief inter-ruptions, a limited radius; murmurs and exclamations, as well as small businesses, kiosks, garages, and vestibules.

In the course of this intensive labor, there was no place he did not visit; grocery shops seemed to be born and develop as an effect of his passing. If the neighborhood had been the unit of measure when he had the car, now it was the block. After a few weeks of walking, he understood the contradiction between these two aims; selling and searching were mutually exclusive, particularly because a sale meant coming back—it would have been foolish to lose a good client—and coming back, after all, meant going to the same place over again. It is true that the car was not necessarily always parked; there was also a chance, albeit a minimal one, of seeing it pass by, although considering this possibility would have meant accepting its ultimate implication: that all they had to do was stand on the corner and wait, though obviously the car might just as eas-ily never pass by. As such, he would dedicate certain days to sales and others to the search. On those mornings, before setting out on his expedition, he would choose the perfect epicenter as our starting point, one that would ensure the fewest obstacles given the enor-mous distance that we would cover. Once there, we would begin to walk in a spiral, inevitably deferring to the shape of the blocks. When, after a few hours, we found ourselves forced to walk in a straight line for several blocks before being able to turn, the notion of progress and expansion left us and we were humbled by a sense of linearity. The loop took on such a wide arc that it ceased to be such; we thought we were simply headed forward, not realizing that we were actually only two blocks to the right or the left of where we had passed, distracted, just a little while earlier. The father was in charge of the turns, and from time to time consulted a street map that was bound like a book—it often forced him to flip back or skip ahead several pages, even when it was only a matter of crossing a street or turning a corner. Finding our location on a map means seeing ourselves from the outside; it has a greater impact on us than looking at old photographs, in which we are caught off guard by a discolored, outdated figure, the memory and foundation of the present, which is recovered as soon as we lean over the portrait. A reality at once uncomplicated and global seems to be present in a map, in such a way that when we coincide, occupying the point observed with our bodies, the only requirement remaining for the map to become truth—that is, ourselves—has been met.

When the three of us stopped to look at the atlas, trying to anticipate natural obstacles—gullies, dead ends, factories, barracks, and the like—to the orderly progress of our spiral trajectory, a deliberation that overlooked the actual object of the walk nearly always occurred: interests and preferences would emerge, the desire to see a certain place or neighborhood based fundamentally on its name. Atlases do not describe anything: they only list streets, ways, and plazas, and public or private facilities that are considered especially large. It would be difficult to imagine their saying much more than that, but in any case our hunger for adventure sought to compensate for this silence by visiting them. It was, precisely, a matter of visiting a name: indistinguishable places and streets marked only by their denomination that added nothing to the landscape, apart from their presence. The vastness was multiplied geographically, but also nominally. Repetitions immediately made the differences between the street in the capital and the homonym on which we stood appear obvious. Others lacked a counterpart in the city, but when one of these, generally named after national heroes or mere dates, so much as suggested an association with a similar name or date, it seemed to be the echo of another street or plaza, and served only as a vague recollection in the topological memory of the people.

We looked like tourists. And, as happens to tourists, when I look back on those walks a surreal nostalgia and a confused feeling of abundance colors their very existence with a sense of ambiguity. Though it may be redundant, it is worth noting the essential scenic value that the landscape, geography, had in the consolidation and development of our friendship. The words scenery or scenic sometimes tend to be taken as a sign of vain ornamentation having little impact on the mysterious series of circumstances that is life; yet scenery is practically everything, and nothing could be less ornamental. I do not mean to say that life is theatrical but rather that, as we pass through it, we erect a stage for its scenes; this is represented by geography. The constellations that M and I believed we formed throughout the day as we connected our individual trajectories needed the space of the city to be understood as such, as the orbit of planets whose course is influenced by the relative effects of mass, force, gravity, and things like that, which define the breadth and depth of their impact as complex equations and reciprocal equilibrium; in this same way, the two of us seemed to bear the weight of the city on the transparent lines that connected our bodies in movement.

It does not matter whether it seems possible for Buenos Aires to exist beyond our influence; what was essential could be found in the diagrams we etched into the territory, which conferred an additional valence upon the known plan of the city, turning it into *more* space, *another* surface, while still remaining itself. The universe would continue to exist if the solar system disappeared, but the solar system would not be the solar system without the universe. The universe is preeminent in appearance only, because the solar system is a category separate from it: without the universe, there would be no solar system, but without the solar system, the universe would be different, other. Something similar could be said about our friendship. The city was crisscrossed by the imaginary lines of our bodies in movement, patterns and designs that became part of the geography; these would not have existed without Buenos Aires—nor, apparently, would our friendship. (Now, and for years, these are also what has been missing.)

As I have already written, a recurring subject of the digressions with which we passed the time was to hypothesize about the essential differences between the city and the suburbs: distinctions whose existence could not be questioned. There is no point in repeating our ideas on the matter, many of which were the belated aftereffects of those walks we took while searching for the car, and which had simply been rescued, or rather salvaged, from the depths of M's consciousness months or even years after the fact. Impressions like the vague recollections being expressed now, in any event. There is no need to clarify that these pages constitute a belated and almost unexpected aftereffect of situations and memories. Compared with the years retained by the average memory, or the span represented by the coming millennium, the choice to recount the few events of this story, not quite two decades after they occurred, might seem a bit hurried. Neither of us would have imagined that, years later, these events would be written down on paper. If we had foreseen this, we would have acted differently, guiding our steps according to our idea of posterity; fortunately, we did not. (This foreseeing should be clarified, however, given that if M knew the reasons why I would end up writing these pages, he certainly would have done what was needed to avoid his abduction, though, in fact, he did nothing at all to cause it. They say that one could avoid innumerable problems, mistakes, and catastrophes if one knew how things were going to turn out, but this is an impossible dream. The most extreme example of this is that we are all certain of death—and even, expanding things a bit, about the decline of civilization, the destruction of the environment, and the inevitable ostracism of the sun—but are still unable to avoid the end. What keeps us from losing hope in the face of this inescapable truth? A belief in the interim, in the fact that, in the meantime, things happen that are worth experiencing.)

No one imagined that, years later, those walks would end up this way, taking the form of words on paper. Still, our steps—as firm and as weightless as the mornings in those days—shone with their own light, without assistance. Those walks through Greater Buenos Aires were predictable, probably boring, and perhaps too speculative. The truth is that very little happened, almost nothing; it was like sailing with a course but no destination. Whoever believes in destiny expects, at the very least, that things should happen; though it might be a mistake, just as no one thinks of tedium as a property of action, no one considers passivity to be the work of destiny, when actually it is. So minor and insubstantial were the events we stumbled upon that the idea of living at the mercy of chance would only have provoked incredulity in M and me. We were contemplative. When not overwhelmed by the desert, travelers see mirages; they expect this, make nothing of it, and carry on accordingly. But to us, saturated by the landscape of the suburbs, the absence of action was intoxicating. We wandered like planets, our orbits well outside the sphere of activity. Events did not affect us; they belonged to an order that was not only absent, but had been effaced, dissipating just a few meters before we reached them.

It was always like that during the time of our walks, one morning after another. And yet one day—which seemed to have been marked to produce, in the space of a few hours, something that had not happened for months on end—would be the exception. We were at the middle of one of those typical suburban blocks with little traffic and unused sidewalks. Because our surroundings kept us from any practical sort of trance, our only option, apart from walking and looking, was to talk. We made bets on finding the car. The father calculated fifteen days, M bet thirty, and I—so as not to discourage them—said a week, when I really thought it would either take more than four months or was simply impossible. Since finding the car depended, at the end of the day, on coincidence, anyone could see that these calculations were just another topic of conversation. The father would say, "In fifteen days we will have covered more than 5,000 blocks, which, added to the 12,000 we had already done, make 17,000," though he did not specify why that was the number required. M, for his part, doubled the figure, perhaps thinking that twice as many opportunities might present themselves that way— as though we might find two cars, or the same car two times. He would take a deep breath and say, "We walk 11,000 blocks every month, plus the 12,000 we've done already makes 23,000. With that many, nothing could get by us." His father would get annoyed and cast him a sidelong glance. "I'd have to be crazy to walk that." Our conversations were of that nature. In my case, I thought we still had something like 44,000 blocks to go—four months, plus the 12,000 that, according to M and his father, we had already covered, or it might even have been that we needed a total of 100,000 blocks, or eight months. But since I did not think it opportune to be honest, I only said, "I think it will all be settled in a week, with the car waiting for us on X as though nothing had happened. I don't think we have more than 2,500 blocks to go." X was the street where M lived. They listened to me as though a divinity were speaking. "From your lips to God's ears," the father said.

At that moment we reached a corner. We saw, due east, a sun that cast no shadow on the pavement on either side of the street. On the next block, M and I thought about the religious implications, for both of our beliefs, of the words "From your lips to God's ears," though they might have been nothing more than another way of saying, "Let's hope," as one might do several times a day. Just as we were crossing the street, we heard a scream, a mix of panic and grief trailing off into a wail; it came from behind the line of doors. To get closer we needed only to keep walking, but we stopped instead of advancing; the surprise held us paralyzed in the middle of the street. Another scream, and someone came running out at full speed, though not in our direction. The man's pants were open and he was having a hard time holding them up. One could see, in his movements, the clumsy syntax of escape: the fear that drew his feet in search of a safe place to hide and the contradictory, apparently mutually exclusive, movement of his body, which froze for a moment with each new scream. The man had raped, but the rape had not reached its conclusion; perhaps this was the cause of the tension between urgency and interruption. People who lived nearby peered out through their windows, others flooded into the street.

Overturned bicycles appeared on the street: people were coming over to watch. It is strange that when something happens, very often something terrible and unexpected, one's first reaction is to wait, as though only another event could bear the tragedy out. People crowded around like ants, circling, exchanging information. And so a somewhat brief period elapsed in which no one noticed the passage of time, all were so absorbed by the gathering. Once it had its fill of words, the tribe regained its disquiet. It wanted facts. A statement, more obvious than novel, was made: The police were slow in coming, and should hurry. It was not hard to gather the details of the story, a familiar series of sordid scenes. The girl or young woman—they mentioned her by name, which left her age unclear—was a victim of the jealousy of her mother, who shut her inside the house whenever she went out, locking all the doors and leaving her without keys. This maternal jealousy had come to be projected through the throat of the daughter, in the form of screams and nervous fits, an echo of itself. That which was sown by one was reaped by the other, it seemed. The lecher, for his part, had fallen back on an old technique—entering through the roof; when he realized he was in danger, he tested the efficacy of another, also old—a leap from a window. Nonetheless, between one event and the next, there was a mystery that was difficult to resolve; at first the lecher thought it was danger he sensed, a threat inscribed in the scream of the girl, but he immediately realized it was a weariness subject to something far deeper, something fairly complex and difficult to gauge. It was the weariness of the limit; it is always exhausting to exist at a limit. It was something related not to time, to the prolongation of a condition, but rather to the intensity—or depth—of that state. To be on the verge of flight, on the verge of invasion: frontiers that, when mentioned in this way, may seem trivial or as light as a cloud, but which weighed the shoulders down with a load that became increasingly difficult to bear, especially when they arose unexpectedly. This weight bent a body in two and leaned over its waist, grabbing on to its hips; and in the midst of it all, there was the urgency of escape. This could last unbearably long.

The women who lived nearby were left at the mercy of fear and consternation, and yet several were less indignant at the incident than at the detestable publicity that had been afforded a private act. Children were running around; every now and then a few would shoot off after receiving an order from the adults. There was also talk that the father, who had been separated from the family for some time, had taken his revenge on the mother through the body of their daughter. Within five minutes everything was possible, even true. There were more hypotheses: that the mother had instigated it, leaving the house at the most opportune moment in order to destroy both husband (or ex-husband) and daughter, for whom she felt no love; this was why she ordered the girl to sleep in her bed, so the father would mistake her for the mother (that is, for her) and both would find damnation through sex. It could also have been that the mother, allied with the father against their daughter, had planned the rape. Many described the house as a living hell: at night, the screams could be heard along the entire street, the neighborhood falling asleep to the recent memory of profanities. They preferred not to talk about the victim, draping over her a veil of suspicion more cruel than even the most aberrant accusation; it was a silence whose fissures gave way to complaints, disdain, slander, and eventually condemnation. Several acknowledged wearily that they had seen her on the corner well into the night, sitting on the sidewalk with boys from outside the neighborhood.

M and I looked at one another; without saying anything, we agreed that if these were the things that had to transpire so that something would happen on our walks, it was better that nothing at all occur. We were not only disillusioned by the situation, empirically speaking, but also by the tenor of the comments. It was disappointing that, in a land as slow, as luminous and, in its way, as elastic as the suburbs, common sense would reign as resoundingly as it did everywhere else, even in the capital. Is the world the same all over? we would ask ourselves later, as we remembered the scene and compared it with others, which were always the same though they occurred in different places.

With the confusion at its height, we started off again on our walk; after a few blocks, we were surprised by the sound of a gunshot. We had been walking and talking about rape in general; M's father was telling a story about a rape that, as far as he knew, had taken place on the train tracks a few meters from his house, when all of a sudden, off to our left, we heard the blast (the shot).

THE FIRST STORY TOLD BY M's FATHER

Shielded by the darkness of the train tracks, a rapist committed a rape. Then he arranged to meet the victim the following night. "Same time tomorrow," he declared as he zipped up his pants, convinced of the fear or the desire this might provoke. The victim did not intend to go. The rapist knew this, but he could not think of a way to prolong the possession, the feeling of power, other than by offering her the freedom to return, regardless of whether she did so or not. (That is what orders are for.) The next day he waited for five hours in the dark, feeling his way along or sitting on the rails with vermin scurrying around him in the underbrush. Her delay undermined his authority and wounded his pride, although, in the hope of restoring them, he was inclined to return to the scene day after day. The following night afforded him proof of the intermittent nature of cold, as opposed to heat, which is constant. They say that waiting softens emotions (an aggravated person will quiet down, an anxious person will show restraint, et cetera) but, in the case of his excessive temperament, it would end up dispelling them completely. The anger of the second night dissipated until it became a vulgar idealization of the first; that which began as an unrestrained desire for dominance ended as a simple exercise in nostalgia. He was falling in love with the memory. He even said, in one of the soliloquies with which he would distract himself, "If she came back, I could forgive her." Moments later, aroused and picturing the liberties he would take, he imagined the details of a struggle rewarded in the end with the violence of possession. He thought of roughness as the most perfect form of forgiveness, in that it was its portent. He talked to himself during the day, as well, trying to understand the force that made him a captive of that place.

In the meantime, the neighborhood had begun to see him as just another resident of the tracks, one of the individuals who set themselves up there, candidates for the voluntary ostracism of the vagabond. Along the stretch of those few kilometers, delimited by the storehouses erected near Palermo Station, on one side, and the shops of La Paternal on the other, his wanderings would achieve, for him at least, a global scale; the space, though limited, could have an infinite scope. The depth upon which he stumbled from time to time, as he committed a rape, mingled with his instinctive knowledge of the place: he knew all its invisible coordinates, both temporal and spatial; what is more, he felt them as part of his body, a perception independent of the senses. At night, or with his eyes closed, he could predict the approach of a train in the distance; a faint buzzing in his ears told him that someone, hidden behind the walls of their house, was about to turn on the faucet and take a bath; a twitch in his eyelid alerted him that he was being watched; he could predict the weather with just a glance. This connection with his surroundings was so evident that it suggested—if not in its scope, at least in its intensity—a precise understanding of the world. This world existed behind the mask of the visual, allowing only its besieged surface—striated, perforated, mutilated, halting—to be seen. The landscape of the tracks, the sight of the storehouses with the cargo containers scattered off to the side; all this remained as a portrait of minute differences. Things rarely changed; at the most, a man might enter his field of vision, cross it, and leave it again on the other side at exactly the same pace. These minute differences also included the vegetation: the length and shade of the grass, the indeterminate height of the stalks and their color, a pale green due to lack of care. Neglect had arrived and would remain, though this formulation is not entirely accurate, as it was clear that it had been there for some time. It all seemed to be consuming itself in an unusual series of death throes, imperceptible because of their pervasiveness. The train cars, like the rest of the picture, continued to wait with tireless resolve. The inveterate rapist could not have asked for anything more: an expansive, almost infinite, space that was invisible to the rest of the city. To occupy those places unseen by others is to conquer privacy, he repeated to himself, not understanding the full meaning of his words.

Several months later, a chance encounter disrupted this harmony late one misty afternoon: on the corner of Corrientes and calle Bonpland, the rapist raised his eyes from a pair of feet that were blocking his way and recognized the face of his victim. The long, feverish wait did not give way to surprise, but rather reverted to bitterness; rapists tend to think they can mitigate their crime by reacting to it in a sentimental way. And so he did: "You didn't come," he said dejectedly, barely hiding his agitation. The victim looked at him, not understanding. "You must have me mistaken for someone else," she said eventually, and walked away.

The shot extinguished its own sound. The fact that, at the end of the day, silence can be chimerical, but that one will nonetheless be surprised by the exceptional weakness of certain noises, is another of the exemplary truths of Greater Buenos Aires. The three believed they were witnessing the first moments after an exodus, when decay begins its impassive conquest. Noises were not only muffled by the time they reached them, they also took the form of forgetting; of a void, even. And yet those slight hollows, those surfaces extending without end, were still occupied—very much so—although some sort of acoustic reticence or a singular effect of the air on the structures made them appear deserted. The scene with the rapist was behind them. When they heard the blast, the three were passing in front of a house typical of the area (there, almost everything seemed typical). It was low to the ground and had a sparse, dejected-looking garden out front. The shot, they imagined, was a kind of void, the mechanism by which matter was stirred and made to vanish. For a moment, they looked at the street as though it were made of nothingness (paradoxically, it was similar to the sensation caused by an abstract silence); this forced them to pause. They did not think of the danger; they were aware only of the din that had sought to dominate the calm of the afternoon. All of a sudden a man appeared, crossing the garden from the depths of the house, his body thrust forward with an urgency that might have seemed theatrical but which proved to be real: agony and trajectory. The last of his strength could take him no further; the simple act of opening the front door had defeated him, and he collapsed. The body that had pulsed with life moments ago was nothing more than a weight drawn toward the earth. There he stayed, slumped over the gate, which held him up like one of those impassive horses in the movies. At that moment, the three all had the same thought: the man that someone had just, as they say, sent into the next life, had made it to the threshold by his own means. (The scene thus had a greater symbolic density: gate and agony, the instruments and disposition par excellence of the threshold coming together in a way that coincidence rendered particularly elegant.) It is not every day that reality unfolds according to chance in such a way that proves how a world plagued by insipid—and unconnected—events can organize itself along the lines of coincidence.

This idea had just taken shape when they heard a scream: a woman coming from the house. When she saw the man, she turned her expression of shock on M, his father, and the other, then ran to embrace the motionless body. And so the three saw a second person cross the garden at full speed. The woman beat at his back as though she wanted to wake him from a dream, restore him to life, re-animate the indifferent matter hanging from the gate like ballast. They, for their part, did not know how to react. One spends one's life waiting for something to happen, and then when it finally does, confusion clouds the mind. On top of this, the chain of events was of such a flexible simplicity that it was rendered abstract: they were not events but rather seemed like the actions of a tragedy, a drama enacted in real time and space. The idea of chance in general and the belief that, around there, chance had a logic all its own—the laws of which had been ignored, or at least unknown, until *that moment—set before them an inconceivable scene, with neither neighbors or onlookers to free them from the obligation of approaching. Yet it would be a mistake to think that their hesitancy was grounded in fear; it was instead due to the distance with which some events are perceived. People die, but rarely in front of us; people kill, but there are rarely many witnesses. When there are many onlookers, all can approach without worry, but when there is no one else there, one would prefer not to be there, either, or at least to escape quickly, to evaporate.*

There is no need to spell out what happened next: the chaos of emergencies, threats, demands, and mistrust. The nature of what had transpired was completely clear and yet, for many, anything at all could have occurred. No one believed M, his father, or the other, each time accepting as true the complete opposite of what they had said. None of it was worth a thing; the situation, though real, was weighed down by a hypothetical significance that preceded the truth of any one of its elements. So reasonable were the reservations of the skeptics that even the three, despite being privileged witnesses to the events, began to question what had happened, though it had been as clear to their eyes as the air.

Of the many types of contact between things, a car crash is the most jarring. It has been said that nothing in the area deserved the name of transportation; it is likely that nothing there deserved known names or words. Though it may seem redundant, things seemed as if they were there for the first time. It should be said that everything appeared to be continually reborn, beginning and beginning with an inexhaustible rhythm. Of that constant peacefulness, the cyclical days on the streets of Greater Buenos Aires—not only on those which he spent walking with M and his father, but also the many others experienced every day, and forever—of that tranquility, the other remembers the people of the neighborhood sitting by their front doors and the surprise that would lift their heads, their eyes captivated by that rare apparition: a car. How movement captivates. They turned their heads less rapidly at cyclists and neighbors; on the lowest tier, there were pedestrians—the three of them, for example—and animals, like stray dogs or horses pulling carts. Those required such a slow rotation of the head that it was barely a movement at all: the perfect state for enjoying a bit of fresh air. This general sense of calm was interrupted by the collision: a car backing out of a garage hit another one, which was parked on the street. It was a stupid accident, but one with unforeseeable consequences. One could walk for blocks on end without seeing a car, yet the only two around gravitated toward one another with the innocence of magnets. They could not believe it: they approached as the car backed up. It was a familiar maneuver that, under other circumstances, would have been completely predictable; circumstances other than these, in which the driver forgot to brake—another idea ran through their minds: the driver might be blind, or drunk, or maybe he was just distracted. In any case, he was unable to anticipate the danger. The collision had not yet occurred (this "yet" means that it was inevitable); shortly thereafter, M's father would tell the brief, though only partial, story of an alcoholic.

THE SECOND STORY TOLD BY M'S FATHER

The man had been out of work for years. The routine of a job is one that is sorely missed; it is also the most obvious and invisible of all. This is because the routine of a job imposes itself upon that of thinking, taking its form and adopting its syntax. People think when they work; outside of work they do not think. This is the nature of the mental drama of the unemployed, on top of all the others. When the man thought of this, the fear of losing his job would send him into a panic before he experienced the loss itself. For some time now, he had adopted the search as a supplementary routine, a substitute, the sort of activity that might rescue him from the blankness of his mind. But it was no use: there was nothing out there to free him from the tedium. Looking for work was a simulacrum that suited the beliefs of the others, but not his own; it was also directed at them. It meant resorting to an exercise in probability until the moment someone appeared who would pay closer attention, would take an interest and ultimately believe the simulacrum, that is, someone who would take it as an expression of truth. In that moment, he would leave the ranks of the unemployed; that person would give him a job and the theater of the mundane would be turned into work. Now, this simulacrum had the same problem as all other games: sooner or later it would find itself subjected to the rule of temporality. It was an order that, though it aspired to symbolic autonomy, had the insurmountable limits of a beginning and an end, moments in which a temporal norm both ceded and imposed itself: the return to normalcy.

It was difficult to fall into step with this simulacrum, precisely because it imposed a false routine; as such, the man wanted to cut it short in any way he could, which meant finding work as quickly as possible. To this end, he promised to change his behavior, even his thoughts. Every morning, each new sacrifice he had been prepared to make in exchange for work seemed trivial and so, at night, alone and without anything to show for it, he doubled his promises. A restricted diet, a fast, self-imposed penance, a vague sense of discipline, et cetera; an entire series of ascetic states was considered. He decided to spend a few nights in the plazas, on the wood or hard stone of the park benches and at the mercy of the police. These gestures of penitence were intended to set a price—that was really what it was all about: paying, compensating for a hypothetical job located hypothetically in the future. In order for the mechanism to function correctly and for the man to remain as one with the simulacrum, these payments had to be intangible. "You don't understand—at least, you can't imagine it," the father explained. Being pinned against the wall with no way out, the streets turning into a space that is not only external and foreign but also, and above all, inimical. That's how it was for Grino until he found a job. Just as the three did now, he would walk around during the day, hoping that something would appear, that someone would believe the simulacrum; they were squalid walks from which he would return at nightfall, overwhelmed by discouragement. He went out every morning without a destination, wandering without a plan but with a great deal of anxiety, and returned in a daze, unable to differentiate that day's travels with those of the day before. A routine, but one that impeded thought. His house lost all the qualities of a house, and turned into something else: a joint, or a hole. It no longer represented a place of his own, but rather the wait before his walk the following morning; it no longer housed a person, but rather someone who, like an animal, traversed the same space day after day, looking for the same prey along different paths. First, his house was no longer a house, then Grino gradually found himself abandoned by the *idea* of house. (And an idea, once it is gone, cannot be recovered; its new place exceeds the word forgetting.)

He saw the sign one afternoon, hanging from a yellow iron gate. He stopped to read it and immediately felt as though he were looking in a mirror. The sign hung at a bit of a slant from a string attached to a hook. They were looking for a *sereno*, a guard. He muttered to himself, confirming his aptitude, that he was a serene person; it was the word that suited him best. He thought of his salvation and even promised that, if they would have him, he would make the ultimate sacrifice: giving up sex and the bottle. They took him, though it was to perform a task whose routine offered no chance of any real change. On the other hand, he thought almost immediately, nothing about it required him to give anything up, nor was anyone asking him to; later on, if the opportunity arose, he would think about it. It was a storehouse that served as a depot. Upon entering, one would have to wait for his eyes to adjust in order to make out the stacked boxes of food, hidden in the dark. On days when the sun was strong, a brutal heat would descend from the metal roof, while in the mornings that same structure was filled with the crispness of a hangar, to all appearances incapable of heating up. At first, they only stored noodles, in cases of twenty-five packets or in sixty-pound bags, to be sold by weight; later they expanded their scope and began to carry tomatoes, grains, and canned goods.

The calm would be interrupted on certain afternoons. In the midst of the silence, Grino would hear an unusually loud noise: an approaching truck. For a moment, the sound of the brakes would drown out the noise of the motor. The driver would get out, knock two times on a panel on the gate, and turn to face the street while he waited to be let in. Grino would slide the doors open and, when it was a big delivery, would help the driver back his truck in. Then they would slowly unload it all, carrying the cases to the back of the storehouse, where there was some space along the wall. They would pass each other halfway, one coming and the other going, but their eyes would not meet. Once they were done unloading, Grino would do the count—twice: once horizontally and once vertically. If the numbers matched, he was satisfied. Then they would climb into the cab and would have a cigarette while they looked forward, that is, at the street in front of them and the house across the way, through which—when the door was open—Grino could always see a girl climbing a tree. As soon as he put out his cigarette, the driver would start the engine; since Grino smoked more slowly, he would throw the butt out the window and sign a sheet of paper with the number of cases that had just been delivered. A busy day presented events like these, but this kind of bustle was uncommon: mostly, his days were spent waiting.

He left at six, when the next shift arrived. At that hour, in the winter, the neighborhood was getting ready for nightfall. Despite the lack of activity, Grino never got bored: laying back against a mat tarp or a stack of boxes, or sitting in the only chair, opposite a small table where he would rest his *mate* and whatever undated magazine he was reading, he spent his days thinking about the same things, usually from the past; events or memories that did not necessarily belong to him, but which could have happened to his relatives, neighbors, acquaintances. There comes a time at which it becomes pointless to situate memories; later, it becomes impossible. Grino found that the clearest memories, those that offered the greatest promise of revelation and which ended up having the greatest eloquence, were the most unexpected ones; a scene, an image that secured its place among the clutter of his mind by virtue of patience and languor, until it emerged from the disorderly tangle of the past and imposed itself with concise simplicity. His memories were not separated from anyone else's; though they did not share a common past, origins are so concealed by memory that the ownership, the origin, of one event or another represented only a trivial nuance. Sometimes he also wondered about the cases of noodles, which would sometimes arrive with one packet too many or one too few. It was a mystery that left him paralyzed—all possible explanations seemed hypothetical and unconvincing—but whose repetition, like the persistent unevenness of the table on which he leaned, signaled the existence of a message directed at him, and him alone.

Grino was also a secret alcoholic; he only drank at home. "You wouldn't really understand," M's father said. Though at first he had been ashamed, his secretiveness was not due entirely to this. He felt that alcohol was incompatible with company, that drinking only worked in solitude. His house, the walls of which he had indifferently been covering for years, cluttering them with clippings from old magazines, almanacs, and with little images of saints— a graphic tangle, the exact meaning and names of which escaped him—echoed the abandon with which he tried, night after night, to disappear into the naively clandestine nature of his drinking. A force from within him allowed this squalor to remain as it was; as such, it was critical that it never manifest itself completely. (They say that people have reserves of hope, of will, of dignity, et cetera, but it would be more accurate to say that they have reserves of malevolence, indolence, and degeneration.) If one saw him as a desperate man, it would seem obvious that he teetered on the verge of desperation, yet that word vanishes as soon as he is seen in another light: simply as a worker.

He drank the same thing for years: the same amount of the same drink. He thought back on the children as they were growing up; the neighbors' kids, whose heads he would pat every morning, and who would get a coin or two from him every now and then. They were adults now, many of them had their own children, and when he would run into them they would speak as equals, with a slight air of mystery. And yet, he thought, clutching the neck of the bottle at midnight, they grew up and I'm still here, drinking the same amount. These associations were arbitrary and had an element of self-pity to them, but he also felt—though this was a product of desperation—that his consistency deserved to be rewarded, and that this reward should be the prolongation of his routine. He buried his empty bottles out behind the house. Later, when there was no space left under the ground, or when he lacked the strength or the motivation to dig, he began to leave them scattered against the wire fence. The bottles formed fairly tall mounds with broad bases; during the summer, mosquitoes would breed in the water that collected inside them. It was unsettling to see so many, with the same faded label and the same colored glass, making up an undefined— but nonetheless clear and uniform—mass. In this way, something as intangible as a routine would manifest itself with all the materiality of a habit. "Just imagine: one bottle every day, over years and years of drinking," M's father elaborated. Grino started in shortly after coming home from dinner. He walked the five blocks from the diner thinking about whatever came to mind, a series of provisional ideas and associations absorbed and shaped by the certainty that, no matter what he might think, what he would do when he got home was open—naturally, as though it were an accidental deflection of his will—his flask, as he called it, assigning benign powers to each new bottle.

There was one fantasy that sometimes calmed him down: that of controlling reality, saying that he didn't need to drink, that he just wanted to. This allowed him to get up and walk around, to see himself as something else or, rather, something better. After about two hours, when he reached the height of his arousal, he would masturbate. *Bitches, bitches*, he would repeat, rubbing himself violently and brandishing the bottle in his free hand. At those moments, just as on his walks or in the storehouse, he thought of nothing in particular. He fixed his gaze straight ahead without actually looking at anything. It had been a long time since he had pictured a specific woman; he thought instead about something at once precise and undefined: a parahuman category, part of reality, a universal female type. *Bitches, bitches,* he would mutter, meaning no offense; he imagined, suspended in the air, a savage femininity in stark contrast to his restrained masculinity. When he finished, he would let out a few deep breaths, less from pleasure than confusion, and the alcohol would gradually stop splashing around in the bottle; the movements of his arm were nervous, electric twitches of the pressure that had finally been relieved. And yet, strangely, he drank from a glass. "I say strange the way one might say peculiar, because during his drinking hours he never let go of that bottle, though every now and then he would forget about the glass." He did not let go of it because he saw in it a genuine importance: the glass was circumstantial—the way one might say, "There are plenty of glasses"—but the bottle was unique. Long before, Grino had read something in one of his illustrated magazines that had stayed with him: the number of bowls, vessels, and containers used by a kitchen was a function of its complexity. Glass, bottle, and sex formed, for him, a complex system that was one part private ceremony and one part daily ritual. The vague charm of the night arose from this duality and continued its work anonymously in the crystalline mounds out back. Between swigs, he might put the glass down on the table half full, but he never let go of the bottle. He went to bed when the liquor ran out. Weighed down by depression and listlessness, he stretched out on his bed and slowly relaxed his fingers, letting the bottle fall to the floor, where it stayed. In the morning, the first thing he would do after waking up was cast his eyes over empty container from the night before: he needed to verify the memory, the guide to the past. He experienced the fleeting clarity that prefigures a moment of recognition: once it has come into being but before it is fully formed. He would see the bottle and immediately remember. There was a kinship between him and the air that had replaced the liquid inside it: a solidarity that joined his confusion to the transparency contained within the glass, which seemed to render it illusory.

One night he has a dream in which he sees the girl climbing a tree. Grino is in the storehouse, watching her. Try as he might, he can't help but notice that the way she stretches her legs has a specific, hardly innocent, beauty to it. Suddenly the girl makes a wrong move and falls; her back collides with a branch before she hits the ground. Grino is alone and does not know what to do, and this makes him feel somehow responsible. He has lived with his impotence his whole life, only now it seems inappropriate, out of place. He is aware of the risk of paralysis: that kind of injury can be dangerous. He does not attempt to revive her precisely because of his fear that she will not respond. He feels his world falling apart. Whatever happens, whichever of the two awakens, he knows that he will be blamed and will lose his job. When he wakes up in the morning, a diffuse sense of guilt keeps him from getting out of bed. Unlike what usually happens, in this case a dream broke the spell of reality. And so began his time out on the tracks.

The driver pulls out of a garage next to a house with yellow doors. The back fender appears first, then the rest of the car. Once he has it out on the curb, the owner gets out of the car and closes the garage door. This action, so often repeated, is almost like doing nothing at all; M, his father, and the other agree that it seems like an invisible operation. At the same point on the opposite curb there is a grey car, somewhat protected from the sun by the shade of a young ash tree. The man closes the garage door as though he were wrestling with a corpse; it is unwieldy, with old ironwork and worn down tracks. He goes back to the car. He seems more absorbed than distracted, as though he were thinking about something other than what he was doing. This is only natural, observe the three, when one repeats something they have done so many times before. They are a few meters away, and are not thinking of anything in particular, either. The three, this trio in search of a microscopic blue car—a metallic sphere the size of a single point lost in a sea of metal—that submits itself to the work of chance; these three realize that something extraordinary is happening (or, rather, that something strange is about to happen). Though nothing had occurred, the stage had been set. The tension of the surroundings collects around the grey car, forgotten in the shade, and makes the street seem inhospitable. And so they—absorbed by the sense of danger and forgetting all else, even themselves—bore witness to the sovereignty of physics when, against all expectations, the driver hit the parked car as he pulled away from the curb. It is remarkable the way reality occasionally makes its own decisions. The collision was slow, unspectacular, and not particularly loud, but it was enough to open the trunk of the grey car at the exact moment the three passed alongside it.

An open door rarely fails to attract the attention of a passer-by lost in thought, awakening in him a curiosity that sometimes ends in horror, as in this instance. As soon as they looked into the trunk they jumped back, their arms raised like the devout. They had come across a nest of rats struggling to escape their confinement. The driver walked over until he was standing just behind them; thus protected, he spoke, or rather yelled, in a nervous voice—a voice that, under other circumstances, would have sounded weary and monotone, but was now terrified—asking them to close it. None of them felt up to anything of the sort, not as long as a frantic rat might jump out at his face. As always, they were at a loss for *what to do; the man urged them on with words that were far too imperious for the occasion. In this fact they found their excuse to postpone their action. They turned around. It would have been better if they had not; they would be left speechless by the new terror that had been waiting at their backs.*

The other would never discuss this with M, but he knows that the three, as they turned their heads to look behind them that afternoon, thought back on fantastic parts of children's stories in which animals have human attributes—clothes, language, feelings—or, conversely, in which the characters have the traits of animals. They were looking at a man whose face had been transformed. This change had nothing to do with the passage of time or with evolution—or, at least, not as it is commonly understood, as aging—the change was related to surprise, mystery, or magic. In the most literal sense, the man had the face of a rat. His features were not approximate, they did not share common traits—the way some say, "He looks like a dog," or, "He looks like a monkey." Instead, each detail of his face combined with the others to compose another countenance, that of a rat. Under different circumstances, this would not have surprised them at all; they might not even have noticed it. But there, with the car turned into a swarm, this face not only confirmed the apparition, it also endowed it with a sense of mystery and menace. "Close the trunk. I can't stand the sight of rats," he begged. For a moment, they thought of turning around and going on their way, leaving him there to face the teeming mass with which he had so much in common and yet rejected. But they did not; in the end, the rule of chance sometimes proves stronger than the will and, fearing that this was one of those occasions, the trio did not want to defy it with their actions.

For a long time, the other would feel the fingers of the man on his back, pushing him toward the car. The man urged them to close the trunk, yet he, barely any further away, was incapable of doing so. M and the other had spoken on several occasions about animals in the city, which were invariably incorporated into its landscape. They began by talking about the way dogs walked, then thought of other animals until they had compiled a long list. Each species could have its specific attributes, but each individual—the cat that only crossed the street on a diagonal, the sparrow that hops to the left before flying to the right—was a cipher unto itself, turning its back on its peers. The meaning consisted of this, of seeing each animal as the atypical emblem of a group. All toads, for example, behaved as though they were toads, yet none could hide the singular disposition that revealed them to be an exception to the species. M and the other thought that animals were too easily distracted, that they were excessively curious, that they often forgot themselves, that they could not measure danger, that they possessed a human sense of eagerness. Animals make selective use of their instinct, M and the other observed, thinking of all they concealed. Yet animals inhabited the city, rendering themselves transparent by living alongside people.

The father, M, and the other looked for a branch, a stick, a pipe— anything long that they could use to close the trunk from a distance. They did not find anything nearby, but a little further along, about fifty meters away, a pile of junk imposed itself on the sidewalk and on part of the street, the way rubble tends to be left in the suburbs. Maybe, thought the three without saying a word, they would find the magic rod in there. As in all triads, there were certain rules: there could not be a fifth element. As such, the fourth—the driver of the car—was erased from the minds of the three so that the stick, pipe, or whatever it was could occupy his place. Meanwhile, the man's affliction continued to grow; he was being taken over by a violent anxiety. The three were infected by his nervous breathing: they heard its murmur, faintly; an articulation preceding a cry, like a dream or a spasm—the picture of reflexive fear. Not so much because of any danger presented by the rats—their sheer

number rendered them abstract, and their lack of place made them seem
clumsy—but due, rather, to the terror of the driver, their role as guard-
ians became clear to them and they acted accordingly.

And so M, his father, and the other began a nervous dialogue filled
with elided and half-spoken words, urgent gestures that were too quick
and tense to actually communicate anything; they, too, had been left
breathless. It was a matter of finding, in that pile of junk, the instru-
ment of their salvation. M and his father resorted to a disjointed, but
apparently effective, language. "Bugs and nails," stammered the father,
pondering the dangers of rooting around in there. He said it too late: M
was already on his way, after replying—though he spoke first—"I'll
get." His words, as sometimes happens, would hang in the air as he
moved into the distance.

I found it surprising, under the circumstances—that mix of disquiet, hesitation, pressure and reserve brought about by the rats—
that M would return, with those two words, to a domestic language
lost who knows when by who knows whom. That "I'll get" had
its own, immediate, referents: in my own home there were those
who said *I'll get* several times a day. Between "I'll get it" and "get
going" or some other variant, those two words emerged, diluting
the meaning by which the phrase was assumed to be conjugated,
imprecisely but with eloquence: a paradigm of ambiguity. It was
only a few minutes before dusk: the horizon was not yet ablaze but
the process of the sunset was already set in motion, tinting the end
of the street with a yellow that grew more and more intense, and
would soon veer toward orange. M looked like a shadow cut out of
that backdrop as he leaned over the mountain of junk, rummaging
through it for the magical lance with the delicate movements of a
rag and bone man.

In this way M, whose form was already slight, seemed to grow even more delicate from where we stood. The intensity of the light blotted out his silhouette, like those moths that grow even more transparent when they come to rest on a lamp. For a moment, we did not hear the rats, the man interrupted his litany, and M was endowed with a distinct plasticity in which magic, something ritual not unlike a dance, combined with beauty, drama, and surrender as we watched his body dissolve like a cloud against the light. His father and I watched as his silhouette, cut through by the line of the street, grew more and more narrow; his feet, restless atop the chaos of objects, tried to gain the balance that would allow him to continue his search, disappearing for fractions of a second at a time. It was then that he levitated before us, our impassive eyes filled with admiration. His father said, "He moves like a frog," or something to that effect, alluding to his tentative movements and his transparency. I did not answer him; I understood the processes of the afternoon that were making M dissolve. Knowing this, however, did not reduce my fascination; on the contrary, it was enhanced because I was able to see this effect as essential, a legitimate confluence rather than something providential. As such, I was left in silent awe.

It would be easy, now, to interpret these incidents like dreams and M's powerful, though fleeting, luminous apogee as the prefiguration of his absence, but this story has been particularly redundant and there is no need for allusions. Just as consciousness registers what is easy, incorporating it in a more or less mysterious way into its workings, it also coexists with the difficult, even the unknown, in order to dispel the field of darkness against which its silhouette appears. Now I am more than twice as old—that is, as many years have passed since M's disappearance as did, for either him or me, before his death—and I simply can't believe it. I can't believe it.

Despite the workings of time, which forces us, among other things, to give up our resistance and yield to its advance, and despite the fact that this "I can't believe it" became, in some way, rhetorical as the years went by, over time this rhetoric acquired, or regained, the full measure of truth contained by the original words. It is against the backdrop of the shallow, dark pit formed by that conclusive reality, the deepest subjective manifestation of which is, after all, this "I can't believe it," that I float, repeating the words. Like all rhetoric, it alludes to a truth in and of itself, though with years of repetition I have distanced myself from the original mystery, from the root of that darkness, to construct another: the foundation of all the time that has passed without M. Event and disbelief are castled, changing places as though "I can't believe it" were the event and M's disappearance the verbal form that questioned it. Sometimes I catch my mind wandering, as everyone's does, only to immediately return to this thought and, if the circumstances are right, repeat under my breath that I can't believe I can't believe it, when so much time has passed and nothing has filled the void of his absence.

One afternoon a few weeks ago I was walking north along an avenue. Sundays in Caracas, as in a good number of cities, are calm and quiet. The light was diffuse; it was somehow fragmented and visibly corpuscular as it was returned by the mountain, as though the sun at its height were not enough and a greater intensity were required, the reflection off the slope, to ignite the air. A trail of marks along the street registered the activity of the people: contradictory, almost always aggressive, marks that spoke of a lack of peace. All of a sudden, a signal blinded me from up on high: someone had probably raised their hand in the foothills and the light from the sun had bounced off the face of their watch. This lasted an instant—a moment more brief than an instant. I observed the slope and thought about how far that particular light had traveled to reach me, guided with greater precision by chance than any other that surrounded me in that moment or this one. That flash had crossed the orbit of planets, illuminated asteroids; it was also the energy that propelled the comets and which had apparently originated in the sun and expanded as light and solar wind before dazzling me. One final moment of concentration, its reflection in the face of that watch, delayed its ultimate dissolution as it fell to earth, promising to make it unique one last time in the form of a flash of light. I don't know why, but that was enough to make M appear in my memory. A cloud floated just above where the reflection had originated, girding the mountain in silence. "From there, Caracas looks like the model of a city," I recalled, and continued on my way.

One day, he told me, he was sent out to buy a few things for dinner; he was given the exact amount of money needed. The grocer rang him up wrong and got confused giving him his change, so M ended up going home with his purchases and more money than he had when he left. His parents sent him back to return the money. At first, the grocer was surprised to see him again; later he understood what had happened, but badly. Leaning over the counter, he muttered his calculations as he scribbled on a piece of paper, as though it could talk back to him. M felt as though he was standing before a giant: broad, strong arms dense with hair, emerging from the creases of a white shirt. When he had finished his calculations, and ignoring M's protestations, the grocer gave him part of the money he had brought with him. At home, his parents are so annoyed by his incompetence that they nearly refuse to let him in. They order him to go back to return it *all*. As in most humiliating situations, they ask him if he knows what the word "all" means. So he goes back, again. M walks the two blocks sensing that it is a ridiculous, foolish misunderstanding, but he does not dare to pursue the idea: the world of the adults is the only one there is, and as such it must be accepted as it presents itself. For his part, having nearly reached the end of his day, the grocer is occupied with cleaning his scale. He asks him to wait; it is a delicate operation. M carefully observes the scale, the weights marked out with short and long dashes, the numbers distributed among them, the red point of the needle, which is going wild at the moment as the grocer lifts and holds the tray over and over; he also reads the brand, written in five gleaming letters that form an arch across the top. Little by little it gets darker and the quiet stampede of cars on the cobblestones filters in from the street. Having finished his cleaning, the man, leaning on the counter as though it were a dividing wall, emphatically explains to M that the money does not belong to him—the grocer—and that he should go home immediately. M understands less and less, though he suspects that he will return several times more. As he is about to leave the store he hears the clicking of the grocer's tongue; M notes that this is the way dogs are usually called, but turns around anyway. He sees the arm emerge from the creases of its sleeve, accompanied by a gesture that, from up high, invites him to come closer. Smiling, the grocer offers him a coin, saying that it is for him and that he should hold on to it. M feels an unprecedented sense of joy: the coin sparkles with its own light, like nothing else. "This is what it must feel like to touch heaven with both hands, as they say; I can feel it." M feels as though he has been awarded an unknown prize—rather, what is unknown is the motivation behind the prize—not being able to explain it, he finds the situation all the more wondrous. Later on, the parents, somewhere between irritation and weariness, would discover that the boy had returned home with more money than he brought with him last time—even though he had taken the precaution of hiding his coin in the other pocket. And so, as he had anticipated, M must return to the grocery, where the man takes the money, performs a few other calculations and gives him back a greater sum. By now the amount is more than considerable; it is a small fortune, as though the money were multiplying on its own. The parents hesitate: every cent the child receives is a sum that must later be explained and returned, which means that it might be better not to send him and avoid his coming back with more money. They argue for a few minutes but in the end make their decision: there is no other choice—M has to return it all. Back at the shop, the grocer stretches a piece of paper out across the counter and does his calculations once more with a pencil; when he is done he hands M an even greater sum. The parents do not know what to do— they ask for an explanation but M tells them only what he has seen: the man speaks to the paper while he writes, then hands him the money. His father is indignant, but cannot resist voicing a paradoxical wish. "If only it were so easy to get rich," he exclaims. They speak a bit more and send M back again, but with more money; this time they also add in, and not just a little: a good part of their savings. This goes on for two or three trips: M goes back and forth, carrying a fortune that might not be great but is not insignificant, his pockets bulging more and more each time, until on one of the trips the grocer, having finished his customary accounting, decides that he is satisfied: Yes, he says, you're right, and he does not give back a cent. M returns home with nothing.

The parents cannot believe it; they have been swindled in the most absurd way imaginable. They get angry and blame the boy: suddenly, at the most innocent hour of the day, that moment between sunset and dinner when nothing ever happens, they have been reduced to nothing, to the most crushing poverty; they had lost years of work and were facing years of privation. The mother cries in silence and the father broods: this is what they get for being honest. The effects of poverty come quickly: the portions at dinner are immediately reduced. The future is different now; it is longer. M's mother says that his father measures time by money: the less there is, the less frequent and longer lasting everything has to be— and there was no end in sight. The three of them are trying to find ways to get the most out of their food when someone knocks on the door. They all go to the entryway, but imagine their surprise when they see that the man standing there is a stranger. He is not the grocer, though he is to M: that's the person who had been helping him from across the counter all afternoon, he insists. The man, before launching into the explanation that all were eager to receive, asks if they would be so kind as to offer him a drink. The parents tell M to fetch the bottle of honey wine and three glasses while they get settled. When he comes back, M realizes that the grocer is already telling his story. The mother serves the wine; they toast, take a quick sip and the other continues: He is a millionaire who amassed a fortune that would take five people more than a year to calculate, but he has made so many mistakes—he calls them *errors* and hopes to have time to recount them one by one and thereby repent them anew—after so many mistakes and being unable to make peace with his conscience, God, through an angel, promised to absolve him if he distributed his fortune among poor and honest families. Saying this, he takes a bag full of money out from behind him and puts it on the table, on the one condition that they set a place for him at the table that night. And so, while the father and the man drink and converse, the mother sets about preparing a meal, the likes of which they had not seen for a long time. Off in a corner, M empties his pocket and watches his coin—as big, heavy, and brilliant as a talisman—spin.

FIVE Despite the hazy origin of our friendship, which lacked a precise moment in my memory and was, like so many other adventures, mixed up in a bundle of circumstances in which very little is clear, I retain a vivid image of the gradual approach or affinity that, following the involuntary and somnolent rhythm of schoolchildren, would grow into a relatively close relationship. And yet sometimes I give in to a false notion: that our friendship began when I received his photo and M mine, not before. I convince myself of this. This conviction is so vivid that it veils all thought in one single color; I am unable to think otherwise until a while later, when I realize my error—that is, when I remember. Like any ceremony, the exchange was meant to inaugurate a new time, to divide a before from an after. Yet instead of indicating a beginning, I see now that it left one behind, forgot it, or something more: that private ritual, which was somehow innocent in that it did not attempt to engage anything beyond the people involved in it, that is, the two of us, set an ending in motion; its culmination was excessive in relation to its trivial beginning. By that time, Argentina was already filling up with the dead. If it had been normal before for them to show up in ditches and vacant lots, they now rejected all sense of measure and took on, in the form of corpses, a central role as the dead (but also as anonymous corpses, which in turn heightened the sinister hierarchy of the whole) in the verist theater that politics had become. When death is common, corpses become commonplace; there is nothing new to them. These corpses, because they were disturbing, seemed more numerous than the dead; thanks to their tragic nature, they also acquired a greater significance. This progression shows how fully their meaning could be inverted; not long before, the dead had exceeded corpses in number and significance. It seemed that there were more dead than living and more corpses than dead.

I am going to recount, as I remember it, something that happened on the night of June 20, 1973, while I walked with M in the early hours of the 21st. Public transportation was not running; nothing moved, in general. The few signs that indicated that the city had not been abandoned spoke of a recent tragedy, or worse, of some kind of catastrophe, incomprehensible and not yet over. Half a block from the avenida del Trabajo, a woman waited for her son, in tears. She was sitting in a doorway and strangely, despite the shadows, I remember her face as being illuminated. She repeated the boy's name; it wasn't enough for her to wait, we thought, she also had to call to him. But there was no reaction, not from the boy or from the people shut away in the neighboring homes, despite the fact that they had probably been listening to her for quite some time. We drew closer. M and I wanted to imagine the interior of the house from which she voiced her living warning and her absent need, though this may sound contradictory. The woman took no notice of us, but we could sense the silence of the home, the objects that, from that night on, would be redundant, useless. A nightstand, a bed, a shelf, a brush.

We walked from Mataderos to Villa Crespo; the same funereal silence inhabited every neighborhood, every block. We met with a dual intimation and an ambiguous beauty in the dark streets. A few hours earlier Perón, the political leader, had returned to Argentina; a throng of people had gathered to wait for him, but the desert around us brought to mind a city that had obliterated its inhabitants. The great mass of *porteños* slept, protected by walls and roofs, on beds tucked behind the façades of their houses, as we walked. Like ships, M and I floated along a surface composed of silence, the rough and the smooth of things, with the disciplined fatigue of the traveler. The shipwrecks were the others, the ones who waited, like the woman with the illuminated face.

That night, M and I talked about virginity. Not about our experience with it—it was still of longstanding relevance to one of us, though I will not say which—but rather, in anticipation of the truth, about the false promise hidden in its loss. One of us attempted to deny any change, and to this end alluded to a number of impossible absolutes. Experience, as the different pressures, sensations, and temperatures to which our skin is submitted, did not matter; the memories that could be etched into the mind on the basis of these circumstances mattered even less. Their triviality was absolute. The moments of a life, which, by the same mystery that allows it to unfold can take on significance despite being the pinnacle of superfluity, cannot be compared with the importance of "that" moment, despite the fact that it is the one truly fated to wane. The millions dispersed after waiting for the leader. Some had gotten there days in advance, but everyone wanted to leave at the same time. They turned and began to walk toward their homes, lost and disillusioned. As is well known, many remained where the bullets found them.

M and I sensed an abyss that divided us from the masses; this might have been due to our natural condition as members of the minority. Of all possible emotions, the masses inspired in us more sympathy than mistrust, more disbelief than fascination. The majority, overwhelmed by its own numbers, was unable to recognize the same essence from which it drew its own strength in the scarce, the brief, and the scattered. Yet one dreamed of joining those vital swells, the very identity of which pulsated in the form of a crowd, because they offered the possibility of giving in to the current and floating along without a care for the truth. Now, as I have been saying, the sea that had been swelling at the outskirts of the city to the southwest of Buenos Aires had dispersed in all directions.

At the corner of Rivadavia and San Pedrito, we relived the sensation of crossing, within just a few meters, a great divide between civilizations: just barely past Rivadavia, we were already nearing Nazca. Someone approached us, breaking our silence. He was poor, probably younger than his appearance let on, with a round face that promised virtue; he did not know which way Ezeiza was. He was walking, like us, which meant that we could have sent him a number of different ways; as such, Ezeiza—without being metaphorical—could be in any direction. "Ezeiza is so far away," we answered, "that you could get there by going this way, or that way, or by heading over there. But the rally's over." "Do you think I could get there before dawn?" "It depends which way you're going," we offered. "To Ezeiza," he answered. M and I looked at each other: "Ezeiza is a big place." "To where the rally is." That place was good only for escape. It had nothing to offer now, hours after the violence; it was of no interest to anyone. "You won't find what you're looking for," we warned him. "I'm going to the rally. I'm going to welcome General Perón. My neighbors told me he was coming tomorrow." He had been on foot since Retiro, where he had gotten off a train and had found no other way to keep moving. We asked him when they had told him this. "Yesterday," he said. "Yesterday when?" "Yesterday, yesterday afternoon." "Listen, it's already over—that was today." "Right, like I said, it's today." "No," we explained, "that was today, or rather, yesterday. Perón already came back." "It can't be," he said, embarrassed. "Yes—in the end he didn't get off the plane at Ezeiza, but he arrived." "So where did he go?" "I don't know," we said, "Morón, El Palomar, who knows . . ." The man walked off to the west; at that exact moment, the temperature seemed to drop a few degrees. The clear sky, the stars, orderly beyond the clouds, the absolute silence, and the cold, pulsating, closing in on us from all directions, even from within our own bones. It all seemed like an illusion, like the morning that follows a night of excess, only the other way around. We stayed on Nazca, crossed the tracks, and a few blocks later picked up our topic of conversation.

Virginity is an abstraction, someone asserted, equivalent to non-virginity. The only concrete thing is its loss; it is never acquired, but since the experience of losing it cannot be prolonged throughout one's lifetime, and in fact generally tends to be fleeting, one is always either within a before or an after, without options or a choice. There should be alternatives: going back, reclaiming it, abandoning it rather than losing it, getting it and losing it all over again, et cetera, like in a game of masks in which each represents a different personality. Virginity is always seen as something unstable, a state that can be abandoned at any time, regardless of one's age, but we should be able to lose it as many times as there are opportunities to be other, to be different, or to be less. Thus the violent anxiety before the loss, armies of adolescents speculating over the inevitability of their condition, turns into a true condemnation when they find they can no longer regain their innocence. "But they can, actually, all of us do," suggested the other. It's true, responded the first. What was in the air was a catastrophe without any outward signs (something particularly Argentine in its insistence on covering tracks, concealing events, and looking the other way).

Perhaps because it was repeated, or because it was somehow unique, the ominous climate of that night has not been easy to forget, though I have often tried to do so. But, as is well known, wanting to forget and forgetting are rarely aligned. Someone might even want to forget, not in order to forget, but to be able to hold on to a memory in a different form, in order to be able to evoke it at will. That night, M had little more than three years to live. Now, as I sometimes evoke that walk and remember more clearly the neighborhood of Flores—calle Bacacay, for example, where the darkness is multicolored under the dense branches of the trees—I also remember the nights in the suburbs, when the whistle of a distant train, as prolonged as that of a ship, offered a textured backdrop of sound. I would go up to the roof of my house, rest my arm on the ledge, and, protected by the darkness, identify different shades of black in the shadows of the foliage, silvery reflections on the asphalt and on distant rooftops. Crickets, a nocturnal bird, a car, and the barking that bounced back and forth across the street suggested a quality much like that of the heavens, upon whose sphere the sidereal abyss takes shape. Before or after this, one might hear explosions or the rattle of a machine gun and be left without words (just as happens now, when one hears shots in the night and there is nothing to say). And so, without noticing—or, noticing, but without realizing—Buenos Aires filled with the dead; they took on a life of their own, an extension of the mark left by their bodies.

As I mentioned earlier, I have on occasion wondered whether someone, should someone read this, might think that I am proposing, or hoping to discover, through the image of M, the logic or mystery through which the people have drifted since those years. The truth is that there is little to propose and even less to discover. Historical meaning was not buried, it was on the surface, there for all to see, saturated with death and unfolding according to an order that was both transparent and faulty, because it was the practical response to another historical meaning that had fought its way into being, eventually becoming legitimate; a practical response, efficient in its way, that ended up replacing the other. It was a macabre substitution that took on a number of trivial embellishments. Nonetheless, I am going to give a meaningful example.

One day, when we were looking for the car, our conversation turned to something like civilizations or cultures in general. M surprised us by saying that, like Borges, he advocated a universal government. "I agree with Borges, I'm in favor of a universal government," he said, exactly. His father maintained a skepticism that was both radical and predictable: seeing as how governments couldn't resolve the problems of their own countries, he could not imagine the efficacy of just one for the whole world. But M, as he immediately clarified, was not talking about a government like the ones they knew, but rather a supreme regulation, an entity on high that would shape great movements and determine the scope of human endeavors. A form of moral government whose authority would be so fully accepted by all mankind that no demonstrations of its force, no evidence or action, would be necessary. Without question, he said in different words, all that would be needed would be to assign human behavior with a precise meaning accepted by all. This government might not coincide with that proposed by Borges, but it was also universal. It would have two central traits: 1) food would be free—like in images of the golden age, people would wait, seated and with their mouths open, for food to come to them; 2) people would be travelers—over the course of their lives they would circle the globe, dying where they were born. Life in the countryside and the cities would go on as normal, as it does now, he added, not aware that he was contradicting himself.

Following a precise order, everyone would work where they could or wanted to, while they lived, went about their routines, whatever, until their next move. In this way, the cities would be cleaner (according to M, no one really dirties a place they will not be staying in for long) and fortunes more modest (travelers cannot accumulate too much). The largest companies would be those owned by laborers and the employees, who, always being temporary, would delegate all control to the users who, provisional in their own right, would create a minute registry of their endeavors so that the future inhabitants would be up to date on what had been done. The population, however, would never be renewed as a whole. There would be no mass migrations, it would all be part of one perpetual journey: from everywhere to all places, each with his family (should they wish to accompany him, according to M) and with his past (inevitable baggage). There would always be a majority in the cities that knew the streets, businesses, public offices, neighborhoods, and the combination of risks, drawbacks, and alternatives that every city has. The same would go for the countryside, towns, hamlets, or smaller cities. The people would travel by plane, boat, train, or on the highway. Whoever wanted to bring their furniture with them would have to find a house they knew could accommodate it all; if not, they would have to leave it. Schools would educate the children—these would be language schools; adults would study where they worked. In every place, the language spoken would be that of the majority (though minorities could also communicate in other languages). The administration of the cities or regions would be the responsibility of elected committees. Everyone, before leaving their place of residence, would cast a vote in favor of one of the individuals or parties that were campaigning; at the end of their terms, the votes cast up to that moment would be calculated. The people voted looking toward the past, but their elections looked toward the future and toward another place: the elected candidates would serve their terms in their next place of residence.

Books, drink, music, tobacco, and television would all be free. Meals would always be regional, just like restaurants, consequently, would be; along with literature, these would be the two principal allusions to the former age of nations. Eating, drinking, and reading—which was the same as sitting and listening—the people would feel the indistinct reminiscences of a lost and vaguely luminous past. This would obviously be a world without nationalities, but it would have towns and families. Religion could go on being collective but would not likely be global, as the idea of the world, the universe, thus materialized, would prove paradoxically imprecise. There would be religions of two or three hundred people, not likely more, and nearly all would adhere to their own private, fragmentary, and often accidental—when not vague or contradictory—cosmovisions. Indigenous tribes, denominated as naturals, would be protected. His father asked if there would be a maximum period of residence in any one place, after which a person would be forced to move himself out—his exact words. M brushed the idea off, that would not be necessary, no one would want to stay on forever; it would be boring and eccentric, practically immoral. The most sedentary would be the elderly and the students, but always for a reasonable time, six or seven years at the most; on the other hand, few in either state would put up with as much.

And yet, the father asserted, in different words, there is a need, a pleasure, or a virtue in living in one's place, where one was born. He was alluding not only to a feeling of loyalty toward one's homeland, but also to the fact that it is necessary to see the world as a mystery in order to be part of it. The earth is a planet that looks a great deal like itself. As such, knowing different places meant noticing the similarities among them; on the contrary, knowing none meant being unique. Between the homogenous and the singular, he preferred the singular. One travels in order to see those who do not as part of the landscape, because they are the ones who possess the unique traits of the region. M did not know whether to agree with his father or not, so he said, "But I'm not talking about the world being different, I'm talking about it being other." They were the same thing, replied his father, and said if he kept on like that, they were going to lock him up. "If you keep talking like that, they're going to lock you up."

It was at these words that I wanted to arrive. In an obvious way, in spite of himself and though it was said with a degree of irony, the father's warning called attention to the violent and trivial substitution produced by so-called historical meaning, the ideological persecution of those years and, a little while later, death. That day, as on many others during the search, we would eat sandwiches in a plaza. We would buy bread, cold cuts, and water or soda, and go eat. Except for the big ones, no one really went to the few plazas there were in the suburbs. Since open space is all around—in the houses and the streets alike—it is unusual to see children playing, the elderly talking, or couples waiting for nightfall in them. Vagrants sometimes wind up there and spend the day; in the afternoons, workers from the production plants nearby prefer them to sitting on the pavement out front. That day we ate on the patchy grass of one of those plazas. We sat there and, though it was not true, we felt as though we ruled the area from on high. The streets seemed to flow downward like the rooftops and façades of the houses. Normally during lunch M's father would announce his sales route, but he preferred listening to our conversations about school, the subjects we studied, our professors and classmates. He felt deep pride and, ironically, curiosity about the scholastic experience of his son, an experience he himself had lacked; any reference made to it, even an allusion to a flaw or an outright failure, sounded to him like a praise or commendation. Evaluations, in all their forms, roll call, "group work," the ways students would cheat off one another, disciplinary measures—the world of the schoolhouse represented a universe that was of a juvenile yet essential complexity, too brief to be taken seriously, given the normal duration of a life, yet too important to be ignored. It was the generous world that kept us occupied and whose routine provided us with a provisional identity (of which, as years go by, only fragments remain).

Sometimes I think about the path my photo is likely to have taken, obviously a variation on the question of M's fate. His is in a box, mixed in with clippings, papers, and objects whose colors supposedly conserve some sort of essence. I usually find the photo hidden and turned over; always intrigued by that piece of cardboard encrusted with dirt, I realize it is M a fraction of a second before reading the half-faded inscription, "Buffeted by the wind." With a turn of my wrist, I examine it. I am going to avoid a second description of the photo—I will add only that M is looking at the camera. If photos say little when one looks at them, there is even less to be extracted from a commentary on them. The truth is, like M, I don't believe in photos—I should say that this forgotten one is one of the few that I have. "Let's keep these photos as talismans, but not as proofs," was what he said, to avoid committing. As inhabitants of that infinite country that is the present, they were both suitable and true; in this sense, assigning them the value of talismans, M allotted them a power that no proof could attain. We often joked about the properties of our photos, which, though removed from the realm of magic, nonetheless frequently immersed us in states of mystery. This mystery, according to M, derived from our belonging to an absent time, that is, either a time long past or one that hadn't yet arrived.

This time belonged to the itinerant past of humanity and the itinerant future of civilization, according to his idea of the society of tomorrow, as he sometimes called it. Jews, gypsies, the nomadic peoples of the Amazon or the Pacific, and the tribes of Mauritania, the Sahara, or Africa in general, existed between these two like floating bridges. M and I, as individuals exiled from reality and transplanted into the pure present, retained (and anticipated) the moral and emotional condition of both our precursors and our descendants. This was why, for example, when he and his father would search the outskirts of the city for the car, I would receive signals, vague but definite, from their travels kilometers away. The noises they heard would reach me—I would actually hear them—despite the distance. Smells would emerge in a jumble but would define themselves, little by little. Distance was not an obstacle; on the contrary, it was a stimulus. There was something powerful at work, I have no doubt, that broke down the restrictions of geography. I obviously could not know, and certainly could not see, what was keeping M occupied at the moment, yet an invisible bond connected us, despite our being spread across a vast territory. The simultaneous, which is unknown, and the visible mixed together in a bundle of partial, intermittent, and accurate impressions. More than once, one of us surprised himself by knowing about a supposedly unknown event, being privy to even the most intimate convictions or feelings of the other. Nothing could explain such knowledge, nothing but affinity, that particular form of communion, the relation of subtle similarity that joined us across space. I would be walking, for example, along San Martín when another me, a second consciousness, drew near to offer me blurred images: hazy embankments, low-set houses, empty lots, deserted streets, cement walls, factories, fences. The trees, identical, accentuated the realness of this dream world; there, the hand of man had settled upon something living. (Because the same mystery that moves the planets also impels people.) This other me would let me know that M was walking with his father in search of the car. On some occasions, this mental communication would be less evident, even imperceptible, though it would still be active, that is, it would be gathering strength. Telepathy exerts the greatest control over the unconscious, though, in those cases, it cannot be proven. One afternoon, however, these two circumstances converged: we were subject to a powerful telepathic influence, the force of which was, in fact, verified.

That afternoon we were walking along streets that had been on the verge of flooding. For days, all we had talked about was the weather. The rain had erased avenues, evacuated neighborhoods, and besieged cities. The television still showed people standing on their rooftops with the few things they had been able to save, waiting for help to arrive. A small, rigid splotch was visible on a roof nearly hidden under the water: it was a dog, paralyzed with fear. A fireman arrived right away and climbed up a short ladder onto the roof to catch hold of it, then dropped it, shivering, into the boat. There were also scenes of the rescued: sleeping in schools or meeting houses, living in freight cars. The images seemed to speak of a new foundation for the city; everything had a touch of the provisional to it, the feeling of camping, a leveled landscape. M and I expounded upon things that might have been platitudes, for example, that *tiempo*—in its most enigmatic sense, that is, when it refers to the weather—is hard to predict, and that even when one can predict it, there is rarely anything that can be done to change it. There was something supernatural in the ability to anticipate the vicissitudes of the weather, not so much for the possibility of foreseeing them, but for the tendency to adapt them to a human scale in order that they might always unfold according to this order, even when they did so in the form of catastrophes. M explained a theory to which he had subscribed throughout his childhood and that even now, nearly an adult, he was unable to discount. This idea postulated the existence of an invisible human race on a microscopic scale. Their time passed much more quickly; a life did not last as long, but to them it was just as long or as short as ours is to us (they could do more or less the same things, M explained); they reproduced at an extraordinary rate. This civilization lived on the surface of the planet and could share our buildings, though no one would know it. The space of a room would be like the entire solar system, of an inconceivable magnitude. Just like us, they would be subjected to catastrophes: the most common, though they would not know the cause, was a phenomenon not unlike an earthquake. These disasters would be produced by people, by us, walking. Megalopolises razed, the countryside damaged beyond repair, roads and channels of communication destroyed. But the lapse between one footfall and the next might represent two generations, or three, meaning that the memory of the disaster would have already faded by the time we stepped down again. It was different when we stood or sat in one place, or where the furniture took up part of the floor: those places were the outer confines, the places where the world ended and things brimmed with mystery and danger. The various forms of cleaning, with their disastrous consequences, translated to something akin to the end of an era. Perhaps, thought M, the weather might end up adapting to the scale of this world; all appearances, however, seemed to indicate that this would be more difficult to achieve. Take an ant in the lightest drizzle: it's not a catastrophe, but it is a greater quantity of water, proportionately.

The two of us walked along an avenue whose sidewalks were covered with tables and whose cafés bore signs that had been made to look like marquees. In front of one of these—passing through meant walking between tables, even though one was still in the street—four men were talking about the weather. They seemed relaxed, having stretched out to fill their seats completely; the table was cluttered with coffee cups, beer bottles, and whiskey glasses. Everything was empty, consumed; there were ashes and cigarette butts. A typical afternoon chat, M and I thought, without needing to say anything. Nothing seemed worthy of our attention, except what we heard. A man with ruddy skin said, "I don't want to know the future, I just want to know what the weather will be like." "Why?" asked another. "So you can lose again?" "Lose what?"

"I don't know. Lose. You must have lost something." "I won what I lost before. I don't lose. I pay." "If you want to know what the weather is going to be, you have to learn to read its signs, like the gauchos do," interjected another. "Signs of what?" they asked. "The signs of the weather," he said. "And what are those?" asked a few. "The smell of the air, the color of the sunset, the clouds, the direction of the wind." "But the gauchos don't do any of that," the fourth intervened, "they just know." Yes, but that's no guarantee," specified the one who had asked. "I knew a guy once who had been living in the country for a long time. He was used to predicting the weather, and he bragged about it. He wanted to be asked about it, to show off his unusual skill. But no one said anything to him. In the country he had been a normal person who knew the same thing as everyone else; here, too, he was just a normal person. Until he went back. The first few times it went well: just like at the beginning, he predicted the same thing as everyone else. They would get together at the bar and talk about the weather—and then the errors began. He stopped being normal. The radar he used to detect the weather seemed to be broken; it seemed to be working in reverse. If he predicted heat, it would be cold; if he announced a drought, it would rain for weeks; the skies never cleared when he thought they would. He finally asked himself, *What good is this skill if I'm always wrong? I'll draw the opposite conclusions.* And so he did, and he was right again, by interpreting the signs as their opposites. He was happy to be normal; the weather once again fell under his purview, if not as an object of knowledge, then at least as one of intuition. One morning a few months later, though, he found himself unable to tell the difference between sign and interpretation: the inversion to which he had grown accustomed had been incorporated by nature, which meant that if he chose the opposite, he ran the risk of being wrong again, though he ran the same risk if he didn't." That was the last thing M and I heard as we passed, before the voices began to grow faint. The coincidence between what we had been discussing and the topic at the table did not surprise us as much as what would happen a few hours later, when the two of us, having forgotten what had happened, experienced a greater mystery than those usually created by the weather.

There was a convergence. A few blocks past the café, M and I said our goodbyes: each was headed a different way. I remember walking along treeless streets that were startlingly quiet, and ending up in a park that seemed to go on forever. I wandered deep into a neighborhood filled with workshops and enormous warehouses, where labor was something certain, tangible. I felt a foolish emotion, as has happened on other occasions, when I saw the rolling cobblestones of a few of its streets, their crests and folds like the workings of geology on a human scale, the effect of the tireless passage of trucks. I kept walking, thinking of things I no longer remember, when, on a corner of avenida Caseros, I unexpectedly ran into M. We stood there, amazed and confused, fearing that the other might have a secret. For a moment, we surrendered to the most painful anxiety. Could there be something to confess? we wondered, for a fraction of a second. Something similar had happened on another occasion, as I mentioned, when we backed into each other a few meters from a newsstand, but the coincidence was greater in this instance, because it had happened again. And unlike before, neither of us was able to justify his presence. Neither was lost, though we realized that each had an urgent engagement somewhere far away at that moment. Guided by mysterious forces, we had wandered for hours and hours until we ended up meeting on a forgettable corner, next to a mailbox. These forces, we saw, formed a point of convergence to which we gravitated, always.

This power brought us together almost every time, protecting us against distance. On other occasions it prevented convergences as though it exerted a negative force, impeding encounters—when it was a matter of bodies—and agreement—when it was a matter of consciousness. In those cases, shared feelings would vanish, as would convictions; the idea of having something in common seemed unthinkable, outside the realm of possibility. M's hope, then, his desire to assign the photos—his or mine, in this case—a power that evaded and yet transcended the affective, is understandable. I have sometimes thought about how the magic of photos, according to M, is not contained by their visual aspect, their ability to provoke genuine surprise in the people who adopt a position of innocence to look at them, even when they know them and what they are of. The magic of photos was that they restored a rudimentary human faculty, though one that may have been forgotten: the inclination to endow an object, its interior or its future hidden by the very materiality of its mass, a logic that transcends all mysteries. "Why would someone hold on to his grandfather's lighter or his father's hat?" Not only because these objects bring them to mind and because the memory is permeated by a bittersweet emotion, but also because a protective energy emanates from them, though it may never prove its efficacy, one which relies on our belief in order to make us feel secure against the evil that threatens us always. This supernatural power, as such, is independent of our conscious mind and our will, and operates without our knowledge. As a result, we can disregard these objects and throw them into a bottom drawer where we never look for anything because they represent those responsible for our misfortune; we can indignantly renounce the things they touched, yet the benign force they exert will continue its work.

On our walk that night, before dawn on the 21ˢᵗ of July, once the topic of virginity had been exhausted and the man who had lost his way looking for the Ezeiza airfields, where he thought Perón would be appearing the following day, was the memory of a fleeting anomaly, M and I ran into Sito. He came from the direction of Ciudadela. Much of avenida Juan B. Justo was still paved with colored cobblestones, and it was there, on one of those sidewalks, that we heard a loud whistle behind us. We turned at the same time—for a moment, M and I must have formed a strange, symmetrical figure—and we saw him coming up the middle of the street, signaling us with his arms. There was a block between us, but Sito did not hurry; he knew that we would wait for him (this sort of assumption inspires friendship). As he approached, I asked M, "How's the mother doing?" "What mother?" he asked. "Sito's mother, how is she doing?" "How is she doing what?" "You know . . . she drank, didn't she?" "Oh. She's the same." As I remembered, she had given up drinking and gone back to it several times, in cycles that were always both drastic and drawn out. So I asked M, "The same as when?" "The same as always. She gives up drinking and then goes back to it." "But how is she now? What is she doing?" I insisted. "Oh, now. I don't know. Let's ask Sito." We had to wait a while before he joined us. The people he had gone to visit had not let him go during the day because of the violence; eventually, after he alluded to the anxiety his mother must certainly have been feeling, he had been allowed to leave. On days like those, and those that followed, danger returned the original sense of uneasiness to the geography of the city, its breadth. Just as in the past, setting out from Ciudadela for another place meant the risk of crossing hostile territory, giving people the sensation of going on a journey when they were only traveling between neighborhoods; movement was once again classified according to the risks it presented.

As he approached us, Sito noticed that we were talking about him; how could he not have, given the unexpected nature of the encounter and the fact that we were waiting for him. But he also knew that we were talking about his mother, despite the fact that we were too far away for him to possibly hear us, Sito confided in me the day we had a coffee after running into each other on Reconquista and Tucumán, as I have mentioned. He told me that he knew right away, that night as he walked toward us after whistling, when he saw us with our hands in our pockets, taking short steps almost in place, practically walking in circles without knowing it, that I was asking M about his mother. Hell is more predictable than heaven, said Sito, and living with her was a disaster, a perfect hell. Not only did he become accustomed to predicting her blows, her seclusions, her delirium, her tears, anguish, and complaints, Sito also grew accustomed to reading, in the faces of others, the appearance of his mother in the form of a question, pity, or disdain.

People made life with her more difficult, he continued. Sometimes he would get distracted and spend hours dreaming of a world in which he would never have to see anyone: he would busy himself only with caring for his mother, not with explanations. In that case, he thought, the alcohol would be less of an affliction than a hobby, since it was the others who saw it as a stigma, not the one who drank. It's always the outside world that ruins family relations; were it not for their contact with the outside world, he and his mother would have enjoyed a tight and lasting, happy bond limited only by the length of their lives. In the same way, his marriage would be absolute heaven if the two of them never had to see or speak with anyone; the same goes for the children. But this is obviously impossible, admitted Sito, and so life turned into a hell. Something in the air told him when someone was thinking of his mother, which created a pressure behind his eyelids that felt as though his eyes were forcing their way forward. It left an impression on him when he was a boy, he continued, the way she would look first at the bottle, then at the glass, right before she took a drink. As though her eyes wanted to leave their sockets, to anticipate the materiality of the drink, pressed on by anxiousness.

Sito learned to monitor his eyelids when daily life suggested that the effect would be repeated. He conserved the reflex after the death of his mother, though it had been stripped of its original attributes. In her absence, this sixth sense had no purpose; but the eyelid, true to character, continued alerting him to other dangers: the change of tone in a conversation, defects in an elevator, someone lying in wait. Just now, I remember the gesture Sito made, of pressing or closing his eye with one hand, when I persisted in questioning his occupation with an attitude between grave and mocking. I don't know why, but this reflex inspires a fear in me worthy of being expressed by one just like it; it seems like a dramatization of the unconscious, and for that very reason a sign that its master has embraced both innocence and cruelty, skirting both territories without exercising control. People like that are capable of the greatest malice, I thought of Sito's tic, but not necessarily of him, as I walked along Bernardo de Irigoyen toward Constitución. We were talking when all of a sudden something went wrong; I don't know what had happened, but I watched him smooth his eyelid with his fingertips every so often, following a convulsive movement of his arm that looked as though he were trying to shake something off. At one point, he knocked over a glass. In fact, he rubbed his eye throughout our whole conversation, and also while we walked down Reconquista and later along Corrientes toward the Obelisk. Sito may not have done anything else. I don't know if I represented a danger, or if he told me that bit about the danger in order to explain a gesture that had no justification; the empty memory of his mother as she caressed the glass or bottle with the tips of her fingers, reading the worn label as though it were a means of understanding the true nature of the drink.

Sito's silences were always unique, always his own. He had learned to live with drama early on, hence the combination of reserve and surliness that emanated from him, particularly from his eyes, when he fell silent. There was a reason that Sito had not stopped talking during our entire encounter; he had even found a way to correct those inevitable silences, when one thinks back or before going on, by coughing or making noise with something or another. As a boy he had been completely withdrawn and his friends had experienced his mortal silence as a burden; he could remain mute and impassive, answering in sporadic monosyllables that only served to underscore his solitude, for hours at a time. But now, with the weight of memory threatening to crash down upon his truth, a moment's hesitation alluded to those past silences, making a fraction of a second seem intolerable; it was in this delicate and simple net that Sito had been caught. As such, despite their difference from the earlier ones in both their duration—these were nonexistent compared to those others—and their nature, Sito found that the value of his silences remained the same: reality seemed to shrink and objects to stretch out as long as the silence lasted. Everything seemed more ominous, there was nowhere to conceal a secret, because everything was brought into focus with clarity and immediacy. (If it had been concealed in the depths before, the truth was now right out on the surface.) It seemed to me that Sito also possessed a mineral obstinacy that equaled his verbal compulsion. The quieter the person, the less stubborn they tend to be. Sito spent much of the afternoon insisting that he couldn't believe I was a writer, until he ended up admitting that he had always thought that the writer would be M. This opinion was so common on the block that his mother—irritated by the silent reproach of her son, whose sadness did not stop her from adding to the growing mountain of empty bottles—would order him, as a way of getting him off her back and as a kind of insult, "Go, go see that writer of yours," meaning M. Sito would go see him, though they would never so much as touch on the subject of writers, or anything related to them. M was never interested in anything of the sort and yet, from early on, he had a reputation as a writer: a partial recognition, of course, but an emphatic one. More recently, after they lost the bond of free time, when they ran into each other every day or nearly every day, as I have said, M and Sito would exchange a few words. Usually when Sito would take the empty bottles out to the tracks at night, to leave them for drifters and vagrants to pick up later.

When we reached calle Esmeralda, Sito asked me to wait; he had to pick something up nearby—it wouldn't be more than two minutes, and then we could keep walking, he said. I stood on the corner, as he asked, and watched him walk toward Lavalle and go into a storefront that was both a hair salon and a candy shop where they also sold fountain pens, almost in the middle of the block. There was traffic on Esmeralda, and the cars took part in a game of patient waiting that could easily last hours; they seemed prepared for that. Thanks to the narrowness of the sidewalk, I could hear the conversation two women were having in the back of a taxi that had stopped in front of me. One said, "I swear, it didn't turn up." "It can't be," answered the other. "But it is. They looked for half an hour, and not a trace." "But it was such a large ashtray, it couldn't have just disappeared." "It didn't all disappear, only half." "Which half?" "Half. It broke when it fell. They looked everywhere, and one half is missing." "That's not possible." "It is. They put the half on the table and stared at it. No one notices an ashtray, but when half of one is missing, everyone is paralyzed with fear." "Why fear?" "Because they didn't see anything supernatural, only its effects." "What effects are those?"

At that moment, Sito left the shop and the cars moved up a meter. He walked toward me with a piece of flimsy pink paper in his hand, on the center of which the number 435 had been quickly scribbled. "It's my lucky number. I always play it, but only sometimes win," he said. Then Sito surprised me further still: he turned the paper over and showed me another number, 733. He was radiant: "*El Pajarito* and *el Uruguayo*, and the two of us meeting, to boot. You'd better believe I'm going to win today!" As we crossed Esmeralda it occurred to me that Sito might be the cause of every bad thing that had happened, particularly and most obviously M's death. It was a ridiculous idea, but I was surprised that nothing kept me from thinking it. Sito talked about the prime sales periods for mattresses; when they sell more, it's not that the prices go up, but rather that there are no discounts. He said: It's our policy. So I changed the subject; I asked him to imagine that he is in a café, having a coffee, when a false move knocks the glass ashtray off the table. He hears the noise—it has broken—but when he bends down he finds only half there on the floor; the other is gone. I asked Sito how he would react if, after looking again and again, he could not find the other half. "I wouldn't believe it," he answered. "But if that's how it was—if you were there and the ashtray had fallen from your own hands," I insisted. "In that case, I would think it had disappeared, but that the part I couldn't see had to be some-where—that it must still exist in one form or another, that there must be some reason for it."

As I have already said, Corrientes slowly took on a horizontal light, compressing all visual perspective. At the far end, in the west, the sun gradually set. The curves of the street hardly mattered; it was as though the rays of light were traveling straight through the buildings. Sito continued explaining, much more interested in his response than I was—I had immediately gotten distracted: I would look in all four directions, and if there was nothing to catch my attention, nothing that something could be hidden under, and if there was no one who could have hidden it or seen anything, then I would say to myself, *it's lost*. It was an unobjectionable piece of common sense. As I walked a while later along Bernardo de Irigoyen toward Constitución, I would think about the different types of tragedy. Nothing stands in the way of taking the disappearance of half an ashtray as a sign, an omen, an effect, a cause, a proof, or a reminiscence. It might also be that the women, aware that some-one was listening, had invented the dialogue in order to trick me, referring to a completely false event. But I was not interested in its degree of truth, only the scale of what I had heard. Perhaps it had not happened to either of them, but rather to someone who had then told them about it, or one of them might even have read it, or it might have been part of a movie. In that case, the enigma would be of a secondary nature, like the final echo produced by a clap of thunder, in whose resonance the singular moment of truth that generated it becomes unclear.

There I was, wondering about the nature of an impossible event and, not only that, trying to find some explanation for its appearance along my path. This might seem ridiculous—all of life's events are certainly interruptions, providential obstacles eternalized later by the course of events itself, and we know that to wonder about chance is to deny the power of destiny. Yet there is something in life that accustoms us to looking for the hidden meaning in things. We see and we touch surfaces, until something suggests a truth oriented in a different way, one inclined to hide its meaning. Sito, for example, told me that he worked as a waiter and, another time, as a mattress salesman, offering proofs that inspired confidence in his being, or being able to be, both those things. Yet without being mutually exclusive, the two activities were incompatible in his case, though not for any reason other than that he had mentioned each as a unique proposition. This compulsive theatricality, I thought to myself as I walked along Bernardo de Irigoyen, seems to be a family curse. The alcoholic is a theatrical individual: he organizes his life around certain prototypical scenes, giving himself over to the habit and immersing himself in a realm of appearances and indirect intentions. Nonetheless, the mother played only one character—her own, though it suffered from great swings—unlike Sito, who felt called upon to play several at a time.

As I crossed plaza Constitución, I remembered a play M once told me about. In it, several characters were played by the same person, as was the case with Sito. It was a piece of Yiddish theater, in which one actor was sufficient to play several non-Jewish characters. Through this unique convention, they demonstrated the secondary nature of the Gentile world and also expressed a sense of superiority;

or else it was a form of disdain, or a simple instance of symbolic justice. A certain young lady is promised to a man who is about to arrive in Argentina from Europe; Rosenfeld is from the same town in Galizia as the young woman's father, named Rosemberg. Because everyone attests to his seriousness, and because the parents respect the savings with which, according to several acquaintances, Rosenfeld will be arriving after many years of work in Vienna, the marriage had been arranged months earlier. The girl expresses her enthusiasm with anxiousness and surrender. Rather than feeling unlucky at the thought of the difficult work of maintaining a home and the imminent daze of becoming a mother, it would have the virtue of keeping her from the difficult passage through adolescence, tedious years in which time seemed to have no meaning and days floated by in pure nothingness.

But Rosenfeld, as soon as he appears, sows the seeds of a vague disquiet: two neighbors, Leike Rosenstein and Jaike Rosenbaum, comment secretly after seeing him pass that he has arrived from Europe after becoming a widower with no descendants—to all appearances, because of his own incapacity. As is well known, to arrange a marriage without being able to have children is to condemn the woman to the greatest misfortune. Raquel receives her betrothed with shyness and affection: her eyes sparkle more than usual, and her lips take the shape of a suppressed kiss. The father, Rosemberg, embraces Rosenfeld as though he were already his son, though in the play he is only five years older (in reality, the actor Rosenfeld is noticeably older than the actor Rosemberg). Behind Rosemberg's affability, one can sense a deference to power, in this case to wealth, that he cannot contain. For his part, Rosenfeld behaves like someone aware of his own importance: he raises his voice without discretion, he addresses recent acquaintances with excessive familiarity (though it would be fair to say that these people feel flattered, and in some way protected, by Rosenfeld's friendship), he demands details about the community and flaunts his worldliness, alluding constantly to Viennese customs. It is true that the many references to Vienna unsettle Rosemberg: more than the Parisians, who are already completely foreign to the restricted world of a Jew from the East, the Jews of Vienna embodied the height of assimilation and the loss of tradition. At the same time, it is also true that, for a poor Galizian family living in a tenement in Villa Crespo, hearing of Viennese customs meant glimpsing a part of Buenos Aires that they had just barely seen, only more.

The marriage ceremony was set for a few days later. As a sign of the change underway, one night the manager of the tenement comes to collect the rent and is surprised by the way Rosemberg pays him without curses or complaints. Raquel grows happier and more beautiful by the day, and is gradually making progress as she is instructed in the work of her mother; she is already able to prepare the most elaborate meals on her own, including the confections. Meanwhile, Rosenfeld entertains advice regarding possible investments of his money: certain friends recommend trade, others, industry. His interest in this stands in contrast to the indifference, even rudeness, with which he receives the wistful comments of his future father-in-law, who lists possible names for his grandchildren, acts out the games and sings the songs that he will teach them, and happily thanks God that they will not experience the privation his own family did. The audience also notices the haughtiness with which Rosenfeld treats Raquel, as though she were soon to be his property. He is satisfied with the quick sympathy felt toward any girl, and with his control over even the smallest—though for this reason, highly significant—details, but never displays the typical affect one feels toward one's betrothed. In these moments, Raquel's bitter, suppressed gestures disclose her melancholy premonitions. Of all social climbers, Rosenfeld is the worst sort because he is rich, though no one is able to pinpoint the source of their aversion and all see wealth as a virtue.

During the preparations for the ceremony, Rosenblum, a young baker from the market on calle Uriarte whom Rosenfeld contracted to prepare the food, on Rosemberg's recommendation, appears. He is shown calculating the budget, indignantly defending his merchandise, being moved by Raquel's innocence, and wishing happy tidings upon the couple. Rosenblum is endowed with many virtues: he is honorable, hardworking, observant of tradition; he even breaks out into irrepressible bouts of lyricism. Thanks to his songs, the members of the family are able to temporarily forget the vague sense of anxiety that is slowly taking them over, and they begin to dance. Yet Rosenfeld is blind to all this; toward Rosenblum he feels only disdain, for his poverty, and suspicion, for his goodness. A series of increasingly unusual events takes place, designed to add to the disquiet; even Raquel, at first so vivacious, charming, and happy, is now—like a defenseless animal that senses great danger in the slightest movement—unable to react even to the simplest of questions, bursting into tears for no reason at all. As a counterpoint, Rosenfeld, completely self-possessed, displays his bounty of ire and arrogance as though he owned everything and everyone there. An example: Rosemberg does not dare to come to the defense of his wife when Rosenfeld insults her cooking, dumping the contents of his plate onto the tablecloth. Raquel, also at the table, looks down and silently cries.

The day of the ceremony, one sees only forced gestures. The threat is palpable, though no one is able to latch on to it and bring it out into the open. The syndrome that has infected the actors, the raising of one hand compulsively to tug at their left eyelid, is an indication of the spiritual chaos that dominates the characters: it is a confusion that can only really express itself through something as mechanical and immaterial as a tic. Eventually, after marches and countermarches, after impossible preparations and essential things forgotten, the moment of the ceremony arrives. Proof that something is not right appears in this moment: there is a stranger among the guests, somebody that everyone asks about, everyone but Rosenfeld, who knows him and watches him with animosity. He is aware that he cannot be the one to let loose the storm and that, in any event, he lacks the upper hand, so he remains silent. The guests try to act as though it were just another marriage ceremony, which does little to justify the martial movements of the actors. The air is filled with forced laughter, with repeated jokes, with sorrowful silences. Finally, at the climax of the ceremony, when Raquel and Rosenfeld are about to exchange rings, the stranger steps forward and, begging the guests' pardon, says that he knows Rosenfeld and asks God not to allow their marriage. He, Rosenthal, the person on whom all eyes were set at the moment, had been the man's father-in-law for many years, fifteen, until his daughter died without any descendents despite having been a healthy woman. Rosenfeld was not able to father a child, he was certain of it. With these words, Rosenthal would produce an unexpected stir, no less real for being spontaneous. Jaike and Leike began to whisper, as did their spouses. Raquel threw herself into her mother's arms; Rosenblum stood paralyzed, with a tray on his arm; Rosemberg began to sweat; and Rosenfeld turned, screaming, toward Rosenthal, overcome with rage. My darling daughter visited doctors and rabbis, and all of them assured her that there was nothing keeping her from having a child, but that man never agreed to see anyone about it, Rosenthal accused, pointing his finger.

The marriage could not take place; everyone knew it, though no one said anything. Everyone—apart from Rosenfeld, that is—except Rosemberg who, surprisingly as pusillanimous as always, tried to be accommodating, saying that everything could be sorted out and that the ceremony should go on. Then Rosemberg's wife spoke, saying that she would not allow it, for her only daughter never to give her grandchildren. The husband fell silent: it was not a comfortable situation for him. Everything was one generalized, collective murmur peppered with shouts here and there. That is, until Rosenfeld, pulling a thick bundle of papers from his pants with a flourish and a look in his eye that consolidated all the ire of which a person is capable, said that if the marriage was not celebrated, Rosemberg had to pay back all the promissory notes he owed. Raquel let out a shriek of terror; her mother fainted, Rosenbaum and Rosenstein would rather not have been there, but Rosenblum kept his calm and, consoling Raquel and attending to her mother, he found time to turn and curse Rosenfeld. This is how the scene ends.

The following morning, Rosenfeld turns up dead. There are so many people under suspicion that it does not occur to anyone that his death might have been a natural one. The manager of the tenement arrives to announce that the police are on their way. A little while later a patrolman walks in—the same actor, dressed in a uniform—who means well but has trouble understanding the situation. He writes in a notebook and says to leave Rosenfeld where he is, that he needs to notify the judge. When the judge arrives, it is the same person as the manager and the patrolman. He closes himself in an empty room in the house with each of the suspects and the guests at the gathering. The judge also means well, but he does not have trouble understanding. In the end he concludes that it is a complex case, and that they should know the cause of Rosenfeld's death before coming to any decision. And so Rosenblum calls the most respected doctor in the community, Doctor Rosenblat, a man of simple yet distinguished stature, behind whose affability one could sense an extensive knowledge of both tenements and palaces, as well as a genuine interest in all Jews, even the most impoverished. When he arrives, Rosenblat greets Rosemberg—they actually know one another—and asks about Resie, his wife. "Resie is Resie," Rosemberg says as an answer to all questions, and leads the doctor into the bedroom.

Rosenblat carefully examines Rosenfeld's body; he asks Raquel, Rosemberg, and his wife, and especially Rosenblum, what he ate and drank the day before. Nothing out of the ordinary, they answered, nothing that they themselves had not eaten or drunk. Rosenthal intervenes once again. He knows a secret: a certain disease, slow and merciless, had been eating away at Rosenfeld for years. That explains the death, Rosenblat ventures; the effects of the illness could be seen on the corpse. Everyone looked at one another, relieved. The judge had the doctor sign the death certificate, wrote a few notes in his folio, and withdrew, though he was not able to resist a glass of honey wine offered to him by Raquel's mother. Raquel and Rosenblum ran to each other and embraced: as the only two young people in the group, the violent tension had, naturally, brought them together. Rosenblum broke into song, Rosenbaum and Rosenstein immediately returned to the stage and all the actors began to dance with joy and contagious fervor.

This was how the play ended, with a resolution that did not demonstrate Rosenfeld's cruelty, but—on the contrary—refuted it: aware of his imminent death, he had decided to marry Raquel in order to leave her his fortune. All the way from far-off Vienna, to benefit a girl in Argentina. It was strange, how distance made certain episodes more enigmatic. If Raquel had lived in Vienna, Galizia or anywhere else in Europe, Rosenfeld's gesture would have seemed like a forgettable eccentricity. But to cross the ocean and go to the ends of the earth to leave his inheritance to a girl he hardly knew! Those thousands of kilometers made of the decision a disquieting mix of chance and goodness, as though the souls of millionaires floated through the air until finding, with a quick and accidental glance, one lucky individual. Everyone dreams of getting rich, M continued; words in which I recognized the echo of similar, but different ones often spoken by his father.

Thanks to Rosenfeld, the new arrival, the insurmountable distance that separates Buenos Aires from Galizia vanished in the minds of the characters, representing itself instead in just a few meters, or in the delicate thickness of the partition that divided the rooms of the Rosemberg home; seeing the play, it was evident that those who were not in one room were in the other (listening). They may also sometimes have felt that they were in the same one, since Rosenfeld was the one who most fully represented the past and, along with it, the diffuse territory from which they all came. Despite the simplicity of his intentions, Rosenfeld appeared to the audience and to the other characters as an enigmatic figure, at once despicable and attractive. The mystery of Rosenfeld. The mystery of Rosenfeld, arising neither from his actions nor his appearance, relied upon something that was impossible to conceal: his status as a traveler. In a manner that was simple and slight, rapid, stealthy, and vaguely heroic, Rosenfeld came from everywhere to end up in one place, but the journey had done little for him and he began to wander again. It would be easy to say that death, had it held off a little, would have allowed him to marry and follow through on his intentions, but the truth is that Rosenfeld lacked absolute time: he was condemned not to finish, to meet his end before achieving anything. He would not have been able to avoid failure, even if he had twenty years. I know this chimerical time, the one that stands still while the other, as the saying goes, slips through one's fingers; I know it well. I know this broken half, explained M, in different words—the real turned to solipsism: Rosenfeld the individual aspiring to attain a totality made impossible by the fact that the search itself was behind him, in a forsaken time and place.

SIX

It was like a solar eclipse, but in reverse. He pictured the night turned to day without prologue or intervention, the urgent din of the animals and then the return of darkness. This is what it would be like not to wake up, to fall asleep like on any other day, but with the knowledge that there would be no dawn. Bad thoughts are replaced by worse ones, he ventured, resting the empty bottle on the floor. Face down on his mattress, his arms hanging to either side, Grino selected from among the few "scenes of abundance" that helped him tolerate his unfortunate situation. It was the sea, the far end of an elongated bay flanked on both sides by mountains that were higher and more uneven on the right than on the left. According to his memory of the photographs, waves appeared like uniform reproductions of the horizon, that remarkable plane from which they emerged, by virtue of a complex mechanism of constant repositioning. They were spread evenly apart and their height was the same; their crests, crowned with airy foam, seemed more like embellishments than crests. Thanks to the photo, the natural world—there is nothing more natural than the sea, with its unchanging horizon—showed its artificial, even mechanical, condition. To Grino's mind, this was the source of the bewildering abundance of the scene. Simple people like him cannot help but feel overwhelmed by nature; yet in a strange, compensatory turn of intelligence and perception, the supernatural appears straightforward to them. This is how the urge to travel that torments so many begins, thought Grino, pinned to the bed by the weight of his bottle of rum and the semen he had freed earlier, caught somewhere between confusion and sleep. Despite the difficulties, he was someone who felt capable of getting up at any moment and setting out on foot in search of that photographic landscape, though in reality it might be impossible to find. Anyone could see that, just as the photo was a partial—and, in its way, false—depiction of an imprecise model, the sea, too, and the waves and the beach that bordered the water like a ring of ash, were nothing more than metaphors of freedom. It is in this second or supplementary nature that, paradoxically, simple souls find their proof, the landscape: anything able to bear multiplication and use, like waves and especially photos, holds a truth that transcends the simple and mundane deep within it. And so, Grino understood, his devotions converged in relocation and religion. The machine that moved the waves was the same one that made photos and guided both planets and people.

No one is immune to deceit, not even their own; take Sito, for example, who I think still believes he fooled me, as I wrote earlier. His mistake was not controlling his impulse to say more than I expected. Excess, in such cases, either reveals the deceit or becomes a falsehood itself, in one way or another. I talked too much, as well, and because of that we both clung to the tiny bit of truth at the mottled nucleus of the stories we told, but at least I can honestly say, as I do now, that *I didn't tell him that* or *I only told him half the story.* Despite his misdirection, he would have had a hard time not telling me something, no matter how minor. Sito has probably drawn his own conclusions, inferred things based on my words and my silences, and thinks that I am much more transparent than my reticence would suggest. In any event, it is important to say this because, though it may seem obvious, certain events remain unknown if they are not brought out into the open. I am referring to something I did not tell Sito, something I was careful to conceal due, in truth, to my own weakness and shame.

I don't know how it might seem—strange, ridiculous, foolish—but I know what it was: futile. To put it concretely, there was a time when I tried to change my name; I wanted to take M's. Perhaps tried is too strong a word, and I should say that I was "inclined" to change my name to his. Since he had the misfortune of being killed, since it was he who had suffered martyrdom, it seemed fair to me that, being the one to have survived, I would compensate for his absence by imposing his name over mine. I didn't think of it only as a compensation; it was something more profound or super-ficial, depending on how you look at it: a balance that needed to be restored. I felt that M and I had achieved an unprecedented and varied sense of unity that should be recovered, if only in a purely verbal or even strictly figurative form. Yet despite the simplicity and precision of the reasoning, and setting aside the justice and dignity of the cause, some things are just impossible.

One day I went to a government office on calle Uruguay, the civil registry. That morning marked the beginning of the final episode, until today, of an adventure that has involved M as an intangible companion. I waited in line for a long time with people who needed to file certificates of birth, death, marriage, or adoption, or who needed to correct errors that appeared in the same, or several of these things at once. (There I learned something I had not known before: that there are errors that can just appear, that may not exist as such at first but can all of a sudden abandon the realm of the correct, moving to another and never being discovered, but rather simply materializing at some point as errors.) Aside from ours, there was another, much longer, line of foreigners waiting to do things with their residency; it seemed as though they had been there all night, with friends and relatives along to relieve them from time to time. I'll say one thing about calle Uruguay: that morning, its wide sidewalk was constantly full.

Inside the building, the line took on a different shape: it zigzagged. When my turn finally came, I said to the clerk, "I'd like to change my name." "What name?" she asked, not understanding. "Mine," I said, "I want to change it." "And may I ask why?" she retorted. "The reason is personal. I want to change it." "But that's a public request and we need to know why. If you don't want to declare your reason, keep your own name." Those words seemed to end the conversation. She was not a beautiful woman, that is, her expression, which had become her features, hid a prior, perhaps more lively, face. "Wait," I said. "If I tell you, is there a chance?" "That depends," she asserted. "Depends on what?" "Depends on the reason." "What sort of reason could it be?" I asked. "Oh, I can't tell you that," she said. "But I need to know if I can do it or not," I insisted. "All right, tell me your reason, and I'll tell you if you can. But not the other way around, because if I tell you, you'll just pick one." According to the card she wore clipped to the pocket of her uniform, her name was Mirta del Soto. "Listen," I said, emphasizing my *porteño* accent and leaning in as though I were about to tell her a secret, "I want to change my name, and don't care what reason I give. What I want is to do it quickly." "All right," she replied, in a weary voice, "tell them that you discovered that your parents aren't your parents. We'll verify it and you can have it changed." "No, that won't work." "Oh, you don't say," she snapped. "It can't be just any name. It has to be a specific one," I explained. "In order to do that, we need to know the reason," she raised her voice, "it's the reason that justifies taking that specific name instead of any other." "But what are the reasons?" "I can't tell you that." "There must be some sort of code, some rule book, where they're all written down." "Yes," she said, "but I don't know where it is." "So how do you know if a reason is valid or not?" "I don't worry about that; I just take the forms. But I'm telling you: without a reason, it won't get looked at." She seemed agitated, but she wasn't; it was just her way of doing her job. She would probably forget all this right away, but I tried to make sure that didn't happen.

When I try to remember Mirta del Soto's face now, it is as though it had dissolved, leaving only the indifferent recollection of an equally unassuming ugliness. Her features, barely defined, appeared to be subject to the order of weariness that had imposed itself on her other traits—traits that, at one time, might have flattered her—flattening, for example, the intonation of her voice or repressing any lively movement of her eyes. Her smock, the identification card, the counter at chest height, and, behind it in the half light, rows of desks, many of which were empty: all these things made her, in my moment of need, seem like a vaguely liturgical figure placed there to perform the ritual of changing my name. But she also appeared to me, more and more tangibly, as an individual, precisely because of her negative traits. (Features, a face: a mystery. I say this in general, beyond the case of Mirta del Soto. A person's face is something brutish, a landscape waiting to be revealed with neither a before nor an after, only what is there in the moment of its discovery, overlooking its enigmas.)

Her way of speaking, inseparable from her foreign-sounding voice and the way her reflexive common sense did away with people's—or, in this case, my—urgency, or at least the importance of their reasons: in her, all of this spoke to me of a sound and self-sufficient universe in which there was no doubt about names, colors, or memories. The unwavering simplicity embodied by Mirta del Soto did not reveal the advantages of a simple truth, nor did it possess the power of minor wisdom, but I was affected by the efficacy of her even, uncomplicated logic that worked like a portable magic kit, turning something complex into something simple and making the obscure transparent. Over the course of two weeks, I went to see her three more times, and on the fourth she let me wait for her near the exit of the registry.

I saw her without her uniform. She dressed carelessly, wearing a brown rain jacket over a red sweater. She wanted to go somewhere far from there, where her co-workers wouldn't see her (she said *colleagues*: "where my colleagues won't see me"). We walked along Uruguay toward Rivadavia. On the way, Mirta talked about her family, or what had become of it. She lived alone with her mother, who was bedridden. She had no husband and no children; her father, who had abandoned them in the distant past, was just a hazy memory. (Right away, I could tell she was lying; something indefinable, impossible to calculate, convinced me of it.) For some time, Mirta had wondered whether her mother might not have been pleased to have her, the daughter, all to herself after her father left. What is more, she could be two, like during the stretches of time when her mother would call her Mirto, as though she were a boy. "So you see," she said, making a gesture in the air, "there are always reasons to want to change your name," alluding to my reticence to give my own. Once we got to Corrientes, it became harder for us to talk—I should admit that it didn't really seem necessary, either—we could not walk next to one another on the narrow sidewalks, so instead we walked with her in front and me behind, our way often blocked by people waiting for buses or leaving stores and buildings.

We went to a café on the avenida de Mayo. As soon as we sat down, Mirta covered the side of her face with her hand, warning me, "That guy over there is the section manager at the registry. If he sees me with you, I'm done for." Far from concealing her, the gesture made her stand out, as did my spontaneous reaction of turning my head to watch him walk past. Mirta was out in the open, but the section manager, surprised and guarded because of our movements, did not recognize her. She loved scenes like that; in those moments she did not just imagine herself to be another, but many others at once; the others were also different—they could be other, too. After a while we cut to the chase: She told me that the only chance I had was to demonstrate my "longstanding use" of the new name, for which I was going to need proof. This proof would be in the form of documents, that is, I needed to present documents that made it clear that I had been called by the name that I wished to adopt. Personal documents like letters could help later on, but what mattered were the public ones: an extended and habitual use of the name that left no doubt as to its suitability to identify me. For example, she said, a photo of your graduation that shows you with the new name. Graduation photos, I thought. It was unthinkable; Mirta seemed to be from another planet. The only photo like that I could remember—and that, on the other hand, I was sure I did not have—was one from seventh grade, which of course showed me with my original name. I told her this, but her fatigue had latched on to the first opportunity to take over her mind and, having proposed a solution, even one that was of no use, she felt absolved of having to think of another. She looked out at the street, and it was as though she were sleeping with her eyes open. I observed the almost imperceptible down that covered her face, glowing in reflection from the window, as it grew more dense around her lips to form a delicate plush. Her neck was rough. Maybe it was true, what she said about her mother, I thought; next to her problems, the idea of changing my name with no justification must seem capricious to her. In that case, it would make sense that she would not want to offer alternatives. Until the very end, I wondered if I should tell her the truth. She might really be able to help me, I thought, but realized right away that it could ruin everything. After a while we left the café and walked in the direction of Congreso.

We got all the way to Montevideo without saying a word. I was thinking about M, about how different that walk would be if he were there, how different the city would be. One did not walk with Mirta; it was an operation that resembled being dragged, as though something had us in tow—if not with our participation, at least with our consent. Mirta acted pensive, but she made an effort to talk even when she had nothing to say, which was, after all, why she had been quiet. Whenever the car motors would allow it, I listened to the plastic rustling of her jacket as she walked. A few meters past Montevideo she said, "Well, this is me. This is where I catch the 56." "All right," I answered, "well, thanks a lot, Mirta."

She looked off to one side and hesitated: I watched the thought that had been forming over the past two blocks take shape in her head. "I thought you were going to take me somewhere else," she finally said. In that moment, I understood that Mirta could not help me if I remained a stranger. We continued on toward a hotel on Rincón.

Once there Mirta's skin radiated heat; it burned and yet, I don't know why, the body did not seem to belong to its owner. A mix of desire and restraint impeded any externalization or connection, creating, as a result, a pitiable delay in movements and gestures, as though she were following orders sent from far away and each maneuver, gesture, or thought were broken down into so many specific, repetitive commands that it was impossible to accomplish anything in an efficient way. Mirta's torpor in bed—which at times was frighteningly ecstatic, as though she were on the verge of unconsciousness or sleep—was similar to her silence as she walked, when she seemed to be at the mercy of lethargy, hard-pressed to move herself. At that moment I was another; not who I thought I was or who she thought I was. Her surrender was so disproportionate compared to my desire or my feelings that I was left with no choice but to concede: to be less, different, a third person. Mirta would get excited to the point of collapse, only to immediately trail off into languor. There was no connection between her breathing and any of this, and her fluctuations produced in me a vague sense of shame. In a moment of particular tumult, I caught sight of her credentials, her identification card, on the rug. "Mirta del Soto, Assistant," it said. I imagined that fate had put her title in front of me to instruct me on the many possible meanings of the word assistance.

Afterward, I walked her to calle Moreno, where she could catch the 56. We had fallen quiet again, but now, as you can imagine, the silence was different. Mirta's availability was no longer as passive; it had become obsequious. She could say the first thing that came to mind, as long as it corresponded to the tone of affectionate gratitude that she felt compelled to express. At the bus stop, across from a hospital, there was a shop that made shirts. As soon as we arrived, Mirta said, "I want to buy you one," and set about looking at the different samples in the window. I stared at the wall in front of me; I sensed the vague memory of something having to do with M. Mirta, for her part, noticing that I had not so much as turned to look at the shirts, as she had hoped, turned and immediately remarked, "The bus is taking forever."

I should say that Mirta's help was essential, though I never did achieve my objective. We met on two other occasions, aside from the days when I went to visit her at the registry. It was impressive, how she could make a routine out of nothing; this certainly derived from a deep-seated need. She fell in love with the café, where we would sit in the same place and order the same drinks, and of course with the hotel, where she never actually managed to ask for the same room. Until the very end, I debated whether to tell her the truth, but I was sure that, for one reason or another, I would regret it. It might even be, I thought, that something similar had happened to Mirta, in fact, it was very possible; at the end of the day, the story about the crippled mother and the absent father could absolutely be one of those that cover up other, more painful, events and, as such, might be no more than the modified version of a less general tragedy. If that were true, however, if someone close to her had disappeared, my wish might be offensive to her.

I know that passivity, I said to myself as I watched her get on the crowded 56 bus as though stepping into a cave of shadows, that dream of peace that seeks out the void, assimilates it, but is flustered by the slightest discord. My confession would be like a thunderclap, which meant there was no room for the truth, though at least I didn't lie: to this day, Mirta does not know why I wanted to change my name. If at any point she had directed the power of her portable magic kit at me, I might either have confessed to her or given up the idea of taking another name; but if, as I have said, I sometimes believed myself to be other, or less, or different, then these states are so fleeting and so autonomous, in their way, that I might not have been subject to her influence.

Once, resting my head on her back, I listened to the sound of Mirta's heart beating; as an echo of her diffuse ugliness, it seemed even more unreal. There is nothing more enigmatic than someone's back, a personal plain that one never sees in its entirety, upon which all strength, weariness, and betrayal converge, and where grease accumulates as it does on a face that's been covered up. Mirta's heartbeat sounded far away; it seemed to reach me from across not one, but many bodies, or at least to come from the depths rather than just a few centimeters beneath her skin. From the other side, I thought, against her breasts all it takes is a bit of attention to hear her pulse, but from this side her heartbeat is relegated to the distance. Lying on her stomach, Mirta did not speak. How I wanted to go on like that, to hold on to the silence for as long as possible and forget that it was her skin under my ear (it was no use).

I did not have to get in line when I went to visit her at work. I skirted along the side of the front door and walked toward the end of an empty counter, where it was darker. Mirta had already seen me come in, and a few minutes later she was with me, though on the other side. She got up on some sort of stool and projected her entire body forward—her arms and chest on the counter, her face in her hands—and looked at me. It was obvious that she was eager to speak. She asked me what I had done that day, commented on the weather, her job, and things of that nature. Her tone was trivial, but it would be a mistake to call it that because, although it was, it is also true that Mirta took great pains to explore the most intricate possibilities of any topic or situation; this, too, spoke of a kind of depth. At one point, she said to me, "I was thinking: since you're a writer, why don't you write a book and sign it with the other name?" I was stunned. It was a brilliant idea: publish a book and then later present it as my justification. Some time earlier, I had told her that I was a writer; despite her great propensity for wringing every word out of any conversation, she reacted, strangely, as though she had not heard me. "She doesn't believe me," I thought; but, at the end of the day, I didn't believe the story about her parents, either.

Maybe she still didn't believe me, and she gave me this idea to bring my deceit out into the open, I thought, as she distractedly folded the back cover of a book, a novel I had with me, as though it were any other piece of paper. As was the case with M, I have great respect for novels, but derive no pleasure from reading them; (in general) I only read for brief periods at a time. Furthermore, the story—like so many others, not worth repeating—did not interest me; yet something, maybe habit, kept me from putting it down, sort of like Mirta, so I carried it around with me anyway, reading it to little effect. How could Mirta do that? I thought. Apparently, books meant nothing to her. She racked her brain for another topic of conversation as she took hold of the back cover, folded it in half, and ran a fingernail along the edge to deepen the crease. Since she couldn't think of anything, she would start in on the cover. The idea she had given me was a good one, the best. What is more, it came from someone familiar with the matter; as such, though there are no guarantees in life, it had a high probability of success. But when I saw her distractedly quartering the book—she was already on her fifth fold—I wondered whether Mirta might not embody an excessive simplicity, a simplicity so dimensionless that her intervention might affect the value and meaning of my endeavor and, along with it, M's memory as a whole. It is true that this very simplicity was, itself, her portable magic kit, the combination of startling qualities behind which I had glimpsed the possibility of a certain freedom, but if I was inclined to change in that direction, to allow that change to take place in the part of me where M was and is kept, that also meant betraying his memory. So I took the book from her hands and said, "Mirta, I have to go." She wanted to know if I would wait for her, she could leave early today. I can't, I said. The idea about the book was a good one, the best, I told her; I never would have thought of it. That made her happy. "All right, get out of here. We'll get together another day," she said, by way of good-bye. When I left the registry, there was a wedding going on across the street, in an annex or something of the kind; they were taking pictures. I turned on to Córdoba and walked west.

Once more I felt, as I wrote several pages back, the lassitude and dissimilation that flowed from people's faces. I knew that I would not see Mirta again; this did not affect me much, but I found it paradoxical that once a solution, the best reason, had been found, I would withdraw without making use of it. I turned right on Rodríguez Peña. I wanted to walk past the Education Library, where M and I often went to consult manuals. At the corner of Paraguay I stopped to observe the plaza. It was veiled in a green and orange mist; behind it, though it was no more than a hundred meters away, avenida Callao looked like the distant backdrop of a landscape, vaguely impressionistic in its colors, the grey stone of the buildings along the avenue and the dappled effect of the branches and leaves intermingled along my line of sight. It wasn't worth it to go into the library, I thought; I was not going to request a book, nor did I have any intention of speaking with the employees there, and I had no doubt that the sight of the furniture, windows, and display cases— and, most of all, breathing in that smell (libraries have a smell)— would depress me. On the sidewalk outside, a long line of people was waiting for the 150 (Lugano or Villa Crespo to Retiro). After spending a while in the library, M and I would light our cigarettes in the doorway, facing the plaza, as soon as we stepped outside. A passive channel of wills: that is what the line of passengers waiting for the 150 was, standing beside the curb. The bus arrived and idled there a few moments; when it pulled away, the line had disappeared. Two or three people remained, at the most.

In that moment I noticed a different facet of M's absence. It may sound self-absorbed and inopportune, but his absence, I said to myself as I neared the curb on Rodríguez Peña, is not only a loss, but also a threat. All these years I thought that the danger had been dissipating bit by bit, and yet, despite the illusion of normalcy derived from the periodic arrival of the 37 and the 150, it was clear that, precisely because nothing made mention of it, no mark or sign or notch in stone or metal that could resist the passage of time in an abiding way, M's absence, the mystery and the silence surrounding his torture and horrible end, remained before our eyes, on the lids, as a threat: the likely blow, shove, or jolt that awaits us tomorrow, on the other side of the page or as we turn a corner. This, the evil that weighs upon us, is a singular truth.

At that moment I also noticed how the slightest setback—if someone spoke to me the wrong way, I stumbled over something, or a car did not let me pass—would be enough to make me feel that everything, the world, was falling apart. I felt myself oscil-late between plenitude and nothingness; I ceased being and was again, quick as a heartbeat. M and I spoke of this often: being, identity, and truth come into view and linger only intermittently; they are never permanent or constant. We would find examples of this fluctuation in synagogues, in the repeated rocking of the worshipers. Most of them were old; the movement might represent submission, disagreement, or rebuttal. It was also an intermittent retreat from mystery. Immobility was more pointless than it was impossible: being needed to travel and faith needed to move. We sometimes went to religious services, for example, on Rosh Hasha-nah or Yom Kippur, either at the synagogue on calle Acevedo or the one on Murillo or, every now and then, at the one on calle Paso. People prayed and many chatted, as has been the case as long as synagogues have existed, and M and I felt like the last representa-tives, not of a culture—since everyone is always the last and every culture is on the verge of disintegration—but rather of a *time* that was coming undone, with too many doubts for enthusiasm or resignation. Something told us that, pointless or tragic, or both, the processes of organic continuity would pass us over, that our bodies were unlikely to give rise to new bodies, but also that our walks, conversations, and voyages, during which we could not tell one from the other, were the tacit proof of an alternate form of longevity. During the service, after listening to the prayers of the rabbi and the redemptive call of the ram's horn, after observing the rites, an imperious reminiscence whose proofs are preserved in a reliquary, a sound forged by pure archaism, a primal gesture able to remain intact due to the brevity of its execution; after observing these ceremonies, M and I would talk about the mistrust that the start of a new year inherently deserved, about the different meanings of fasting, and, of course, about the implications of absolution.

I asked myself, on the corner of Rodríguez Peña, off to one side of the Education Library, how it could be that, having managed to find my justification and having garnered some degree of support, I would abandon the endeavor and want to forget about the whole thing. This might all be highly paradoxical, but faced with the real possibility of changing my name, I became aware of my own fear—not of what might happen to me, since, as is well known and easy to imagine, one never knows what is going to happen; the future is a true unknown, and it is precisely because of this that one resigns oneself to its mystery and actually prefers it—not of what might happen to me, but of what might happen to the memory of M that I held inside me. And so it becomes clear why one sometimes chooses inaction over change, though there are risks—the degeneration into futility, in this case—things dwindle and come to an end; it happens to everything.

And so, with the passage of time and the unavoidable changes to people and things, it was inevitable that I began to lose track of the traces left by M. Fewer and fewer things remind me of him. They remain only as memories, but there comes a time we can no longer be sure of the real value of what we retain because, just as we can mean so many things when we say forgetting, many of which are contradictory and some of which are complementary, it is also true that we should not be overly credulous when we say things like recollection, memory, or simply evocation: there, too, a cave of shadows lies hidden. At the time, as I have mentioned, my encounter with Sito snapped me into the present. But the flash caused by that impact illuminated the impossible; the truth is, there comes a time when the recovery of memories becomes a path riddled with obstacles.

I recently began walking along avenida Dorrego again, the way I did right after the abduction. Sometimes I would start out from Corrientes and other times from Warnes, or Martínez Rozas. I've even stopped by his block, where, as Sito would say, time has stood still. Each time I sensed a waning nostalgia, the echo of an increasingly tenuous presence. The walls might remain the same, as is the case on his street, but the heat or the cold we felt as we leaned against them, the sideways glances we used to cast at them, the way they absorbed the sweat of our bodies year after year, the thickness of our voices and the meaning behind our looks: all that has faded away. It exists only in the form of traces that grow more and more faint. If this is the future of all things, if this is the future of the past, to mingle with the many forms of forgetting, distort recollections until we wear away the very traces we leave and are left on us, the ones that keep us on our feet, I can't help but wonder what our role really is. I am not complaining about the withdrawal or disintegration of bodies or memories, of ourselves and of the part of us that lives in others; these are operations to which we all are condemned and there is no reason to address them. Still, it seems to me that if this all belongs to the natural order of things, as it appears to, it should be challenged by means of a new position, different proofs, and another kind of action.

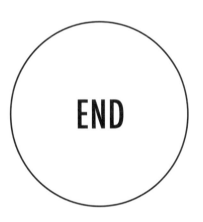

SEVEN *"Of all invisible countries, the present is the most vast."* For some time, this statement seemed more accurate than misguided; then something changed and it seemed more clever than accurate. Now I have returned to my original opinion: Of all invisible countries, the present is the most vast. We cannot think about an idea without modifying it; though this is, in part, the essence of an opinion, I would like to distance myself from it. We inhabit different countries at the same time, lands of such crystalline transparency that they are invisible, all but the most luminous one. The present moment is the longest, the most lasting, sentence passed on us. Since M has been gone, not only I, but several others as well, have lived in a dimensionless present uncoupled from reality, within a territory whose borders, if they exist at all, are undefined and rely on our movements, yet within which stillness is the only viable option. Our place advances with progress and recedes with retreat. We cleave the air without moving, wrapped in our enclosure as by a skin. It has been impossible to free myself from this smooth and transparent time; I wander, I walk within it, remembering and sensing M as a figure fossilized by memory, transformed into a purely temporal substance, until I return to wakefulness and discover the mark of his body on mine. Then I see him, sitting up in bed. He has just woken up and is leaning on his hands, which are open behind him: tensed arms, ash-colored skin, a smooth chest, and a few drops of sweat on his forehead as he opens his eyes wide, not understanding his restlessness.

The mark of his body on mine. A few nights ago I had a dream that we were on a train headed for Moreno. As nearly always happens, the closer we get to the end of the line, the fewer people there are; after Merlo, there is practically no one left in our car. Someone comes from up front, walking carefully because of the movements of the train, and sits four seats ahead of us. Immediately, someone comes from the back, walking carefully because of the movements of the train, and sits four seats behind us. M and I are sitting across from one another, but we have the impression that the same things are happening outside the window on his left that are happening outside of mine, though this is impossible; the houses are the same, the cars are the same, to say nothing of the streets. We have identical landscapes to our left. A while later, once we leave Paso del Rey behind us, someone comes from up front, walks past us, and sits three seats behind us; right away, someone comes from the back, passes by us, and sits three seats in front of us. After that, when someone walks past us toward the front, someone else immediately walks past us toward the back. M and I do not speak but, in the memory of the dream, this silence is the expression of a truth. With just a bit of imagination, one could infer that if reality as a whole were symmetrical for several meters around, with us at the center, there was no reason that the rest of the planet should not be symmetrical, too. This idea, which was certainly the culmination of many of our aspirations, insinuations, and beliefs, pleased us, because it allowed us to imagine that we were the same. The importance of this equality was not the establishment of an equivalency, but in the revelation of a new identity. For the short time it would take the train to go a few station—short compared to the normal span of a life—we would be conjoined in mutual indistinguishability.

After a while, as the train slows before reaching Moreno station, the last on the route—the deceleration more obvious than at the ones before it, due, as M and I agreed, to the fact that the passengers all know it is the last stop and this makes it all seem more conclusive—the dream comes to an end. But Moreno is not Moreno. We are actually arriving at Palomar station. This confusion is not disconcerting in the least; there is no need to retreat from any mystery. It is El Palomar, under the name Moreno. As we approach we hear birds squawking in the trees near both platforms, even the one by the freight line, and from the thousands that surround the station; this masks the sound of the slow-moving train for a moment. Then, as soon as we come to a stop, once the motionless car has turned into the promise of the next journey, I look at his profile as he stares out the window and say, "This has been our greatest adventure." At which M turns and answers, smiling, "Yes, our greatest adventure."

Caracas, July 1994

227

Sergio Chejfec, originally from Argentina, has published numerous works of fiction, poetry, and essays. Among his grants and prizes, he has received fellowships from the Civitella Ranieri Foundation in 2007 and the John Simon Guggenheim Foundation in 2000. His books have been translated into French, German, and Portuguese, and he teaches in the Creative Writing in Spanish Program at NYU. His novel, *My Two Worlds*, is also available from Open Letter in English translation.

Heather Cleary is a translator of fiction, criticism, and poetry, whose work has appeared in journals including *Two Lines*, *Habitus*, and *New York Tyrant*, and in the edited volumes *Revealing Mexico* and *The Film Edge*. In 2005, she was awarded a Translation Fund grant from the PEN American Center for her work on Oliverio Girondo's *Persuasión de los días*.

Open Letter—the University of Rochester's nonprofit, literary translation press—is one of only a handful of publishing houses dedicated to increasing access to world literature for English readers. Publishing ten titles in translation each year, Open Letter searches for works that are extraordinary and influential, works that we hope will become the classics of tomorrow.

Making world literature available in English is crucial to opening our cultural borders, and its availability plays a vital role in maintaining a healthy and vibrant book culture. Open Letter strives to cultivate an audience for these works by helping readers discover imaginative, stunning works of fiction and by creating a constellation of international writing that is engaging, stimulating, and enduring.

Current and forthcoming titles from Open Letter include works from Bulgaria, Catalonia, China, Germany, Iceland, Poland, and many other countries.

www.openletterbooks.org